THOMAS CRANE PUBLIC LIBRARY
QUINCY MA

CITY APPROPRIATION

JUL

2011

Praise for *Volk's Game*

"Brent Ghelfi writes like Dostoevsky's hooligan great-grandson on speed. Highly recommended."
—Lee Child, *New York Times* bestselling author of *The Hard Way*

"State of the art…[the novel's] characters are colorful, its descriptions of Russia are vivid, and its suspense is palpable. In terms of sheer entertainment, *Volk's Game* is an impressive debut."
—*The Washington Post*

"Impressive debut…the twists and turns accumulate at an almost dizzying pace….This thriller could mark the start of a successful long-running series."　　　　　　　　　—*Publishers Weekly*

"This is a novel that could appeal to two audiences. At a visceral level, it will please readers, mostly men, who get off on guns, war and extreme violence. At a more elevated level, it could impress others with the excellence of its storytelling."
—Patrick Anderson, *Washington Post*

"Stunning and brilliant…Ghelfi's prose is like a dark drug that pulls you further under its spell with each taste, so that by the end of the book, the reader is exhausted and, though satiated, ready and frantic for more."　　　　　　　　　　　—Bookreporter.com

"I have to give it up to Ghelfi for carving out a singular voice for his broken hero….[Volk] has enough heart and steel to become something really special."　　　　　　　　　　　—Bookslut

"Moving at breakneck speed through Moscow, St. Petersburg, and Manhattan, leaving a slippery trail of boy parts and exploded vehicles, Ghelfi handles the conventions of his genre like a pro. The violent derring-do is anchored in a portrait of contemporary Russia that is compelling and brutal on its own terms." —*Newsday*

"*Volk's Game* is no ordinary thriller: it's a 500-horsepower Mercedes blasting through the Moscow night. Alexei Volkovy is the most original thriller character to come down the Russian pike since Arkady Renko, yet he inhabits a Russia that Renko might have difficulty surviving. Volk moves through this frenetically paced novel like an avenging angel in the employ of both God and Satan. Brent Ghelfi's insights are rapier-sharp, and his prose seems to illuminate the page. Be glad, because you'll be finishing this novel at four a.m. I'm ready to read the next installment NOW."
　　—Greg Iles, *New York Times* bestselling author of *Turning Angel*

"Everything we look for when we read—freshness of setting, intriguing characters, vivid prose, new understandings—is well and truly here. Brent Ghelfi may not know Vincente Huidobro's work, but on his own he does exactly what that poet counseled: Invent new worlds, and be careful what you say."
　　—James Sallis, author of *Drive*

"Hypnotically suspenseful and ballistic paced, *Volk's Game* by Brent Ghelfi is fascinating journey into the dark world of international intrigue. From a plot full of surprises to crackling dialogue and often lyrical prose, this masterful debut novel belongs on every thriller-lover's bookshelf."　　—Gayle Lynds
New York Times bestselling author of *The Last Spymaster*

"It's rare to find a thriller this fast-paced and breathlessly dangerous that is also beautifully written. Ghelfi hits as hard as his hero Volk. Like staring down the barrel of a Sig-Sauer, you can't look away from *Volk's Game.*"　　—David L. Robbins, author of *The Assassin's Gallery*

Praise for *Volk's Shadow*

"In Ghelfi's mesmerizing second Russian thriller (after *Volk's Game*), Alexei "Volk" Vokovoy, an ex-army colonel with a prosthetic leg who does the dirty work for a paranoid Kremlin official known as "the General," received what appears to be a simple assignment: find a missing Fabergé egg. The hunt quickly leads Volk into a raw, uncivilized world in which even the most basic needs of common Russians go unmet. Crime bosses work hand-in-hand with the government. The riches of oil trump all other priorities. Sexual violence surges uncontrollably....crisp characterization and strong visual prose keep the story moving to its harrowing climax in Chechnya. Those seeking a tour of the dark side of contemporary Russia will be more than satisfied."   —*Publishers Weekly*

"Like a bullet, Col. Alexei Volkovoy (*Volk's Game*) goes where he is pointed and doesn't stop until he hits something. Brutalized by training, war, and captivity, he has criminal tendencies and a capacity for explosive violence that hide a deep loyalty to Russia and to the few people he trusts. When a series of seemingly unconnected crimes begins pointing to a single source, Volk (Russian for wolf) takes on Kremlin power players, the Russian mob, and Chechen rebels to resolve them. Volk is less Arkady Renko than a Russian Jack Reacher, making *Volk's Shadow* as noir as a winter night in Saint Petersburg."   —*Library Journal* starred review

"Alekei 'Volk' Volkovoy hits the ground running and doesn't get a chance to catch a breath in Ghelfi's sequel to *Volk's Game*. A terrorist attack on the headquarters of an American oil company appears to be the work of Volk's nemesis, Abreg. Toss in a Fabergé egg, a senator's daughter with a secret agenda, a missing little girl, a mysterious murder, and the reappearance of the love of Volk's life, and it's no wonder that the Russian black marketeer and covert military operative is such a tortured soul. The Russian underground is no field of pretty flowers, and the hard, brutal reality of Chechnya, where Volk lives and works, provides a cold but fascinating setting."   —*Booklist*

Praise for *The Venona Cable*

"Brent Ghelfi's Volk is back in *The Venona Cable*, lethal as ever, this time plunging headlong into the heart of LA to follow a trail rooted in the closing years of World War II. This is Volk—damaged, intense, perversely moral—at his compelling best."   —Erik Larson author of *Thunderstruck* and *The Devil in the White City*

"*The Venona Cable* packs more punch than a truck full of C4. Action, suspense, and international intrigue are masterfully interwoven in an intelligently written, pulse-pounding thriller that everyone will be talking about. Brent Ghelfi is the new Le Carre."
—Brad Thor, #1 *New York Times* bestselling author of *The Apostle*

"Ghelfi expertly portrays the seamy undersides of Moscow and LA....A sure bet for thrill fans."   —*Library Journal*

"Ghelfi keeps the Cold War hot with the intrigues of various Russian and US agents, double agents and a slate of characters who are seldom what they seem....Swift, sharp character descriptions and atmospheric evocations of gray, melancholy Moscow and the seedier streets of Los Angeles add style and color to a delectably complicated plot."   —*Kirkus Reviews*

"The accolades Ghelfi has received for Volk novels are well deserved, and this will only add to his acclaim."   —*Booklist*

The Burning Lake

Books by Brent Ghelfi

Volk's Game
Volk's Shadow (Shadow of the Wolf)
The Venona Cable
The Burning Lake

The Burning Lake

A Volk Thriller

Brent Ghelfi

Poisoned Pen Press

Copyright © 2011 by Brent Ghelfi

First Edition 2011

10 9 8 7 6 5 4 3 2 1

Library of Congress Catalog Card Number: 2011920302

ISBN: 9781590589250   Hardcover
       9781590589274   Trade Paperback

All rights reserved. No part of this publication may be reproduced, stored in, or introduced into a retrieval system, or transmitted in any form, or by any means (electronic, mechanical, photocopying, recording, or otherwise) without the prior written permission of both the copyright owner and the publisher of this book.

Poisoned Pen Press
6962 E. First Ave., Ste. 103
Scottsdale, AZ 85251
www.poisonedpenpress.com
info@poisonedpenpress.com

Printed in the United States of America

PART I

"Everything she wrote was on the edge."

—Vitaly Yaroshevsky, deputy editor of *Novaya Gazeta*,
eulogizing slain journalist Anna Politkovskaya

Chapter One

Dead of winter in Moscow, darkening skies, the day fading to night behind storm clouds. The city crackles under layers of ice and wet-packed snow as I crunch along the pathways between the pines and silver birches in Victory Park. The park is nearly empty. My breath trails behind me in lonely streamers.

I have a sense that something evil is about to hatch. Another mass grave spilling bodies, maybe, one more reminder of Stalin's reign of terror. All these years later, the horror of those times should linger only in aged memories, yellowing documents, and sepia photographs. But rotted flesh and broken bones keep blooming from the soil to remind us that the past never ends.

A cold shiver passes through me. How many times in my life has a premonition of evil been followed by the real thing?

Ahead looms the obelisk atop Poklonnaya Hill, marking the spot where Napoleon gazed over the spiritual capital of Russia while he waited in vain for news of the Kremlin's surrender. Moscow burned on that long-ago night, engulfed in flames before Napoleon could occupy his prize. Now in the gathering darkness the first lights of the city provide only the illusion of warmth.

I find a bench overlooking the golden domes of an Orthodox church and settle in to wait.

Nightfall comes quickly. The cold drives away all but a few of the remaining visitors. Orbs of light from the streetlamps punch yellow holes in the darkness, growing progressively larger as they march up the hill toward my spot on the high ground.

A man appears in the lit cone beneath the farthest lamp, a wavering shadow that firms into a dark silhouette as he passes from one island of light to the next, head down, shoulders hunched against the chill wind spilling down the hills in waves broken by naked trees. His image hardens as he draws nearer, resolving itself into the stooped shape of one bent by time and hardship.

Ilya Jakobs.

The pale smudge of his face hovers between the upturned collar of his overcoat and the brown fur of his sable hat. Saggy skin, downcast eyes, pink lips visible beneath his ragged mustache. His hands buried in his pockets, he lowers himself onto the bench next to me, groaning under his breath when the bench takes his weight. The sound seems to emanate from the cloud of steam in front of his mouth.

Neither of us speaks for a long time.

"The cold aches my bones," he says at last.

Ilya's voice is soft. No sharp edges or inflections. A prisoner's murmur, a low sound meant for one pair of ears, intended to fall softly from his lips to be borne away by the wind. The Gulag's hardest lessons are never forgotten.

I finger the note in my pocket, written in pencil on brown paper torn from a grocery bag and left with the counter man at Vadim's Café. *Victory Park, the bench nearest the obelisk, tomorrow, 6 o'clock. Don't tell the General.* The letters are crooked, blurry where his shaky hand smudged the writing. Signed *Ilya*, the same way he signed his samizdat manuscripts fifty years ago, risking death or imprisonment by attaching his name to forbidden literature.

He shifts his weight and sighs. "You've been away."

I sweep my gaze around the park, looking for moving shapes in the gloom, for a flicker of light from a camera lens or a cigarette, for anything that doesn't belong.

"America. Los Angeles, mostly. Chasing phantoms from the Soviet days."

On the trail of a decrypted World War II-era cable and the photo of a man who turned out to be my long missing father, a Cold War defector. I still don't know what to make of that episode, or whether I made the right decision in the end.

"It's warm there all the time," I add.

Ilya nods. The movement makes his coat rustle against the rime on the back of the bench. "We don't fit in places like that. Just as they aren't suited to here. Cold changes a person."

The sound of heavy footfalls and labored breathing carries to us before a woman appears on one of the paths, chugging toward us. Rumpled, bundled into several layers of clothing, old or injured by the looks of her tottering gait. She passes without a word or a glance.

A sliver of moon finds a gap in the clouds and brightens the evening gloom. I blow into my gloved hands to warm them, waiting for the woman to disappear around a bend in the path.

"Are you still writing?"

"Bah. Who is left to publish what I have to say? Worse, who will read it?"

"*Novaya Gazeta* might print it."

"Not since Anna and all the others. They are afraid, like everybody else. I don't blame them."

A nighthawk flits overhead, chasing the moon behind a claw-shaped cloud, blacking out the silver light. I think of Anna Politkovskaya, gunned down in her apartment building. And of Magomad Yevloyev, another fierce Kremlin critic whom I got to know during my years on the border of Chechnya and Ingushetia, shot in the head while "resisting arrest." And Natalya Estemirova of the human rights group Memorial, abducted and killed outside her home in Grozny. So many others. One after another they disappear, beacons of light snuffed out by an ocean of darkness.

I turn up my collar. My nose and cheeks feel frozen. "How many dead journalists now?"

"Since Putin took power? Twenty-one. More if you count unexplained accidents. Shot, stabbed, beaten, poisoned, pushed out of windows. Who knows how many others have been bullied or harassed into silence?"

He drags a crumpled handkerchief from his pocket and uses it to wipe his nose. The handkerchief looks old, red faded to pink from many washes

"And now one more. That's what I want to talk to you about."

The premonition of dread I felt before hardens into an acidic lump in the pit of my stomach.

"Who?"

He stands with a groan. Weakly stomps his feet against the frozen path, like a small child throwing a tantrum.

"Walk with me," he says, and I do, limping a bit as we wander slowly along the path toward the Orthodox Church, my stump grinding uncomfortably into the socket of my prosthesis. Sitting too long in cold weather does that now.

"Not *only* another journalist." Ilya's breath balloons from his mouth, lit like a mustard cloud by the overhead lamps. "Four were killed. Three of them students sent to a village called Metlino to study the geographic features there."

I try not to react, but his gaze sharpens as he reads something in my eyes or my posture.

"You know that place?" he says.

"I heard it mentioned not long ago. Metlino has interesting geography?"

He coughs for a long time, a wet, hacking sound, waving away my offer to thump his back to clear his lungs of phlegm. Icicles of condensation glisten like slivers of light in his gray mustache by the time the fit passes.

"Maybe the students were there for another reason."

"Such as?"

"Metlino is near the site of a radiation explosion. It was one of many villages contaminated with the fallout when a nuclear plant called Mayak blew."

My fear hardens into near certainty. I don't have enough spit to swallow. My gaze drifts to the golden domes of the church. They remind me of the view I once had from the window of a room in the Astoria Hotel in St. Petersburg. A different dome threw golden rays through the parted drapes that night.

Ilya clears his throat. I realize he's been staring at me.

"So?"

"Yes, *so* is always a good question." He offers a fatalistic Russian shrug. "Maybe I make too many connections these days. Think too much, allow events that don't really belong together to blend into something sinister in my mind."

He coughs again. Moist air billows in jaundiced clouds around his cupped hands. When the spasm ends he wipes his nose with the handkerchief.

"So these four, this journalist and these students, they made problems for someone. I don't know who, but he"—Ilya knits his shaggy eyebrows while he considers the word—"or *she*, maybe. More than ever they are women now, like Valya, yes? The point is that somebody didn't like them being there."

"How?"

"Shot. Executed."

I stop. Turn a slow circle to make sure we are still alone in the night.

"Why should I care?"

He waits until my gaze catches and holds on his. "The three students? Who knows? Perhaps just the wrong place, wrong time? But the fourth victim, she is more important to Russia, and to you."

I know the name on his lips. But for some reason I need to hear him say it. I don't know why. I need to hear him say her name.

So I ask.

"Who?"

He wipes his nose, regarding me with an expression that borders on sympathy. His eyes are rheumy, red-lined, sad.

"Kato."

Chapter Two

Kato.

Her real name was Katarina Mironova, but she wrote under the nom de plume "Kato." She covered the second Chechen war as a correspondent for several Western news magazines. Later I learned that her byline appeared in *Time, Newsweek,* and *The Economist,* along with numerous daily newspapers around the world. But I didn't know any of those things the first time I met her a decade ago.

She was traveling with a mechanized Russian column that appeared in my binoculars as it wound along a muddy road clinging to the side of a mountain somewhere between the rubble of Grozny and the high village of Shatoi. I'd been on solitary patrol for more than a week, searching the steep-walled valleys and craggy redoubts for Chechen rebels. Shatoi being the birthplace of a rebel leader with hundreds of men under his command in those days, the region seemed as good a place as any to look.

I spied the convoy near dusk. Ten Russian GAZ Tigers—vehicles similar to American Humvees—interspersed along a line of armored personnel carriers, eight-wheeled Zils mounted with surface-to-surface artillery missiles, and MAZ heavy haulers with T-90 battle tanks on their back. Frozen clods of mud fountained into the air behind the tires and tracks. Soldiers huddled on top of the armor in clumps, like wrinkled boulders in their green slickers, seeking meager shelter from the cold and wet.

I scrabbled down the rough granite side of a ravine and waited in the middle of the road with my Kalashnikov at my side. I was dressed in a gray-and-white camouflage smock, and I had to unwind the woolen wrap on the lower half of my face to talk. Gaunt, tired, weathered by exposure and armed with enough weapons to fight the war by myself, I must have appeared as an unholy apparition to the major who climbed out of the lead Tiger to demand my papers and a password.

He listened while I established my bona fides, the two of us standing there at the head of his column in a muddy road darkened by the shadows thrown by the mountain ridges and scudding clouds. Then he retreated to the Tiger to use his radio.

When he returned, he saluted smartly and asked what I needed.

Food and provision, I told him, ticking through my list while his adjunct took notes. Exchanging few words, I gave him a sealed report with instructions to put it into the hands of his superiors. I knew they would see that it got to the General.

The sun melted into a blood-red pool behind the mountains while we talked, coloring the bottoms of the clouds a lighter shade of rose, dropping the temperature to bitter cold.

When we finished, the major ordered his men to bivouac there for the night.

I found a fire and warmed a tin of sardines, then squatted with my meal in the gloom outside the circle of firelight. Punched the blade of my combat knife through the lid of the sardines and a tin of condensed milk and ate with my fingers, using crusts of bread warmed by my body to scoop out the milk. By habit I ate slowly to fool my stomach into believing it was getting more than it was.

I saw the woman before she saw me. She didn't stand out because of her clothes. Knit cap with earflaps, a man's greatcoat hanging loosely from her shoulders, hard-shell outer pants tucked into fur-lined boots. What caught my eye was the graceful way she moved. Her first flowing step set her apart from all the others around the fire.

One of the men sitting near her cocked his head toward me and said something I couldn't hear. They talked for a few minutes while she studied me, her features indistinct in the firelight. After a moment of hesitation, she plucked a kebob off the rack over the fire and picked her way across the frozen mud between the rocks and the scrub brush. She stopped a few meters away and leaned against a boulder.

"You are *spetsnaz*, Special Forces?"

Backlit by the fire, still only a shape and, now that she was so close, a smell. Wood smoke and pine and lavender soap. Eyes that gleamed in the faint light of the moon and the stars peeking between the clouds, but I couldn't tell their color.

"Alpha Group?" she said, naming one of our counterterrorism units. "Vympel?"

When I didn't respond she pushed away from the boulder and squatted near me, resting her haunches on her heels, elbows on her knees. The Chechen way. She handed me the kebob she'd carried from the fire.

"One of the men told me you didn't take any food. They have plenty for now. They restocked in Gudermes."

Our hands touched when I took the stick. Hers was warm, and when she withdrew it mine felt colder than it had a moment before.

She took off her cap and raked her fingers through shoulder-length hair, making a sound akin to a purr as the tension eased in her scalp. Black hair streaked with red highlights. Or maybe the reddish streaks were no more than reflected firelight. I couldn't be sure. Dark brows, straight nose, full lips. High cheekbones that shaped her face into an oval.

"My name is Katarina. People call me Kato."

I bit into the kebab. Onions and goat meat still hot from the flames. I licked my fingers. "Kato. Like Stalin's first wife."

A flash of pearly teeth when she smiled, nodded. "'Sweet and beautiful,' Stalin called her."

"So sweet I can smell you from here."

She pouted her lower lip. "Not beautiful?"

I didn't answer. My camouflage gear chafed my skin, which felt uncomfortably hot, although an icy wind blew off the mountains. The last time I'd been with a woman was six months before in Mozdok. A widow, her face etched with grief and despair. We each drew a measure of comfort from the other that night, but when we parted the next morning I think we both still carried the same scars and were haunted by the same demons that had pushed each of us into the arms of the other.

Kato shifted her weight from one heel to the other. A small, natural movement, as if she were swaying to the sound of music in her head. She didn't say anything more for a long time. Just studied the glowing stars and rocked on her heels and rubbed her hands together to stay warm. But each small shift brought her a little closer to me.

And closer to my pack, which leaned against a rock at my feet.

One of the soldiers approached from the fire and offered her more to eat. She looked at me and raised her brow. I shook my head, and she smiled at the soldier and said no. When he left, she angled her gaze toward me.

"Your name is Volk."

The major hadn't told her that. He wouldn't have dared. Most likely she'd overheard the soldiers talking. Speculating the way they tend to do when they know some small part of something they see. Pebbles crunched under her boots as she shifted her weight, advancing a few centimeters closer to my pack.

"Don't answer, then. But I hear stories. An assassin. Always alone. A patriot protecting mother Russia, true? But who do you think you're protecting her *from*? And who are you protecting her *for*?"

Firelight traced the line of her jaw. Eastern features, olive skin, eyes tilted up, still impossible to see their color.

"We just left a village near Shali," she said quietly. "Do you know that place? These troops and others executed a sweep, a *zachistka*."

Her face twisted when she said the word, an ugly one in this context, where it means that the people of the area were marched through a filter of interrogations, strip searches, and body-cavity probes. Sorted and sifted and examined. Treated with cruel indifference at best. Abused, tortured, killed and ransomed in the worst cases. *Zachistka*. Think of an enormous metal grater slicing through the soft cheese of human flesh.

"The village was surrounded and secured. The soldiers conducted house-to-house searches and ID checks. They arrested all the men aged fifteen to sixty and loaded them onto transports. I don't know where they took them."

I kept my features flat, expressionless, and said nothing.

"A sixteen-year-old girl was murdered," Kato whispered. "A lieutenant colonel named Baburka dragged her into the woods. Raped her all through the night. Strangled her at dawn, then buried her."

"You witnessed this?"

She shook her head fiercely. "No. They held me at a base camp outside of Shali. I learned the story from two of the men who were there when the girl was abducted. Another heard her cries in the woods and saw the freshly turned earth."

A fine scar adorned the soft skin below her left eye, visible in the dim light as a silver line. I gazed at the camp, where the fires still burned and the men were carving out their hollows for the night, then I stared off into the distance.

"Why tell me?"

Now she was close enough to reach out and catch my sleeve, forcing me to look at her again. Green eyes, I saw for the first time. Wide and imploring.

"I know people who know things. They talk to me. That is my job, you see? To persuade people to talk." She tightened her grip, pulled herself closer to me. "They say you're not like the others."

I broke her hold and stood up in one smooth motion. No stab of pain, no wince, because I was still whole then, my left foot still years away from being mangled, crushed, amputated. She looked small and vulnerable below me, staring at me while she worked the zipper on one of the compartments on my pack.

"You're in danger here," I said.

She pushed off the top of my pack with her hand as she stood. Her gaze never left mine.

"I've written an account of what happened. I can't keep it, I'll be searched, and censored. I need you to see that it gets to my editor in Moscow."

"No."

"Then you're not the man they say you are."

Cloaked in darkness and with the black slope of the mountain behind our position, the soldiers wouldn't be able to see us. But they would know we were still there, and they would be curious.

"Go. Tear up your story. Write it again when you're safe, if you must. Those aren't the kind of messages I deliver."

Her lips twisted, and her eyes flashed, sad to angry in an instant. "How true. You deliver bullets and bombs and missiles."

We stood staring at each other for several seconds, her breath warming my cheek. Then she wheeled away, her back stiff, her hands clenched at her side. Seconds later I slung my pack over my shoulders and slipped into the night, climbing higher at a steady pace until I reached an outcrop that overlooked the camp.

I couldn't see Kato. Only circles of firelight and drifting shadows and the reflected copper glow from the armored sides of the transports and rocket launchers. Whorls and lines of orange and red, like lava welling in the cracks of the earth.

I wouldn't see Kato again for nearly six months. But I thought about her all the time in those days. Before Valya, I was always alone. Lonely in the mountains, lonely on leave, lonely in the company of others.

That night on the outcrop above the camp I searched my pack. Found a hand-sized notepad in the outside pocket where she had placed it during her rocking dance on her heels.

Held it. Turned it in my hands.

Blue cover. Perforated pages and spiral wire at the top. Most of the pages already torn out, only seven remaining, all of them covered with a neat cursive. Her lavender scent clinging to the paper.

I didn't read it then. The moon and stars offered too little light between the clouds. I would read it later and make up my mind then.

Ilya stomps his feet to warm them, the sound gunshot-sharp in the cold night, awakening me from my reverie. I scan the area. The closest people are over a hundred meters away, shadows in the night. My companion says Kato's name and then something else that I don't catch.

"What did you say?"

He hunches his shoulders, this small, gnome-like man with a grim message.

"I said Kato makes *twenty-two* dead journalists."

Chapter Three

Grayson Stone picks his way through the tables on the casino floor, his gaze locked on a knot of men and woman standing around a craps table.

Delveccio and his entourage.

The men in their thirties and forties, the women much younger, late twenties at the oldest. The whole group liquored up after nearly twelve hours of hard partying that started on the first tee of the Wynn course. All of them hooting loudly as the dealer's voice carries over the din.

"Hard eight, winner!"

Delveccio stretches on tiptoes to reach into the pit for his money.

Five-five, two-fifteen, according to his FBI file.

Bullshit.

To Stone's trained eye Delveccio looks two inches shorter and twenty pounds heavier. Daphne Graham—formerly attached to an elite unit within the NSA, now one of Stone's hired hands—stands four feet behind Delveccio, wearing a tiny earphone. She had described the man more accurately during last night's planning meeting. "Two hundred and thirty pounds of hate," she'd said, biting into a one of the carrot halves she carried in a plastic bag in her purse.

Stone cruises the gaming area, scanning for members of Delveccio's security detail. He spots three, all men. One seated at a blackjack table, paying more attention to his cards than to his boss. Another, a black guy wearing low-slung jeans and a hoodie, propped against the metal railing near a row of flashing slot machines. And, standing near Graham behind Delveccio, a fiftyish man in a blue windbreaker and a Panama hat.

All accounted for.

Stone keeps sweeping his gaze, looking for unknowns. Those are the ones that get you killed. But everybody else appears to fit in.

Cocktail waitresses in togas, all tits and ass and long legs. Harried dealers eyeing cards, dice, and bounding metal balls. Pit bosses watching the dealers and eyeballing the players. Crowds flowing between the ropes, looking for an empty seat at a table, a mark, a flash of thigh from a hiked-up skirt, or just plain gawking. Near one of the bars a couple of hookers nurse their drinks, waiting to relieve a lucky winner of some easy money.

Little has changed in the time it has taken for Stone to make his way down to the casino floor from the observation center. Up there, a multitude of cameras records every movement for the watchful eyes of the casino's staff and another member of Stone's team.

One player at a craps table near Delveccio's looks like a cornfed Nebraska girl, complete with a yellow ponytail sticking out the back of a red Huskers hat. But she's no college student. Casino spotters ID'd her an hour ago, when Stone was still upstairs. They zoomed the cameras for him. The bottom of her glass is coated with a sticky substance. Every so often she casually rests the drink on the racked chips of the player next to her, then lifts it away with a load of black chips stuck to the bottom, pockets her take, and moves on. Casino security hasn't moved in to stop her little swindle. Not yet, at least. Not for another few minutes.

They're under strict orders to stay the fuck out of the way until Stone and his team finish their business. Which at this moment means pulling Delveccio out of the casino the same way you yank a rotten tooth out of an infected gum.

Stone settles into position behind the black guy in the hoodie and says "Go" quietly into the mic in his lapel.

Nothing happens.

But Stone knows that somewhere below his feet in the parking garage a van is firing its engine, pulling ahead to the service elevator, sliding side doors open to receive cargo. Graham, Gibson, Jackson and the others are on hyperalert, focused on the target and any person or thing that might get in their way.

And, from the pickup station in the bar, a spiky-haired cocktail waitress wearing a name tag that says "Miranda" is heading for the table with Delveccio's last round of the evening.

Maybe his last ever.

Ten seconds later Miranda rounds an enormous column, serving tray balanced on her shoulder, prancing like a runway model with a swaying stride that causes the guy in the hoodie to straighten and crane his neck to get a better look.

Her real name is Rachel Parks. Stone plucked her from a group of promising candidates at the CIA more than a year ago. Money bought what he needed—looks, brains, talent—and building a strong team was one reason why Stone got ahead. Delveccio wasn't on his radar then. Who'd have thought he would someday have to live *and* work in this desert cesspool? Low taxes and easily purchased politicians made the decision to locate here inevitable, not only for Graystone Security but for Echo and Blackhawk as well. But none of them like doing jobs on their own turf.

Stone tracks Miranda's progress, looking for signs of a fuckup. Sees none. Miranda had proven to be a fortunate choice. Because, although Delveccio swings from both sides of the plate—a fact he goes to great lengths to conceal—he usually goes for women. And with women he likes busty redheads.

"Where you been, baby?" Delveccio shouts at her over the din.

He's still rolling, been at it almost fifteen minutes so far. He thinks he's on a hell of a streak, that much is obvious by the way he shakes the dice and pounds them onto the table and mutters some sort of incantation before each throw. Stacks of chips everywhere on the blue felt of the table. All the gamblers in Delveccio's retinue keep raising the stakes. "Great fucking roll, man!" one of them shouts, and another, nicknamed Jimmy D, whoops and slaps the girl next to him on the ass, their greed fueled by alcohol and God only knows what drugs.

But Delveccio's good fortune is simply part of the plan, his run kept alive with the help of the dealers and rigged dice. He won't seven-out unless Stone tells someone he should.

Miranda hands Delveccio his drink. A sweating crystal rocks glass filled with vodka and knock-out drops. Some kind of nasty barbiturate. "Drop a horse on its ass," according to the M.D. who gave the drug to Stone a few hours ago.

Delveccio kills the drink in one gulp, just as he's been doing all evening. Miranda takes the empty glass and hands him a full one.

This one he sips, talking to her between swallows. His left hand drifts down to her thighs and ass, then scrapes over the front of her sequined crotch, lingering there as she presses against him with a vampish giggle. His heavy eyelids are half closed, his rubbery lips parted as he concentrates on what he's feeling.

Then he stops caressing her. Drops his glass. Drags one hand on the rail of the craps table for balance. Sways. Closes his eyes and then opens them suddenly, like a sleepy driver realizing he's about to nod off.

The hoodie-wearing watchdog in front of Stone straightens. Says, "This ain't right" under this breath.

Stone pulls a Taser from the pocket of his jacket and, holding it low, tazes the hoodie watchdog in the small of his back. The man stiffens, groans, topples all in one piece like a felled tree. Gibson catches him under the arms and hauls him off.

The same thing happens at the same time to the others in Delveccio's security detail. Each taken out with surgical precision at exactly the same moment, all sound absorbed by the clamor of the casino, all movement lost in the swirl of gamblers and waitresses and shift-changing dealers. Delveccio's bodyguards are there one moment, gone the next.

Meanwhile, Delveccio appears to be choking. His face has turned the redness of a baboon's ass. One of the women in his entourage says something to him, then turns and shouts at the boxman sitting on the other side of the table in front of the rows of colored chips. Stone can't hear the words, but he can read her lips easily enough.

Get a doctor.

The boxman—Special Agent Jackson, on loan to Stone from the FBI—signals immediately to the pit boss, who picks up the white phone mounted on the podium behind the table. Two paramedics arrive within seconds. Too fast unless they'd been waiting nearby, but nobody will notice, not right away. They clear the area, strap an oxygen mask over Delveccio's sweaty red face, and load him onto a stretcher.

Stone circles the casino floor. Sixty seconds in. None of the men and women in Delveccio's group—apart from his security detail—seems to suspect anything's amiss. They're milling around, concerned for their boss, questioning the paramedics.

Wait. What about Jimmy Diamonds?

Jarco Dabizha, called Jimmy Diamonds or Jimmy D because of the jewelry he wears like encrusted armor, pieces of which he leaves behind with the bodies of his victims, is peering around like a rat sniffing for food. No dummy, Jimmy D. His antenna are up. He knows something's going down.

Stone steps closer to the craps table. Keys the mic. Says, "Watch Jimmy D."

Jimmy fucking D. Got his start as an enforcer for one of the gangs in some jerkwater Siberian village that was a crossing on the trade route into Asia. Body count so high even the degenerates got sick of him, sent him overseas a decade ago. Three kills in Vegas the local police know about, probably half a dozen more they don't. A left arm in a dumpster off Industrial Boulevard was all they found of the last guy. A diamond clutched in the blackened hand. Turned out to be CZ, Jimmy being notoriously cheap except when it comes to his tailored clothes and jewelry.

Ok, he looks suspicious. No problem, he won't recognize anybody on Stone's team.

Or so Stone tells himself.

But all of that changes in an instant when Jimmy spots him and his eyes grow big. Jimmy's prominent Adam's apple bobs, and he reaches beneath his jacket.

"Graham, take him down. Now!"

Daphne Graham has already moved to within a yard of the lanky killer. Primed for the order. She fires her Taser into his back before he can pull a gun. Razor-thin and tall, Jimmy D arches his back and cuts loose with a howl that sounds like a cat with firecrackers tied to its tail, then drops. Everyone except the paramedics working on Delveccio turn to see what happened, but Graham is gone, already melted into the crowd.

The pit boss makes another phone call. Just as the paramedics load Delveccio onto the stretcher and haul him away, a second set appears and takes charge of Jimmy D. Casino security personnel are all around, covering the craps table, reassuring all the patrons, telling them that things will be just fine now, not to worry, have another drink, both the gentleman are in good hands now, they'll be fine, relax, enjoy yourselves.

Stone disappears behind a column as they herd the remaining members of Delveccio's entourage toward the exit. Once he's out of sight of the casino floor he walks faster, each long stride eating up ground.

By now Delveccio will be in the van. In ten minutes he'll be on the Interstate heading northwest to a private residence in the Vegas suburb of Summerlin. Stone had rented the place after he found out it had a basement that could be soundproofed.

Nobody will be able to hear Delveccio scream.

They'd gotten their man. Time to get down to business. Focus on what must be done. Rip Delveccio apart, if need be. Do to him what he did to the two coyotes in the desert.

But one question looms large: How the fuck did Jimmy D recognize him?

Chapter Four

By the time Stone arrives at the Summerlin house, the two "paramedics," Special Agents Carson and Baker, have chained Delveccio spread-eagle to the bare metal frame of a double bed in the basement. The springs sag and creak under his weight. His arms and legs are stretched to their fullest. Six-inch lengths of chain attached to each ankle and wrist are needed to complete the X.

Five-five my ass.

A red ball gag with a wide leather strap prevents Delveccio from talking. But his eyes are goggling, frantic, one of them so bloodshot that the brown iris appears to be an island in a sea of red. The room smells of wet concrete and the sharp tang of fresh urine. Delveccio has pissed himself.

"We gave him a shot of adrenaline to wake his ass up," Carson says.

Carson is almost as tall as Stone, but softer. Where Stone is thick-skinned and thick-skulled, built for violence, Carson looks like a former college athlete gone to seed. Which he is. He is also an FBI field agent who's been keeping tabs on Delveccio for three years. Stone didn't pick Carson for his team. Carson was assigned. But the man has the right mentality to suit this operation.

Daphne Graham enters the room behind Stone. Regards Delveccio with an expression bordering on pity.

"This is terrible. Drugged, chained.…It's not right."

Stone feels the familiar slow burn of rage, even though Graham is parroting a script they prepared two days ago. Mealy-mouthed bullshit. Fine for politicians and the press, the kind of people who have the luxury of high-minded morals. Not so good in the real world.

How else does one defeat evil?

He once asked that question during a private briefing to one of the Congressional oversight committees looking into the question of torture at Afghanistan's Bagram prison and elsewhere. He'd wanted to laugh in the face of their righteous indignation. Where in the history of the world was torture *not* a commonly used tool? What country would *want* its military and intelligence operations to fight with one hand tied behind their back against an enemy that used children as shields or high-value targets? Nobody was able to give him an answer that day in the hearing room.

So he answered his own question.

"Two situations," he told them. "First, a ticking time bomb strapped to the person you love most in the world. Everybody— you, me, and Mother Theresa—would do whatever we needed to do to save our loved one.

"The second case is a little tougher. Your prisoner has information about an attack that could kill thousands, tens of thousands. You don't know where or when, but the threat is real. What then? I say the people charged with defending this country have a moral imperative to act to save its citizens. And if someone righteously disagrees with that course of action, I respect their opinion in the same way I respect conscientious objectors. They can and should be exempt from combat duty and the business of intelligence. But don't put them in charge of Centcom or the CIA."

Delveccio writhes. His eyes roll in his head as he strains against the chains.

"I'm not going to cover anything up for you, Stone," Graham says, and Stone smiles grimly at the echo of the question asked of him at the end of the Congressional hearing.

"Why would we put a man like you in charge of anything?" said a congressman from Vermont who'd gotten rich suing doctors.

Two months later, the congressman got his wish. Stone was out. A free agent.

He'd have done it ten years ago if he'd known the money was so good. But the part he liked best was the freedom from rules. The rules apply inside out, but not outside in.

"You tell me, Graham," Stone says, following the script. "How many lives are you prepared to sacrifice in order to spare this asshole a little distress? Fifteen minutes, that's all I need. Fifteen minutes to treat him the same way he treated those two coyotes out in the desert."

Coyotes meaning people in this case.

Two men driving a box truck stuffed with fourteen illegals and three hundred pounds of uncut heroin. Street value of more than $17 million. Bound for Vegas. Delveccio and his men wanted the heroin. They didn't want witnesses.

So they lined up the illegals and shot them one by one in the back of the head.

One tried to escape.

They ran him down with an SUV. Hitched him to the bumper with a chain. Dragged him through the rock and scrub brush and cholla for a few hundred yards. They didn't stop until the chain got wrapped around a mesquite tree and ripped his feet off. What was left looked like a chunk of raw hamburger. Barely identifiable as human.

But what they did to the two coyotes was worse.

They tied ropes to their wrists and ankles and stretched them off the ground between the SUV and a pickup. Played with them for a couple of hours. Cut them. Stripped skin in long curlicued ribbons of flesh. Burned them alive.

Too much to attribute solely to latent viciousness and mere sadism. Something more at work. Something personal.

One of the cameras on a satellite used by the National Geospatial-Intelligence Agency to pinpoint narcotics traffickers, human smugglers, and terrorists caught the scene on a surveillance photograph. Must have been during the middle of the festivities, according to the NSA analyst, because the men were still suspended between the vehicles at the time the picture was taken.

Stone loses no sleep over the fate of the coyotes. Modern-day slave traders. They can kill one another off any way they choose as far as he's concerned. But the memory of their mutilated bodies still causes his stomach to flip and crawl up his throat.

Carson hands Stone a long-bladed hunting knife.

Delveccio's eyes widen. He thrashes. Tries to say something through the ball gag. Stone slaps the flat of the blade into his palm, making a sharp, cracking sound.

"Just like those poor bastards in the desert, Delveccio. Couple of notches in your chest, then tear away the skin. See how long we can make each strip. What do you think? Couple of feet? Maybe I can peel one all the way from your throat to your heel."

Delveccio writhes and rattles the chains. Bug-eyed. Drenched in sweat. Wet stains under his arms and at his crotch. Keening around the gag.

"Cut off his clothes," Stone says to Carson.

"I'm out of here," Daphne Graham says.

"Me, too," Baker says.

Baker looks like a bookkeeper. Horn-rimmed glasses, his hair oiled and parted on one side. But he's smart, dedicated, ruthless—nowhere near as squeamish as he's acting. A few hours ago he had himself volunteered to take the knife to Delveccio. That was one of the reasons Stone had assigned him to leave with Graham.

Doing it is one thing. Liking it is another.

"Fine, go. What about you?" Stone says to Carson.

"I think I'll stick around," Carson says. "Long as I get a turn, too."

Delveccio squirms some more, grunting and writhing as Graham and Baker leave.

Carson cuts away Delveccio's clothes while Stone watches like a butcher inspecting a hog. Fat ripples, gooseflesh, shriveled pecker. *More like two-fifty*, he decides.

"You're a fucking mess, Delveccio," he says conversationally as he approaches the bed.

He makes a two-inch incision through skin and fat just above Delveccio's pectoral muscle. Delveccio screams, but the sound is muffled by the gag, so it seems to emerge from the cut in his chest rather than from his mouth.

Stone notches another cut, forming a bloody V and creating a flap to grip and pull, like tearing open a delivery package. Delveccio struggles so violently that the bed frame scrapes a few inches across the concrete floor. Carson slaps him, drawing blood from his lip. Delveccio's choked scream turns into a moan of terror.

Stone puts his mouth next to Delveccio's ear.

Whispers. "I want to know about the dead coyotes."

"Ummhumph!" Delveccio nods so hard the bed moves again.

"This is a one-time offer. You're going to tell me everything the first time, right? Any sign of bullshit, I'll skin you alive no matter how much you talk. I'll do it for sport. Nod your fat fucking head to say you believe me."

Delveccio shakes the entire bed when he nods.

Carson looks disappointed. Stone motions for him to remove the gag.

"Tell me you believe me, shithead."

"I believe," Delveccio moans. "I believe you, man."

Soft. How the hell does a guy like this last for so long?

Stone pulls Carson into a corner. "This is the guy who's been running you people ragged for three years?" he says under his breath.

"Who the hell are you to take a break from your cushy overseas gigs and lecture us?"

Stone shakes his head, returns to the bed, and squats next to Delveccio's ear.

"First thing I want to know," he purrs, "is what the fuck were two Russians doing in the Nevada desert with a cargo of Mexican illegals and heroin?"

Chapter Five

Ilya and I leave Victory Park together. He takes the train south toward his home in the Konkovo district, and I ride the line to central Moscow.

A pack of kids crowds into the car just before the doors close. Young, freshly scrubbed, mostly male. The boys with their heads shaved or cropped short, two of them arm in arm with girls wearing tight jeans, sweaters, and leather jackets.

Nashi Youth. *Nashi* meaning "Ours!" The right-wing incarnation of Komsomol, the youth wing of the Communist Party. Created and funded by the Kremlin to conduct violent campaigns against opposition leaders, but now withering away in the wake of the latest elections.

"Nothing short of a paramilitary force to harass and attack enemies of the State," Kato had said bitterly during their heyday. "One more sign of our slide into fascism."

I close my eyes, holding the bar above the seats, swaying in rhythm with the train. I last saw Kato three months ago. Late in the afternoon we had sat and talked at a plastic table set on the outskirts of an open-air market, her words serious and direct, as always.

"Russia has a problem."

"Only one?"

"This is not a time to be funny."

A waiter passed our table, carrying a loaded tray. He cocked an eyebrow at us, and I shook my head, declining food and drink. Kato said, "Soup, bread." I don't think he recognized her.

She toyed with her spoon, looking down as she turned the silver bowl to examine her own reflection. Serious, almost brooding, her features shaded by her black hair hanging like a veil on either side of her face. No red highlights. I never saw them again after that night by the convoy in the mountains.

"I've been commissioned by the editor of Epilogue to write a story about Russia's nuclear program."

"Big topic," I said, trying to keep my tone neutral. *Dangerous topic*, I almost said.

Somewhere in her family history Kato had Japanese ancestry, and it showed in the olive luster of her skin and the angle of her eyes. She scowled at her reflection, lowered the spoon, and polished the shallow bowl with her thumb as if she were trying to erase the image there, her lips tight in concentration.

"The story begins in 1942," she said, earnestly rubbing the bowl with the pad of her thumb. "That's when Stalin launched the program he called *Uran*—probably meaning uranium, but maybe Uranus—in response to the Americans' Manhattan project. And it ends…well, the ending hasn't happened yet."

"Long story."

The waiter slid a steaming bowl of borscht and a plate of black bread in front of her. Kato stirred the dollop of sour cream into her soup, turning it from red to pink. She broke off a chunk of bread, dipped it into the soup, and shoved it into her mouth. Nothing dainty about the way she ate.

"Maybe long enough for a book," she said, chewing.

The waiter hovered near a long table crowded with a family of twelve. The adults stared in our direction, then looked away when they saw me notice them. Somebody at the table had recognized her.

"Stalin built ten nuclear gulags," Kato said. "Scattered from the Urals to Siberia. Given code names like Arzamas-16, Chelyabinsk-65, Krasnoyarsk-26, and Tomsk-7."

She narrowed her eyes, concentrating.

"Those nuclear gulags were the places where Soviet teams conducted research and produced the fissile materials for the Soviet bomb. 'Closed cities,' meaning their existence was kept secret. All of them have a history of nuclear disasters, environmental contamination, and public health scandals, all of it suppressed by the Soviet government."

"You want to write a history book?"

"Funny."

She tilted her bowl, scraped the lines of soup and bread crumbles into a spoon-sized pile, and ate the last bite with her eyes closed, her lips holding the spoon for a long time before she slowly withdrew it.

The look on her face reminded me of the summer night in Grozny when we saw each other for the first time after she gave me the notepad. We made a makeshift meal in the phosphorous white and green light of Russian flares and tracers, and we shared a mattress thrown onto the wooden floor of a gutted warehouse. In the morning I watched her eat potato pancakes and eggs fried in an iron skillet. Big bites, absorbed in her meal, doing everything but lick the skillet to get the last crumb.

Now I wish I had reminded her of that night and morning while we were there at the outdoor market with an evening filled with possibilities in front of us.

But I didn't.

"Those stories have already been told," I told her instead.

"Some of them, yes. But not all. People are still dying. Our water and crops are radioactive. And Europe uses Russia as a dumping ground for its nuclear waste. Out of sight, out of mind for them. Then they congratulate themselves on how environmentally friendly they are, as if an environmental disaster here means less than one in the south of France. How convenient for them. How superior they must feel."

She kept up a running monologue for a long time, pausing whenever someone came within earshot. I didn't say anything, just listened with half an ear and let her vent. I was preoccupied with my own problems then. Now I wish I had paid more attention.

All I can remember are snippets of what she said that day, like the broken words of a political speech recorded on 1940s-era audiotape.

Hundreds of square kilometers contaminated with radiation. Uranium, plutonium, and other radioactive waste discharged into our waterways. "High-level waste," she called it, those words carrying clearly through the distorted pops and gaps in my memory. Decommissioned facilities from which the radio-active material was never removed and never reduced to safe levels. Dispersal patterns and their effect on crops, livestock, and people. The symptoms of radiation sickness: nausea, vomiting, and diarrhea, followed by hemorrhaging and inflammation of the mouth and throat and, in severe cases, death within as few as two weeks.

Instead of listening closely, I watched her talk, admiring her, and not just for her bravery. She'd proven her courage many times in Chechnya. No different from Ilya writing his samizdat papers by flickering candlelight all those years ago, then sending them out to the world where they could come back to harm him in so many different ways.

No, I admired Kato for more than mere bravery. She harbored something more elemental than that, an abiding passion that drove her to shine a light on corruption, abuse of power, injustice.

Maybe I should have tried to talk her away from the story, just as a police negotiator tries to talk a suicide down from a ledge. But I think the truth is that whatever warning I might have given would have fallen on deaf ears.

The train sweeps into the Lubyanka station and sways to a stop. One of the Nashi Youth uses the toe of his boot to prod a man who has fallen asleep, then kicks him harder when he fails to get an immediate reaction. The man startles awake, realizes where he is, and scoots over to make room as more passengers enter and half a dozen get off. His cough is so deep in his lungs that it seems to collapse his chest.

The boys and their companions snicker. One of them points his chin at the man's jacket. It is dirty, with holes at the elbows and shoulders and frayed at the collar, the patch of the 506th infantry sewn onto the sleeve. The 506th was among the first troops to advance into Grozny during the first Chechen war.

"A fucking black," the first boy says.

The former soldier stares straight ahead and says nothing. Like most of our veterans, he must have heard the expression a thousand times, that or the word *Chechen*, always dripping off the contemptuous lips of his countrymen who remained safe and warm when the rest of us went south to fight the wars of Yeltsin and Putin.

One of the passengers starts to say something, then compresses her lips and looks down at the rubber mat on the floor of the train, her knuckles white from squeezing the handrail as we pull out of the station. Probably the mother, sister, or wife of someone lost in our dirty southern wars. The mother, sister, or wife of a *black*.

The Nashi who was so free with his boot steps closer to the soldier and leans over him, using the rail for balance.

"The world owes you a living now, eh? You go down there, you murder, rape, and steal, and then you come back here and tell us how bad you had it. How you're fucked in the head and need a pension for the rest of your worthless life."

While the Nashi has been harassing the ex-soldier, I've edged closer to him through the ranks of the other passengers. Now I'm near enough to touch him.

He starts to say more, but I don't give him a chance. I pretend to stumble, putting my back to all the other passengers except the soldier and him, and all in one motion I drive my rigid fingers into his throat. He staggers back, knees buckling, eyes wide with shock. I grab him before he can collapse, pulling him against me like a lover, with my mouth next to his ear.

"The black earth of Chechnya was drenched with blood," I whisper harshly. "We left our legs, our arms, our broken bodies. We left our fucking *souls* there."

He can't get enough air through his mangled windpipe. His body is stiff in my arms. The other passengers, including his friends, know something is wrong, but nobody is quite sure what's happening, and no one can hear me except the young tough in my arms. I squeeze him harder, like a Heimlich maneuver done face-to-face, forcing air into and out of his lungs. He starts breathing on his own again just as the train rumbles to a stop at Kitay-Gorod.

"You think about that the next time you want to kick a man," I whisper.

The soldier stands. I shove the Nashi into the empty seat. The back of his head smacks the window, but his expression doesn't change. He still can't control his own movements.

He may be badly hurt.

"He'll need a hospital," I tell his friends. They're still stunned, silent in the face of this quiet and unexpected violence.

I motion for the soldier to follow me onto the platform. One of the girls yells after me, "Hey, what did you do to him? Asshole!"

"Happens all the time," the soldier says as we watch the train pull away. He coughs again, his whole body shaking. "What can you do? Other than what you *did* do, of course."

I gesture toward the patch on his jacket. "How long were you there?"

"One year the first time. Then I re-enlisted. I don't know why, just stupid and crazy. Second time around, most of the good ones were gone. The ones who thought service to country was a duty. By my second tour, half the men in my unit had enlisted just to avoid prison sentences. But it didn't matter anyway. We were all fucking *vouchers*, there to be spent for the price of an officer's promotion or a goddamn tub of butter." The soldier motions over his shoulder at the departing train. "He's right."

I nod slowly, not agreeing or disagreeing, hardly seeing him at all anymore, already thinking of what I need to do. Arrange travel to Metlino, the place of Kato's murder. Gather the things I might need there.

And I'll need to talk to Valya about Kato, a difficult topic, to say the least.

The soldier says something to my back as I climb the stairs. I can't make out the words. He yells, "Thank you!" as I reach the landing, but I don't respond.

Something's been niggling at the edges of my consciousness ever since Ilya said Kato's name. Elusive, ill-defined. On the train, remembering Kato eating lunch at the outdoor market, the thought seemed closer, but it keeps slipping away.

And then it flowers fully in my mind.

Something Ilya said that would have struck a chord immediately if I hadn't already been so alarmed by the news I was about to hear.

"But the fourth victim, she is more important to Russia, and to you."

Ilya shouldn't have known that. *Nobody* was supposed to know that one of the men most trusted by the General—the commander of the 58th Army during the second Chechen war—was a source for one of the war's most vocal critics.

Chapter Six

Leaving the crowded metro station, I try to think of any way Ilya might have known about Kato and me.

Nothing comes to mind.

I recall Kato's last words to me as we said good-bye in the bustling throng in the market, standing so close together I could smell shampoo in her hair.

"I can't ignore this, Alexei," she said. "And I won't let other people ignore it, either. If the Western media pick up the story, the Kremlin will listen, and if not the Kremlin, then the United Nations."

She moved even closer and stared up into my eyes, our noses almost touching.

"My publisher wanted a working title for this, this…mess we've created. Something that would suggest the theme of the book, give readers a quick handle on the content."

"What did you choose?"

"I told them to call it *Slow Motion Chernobyl*. You get it?"

I nodded to say yes, go ahead.

"We're poisoning our air, our water, our food. We have been for decades."

"Look, Kato—"

"Listen to me! The story begins at Arzamus-75, a town built mostly by German prisoners of war 75 miles outside the city of Arzamus. Now it is called Sarov. Since 1946 it has been a nuclear weapons design facility. I went there last month and started asking questions. Instead of answers, the man I met with there fed me half-truths and lies."

"Who?"

"The people at the facility I visited called him Solo. Just that, Solo. No *sir*, no *doctor*, no *mister*. I don't know whether he is civilian or military. I don't even know whether that is his real name."

"Why are you telling me this?"

She held my gaze with fixed intensity, her brow furrowed.

"In 1957 an explosion occurred at Mayak, in the area north of Chelyabinsk. One of the reservoirs holding highly active liquid radioactive waste was defective. Radiation overheated, exploded, created radioactive clouds a kilometer high that were dispersed by the wind. They named the contaminated area the East Urals Radioactive Footprint, as if the limits are defined, the problem contained." Her voice dripped with contempt. "According to the authorities, the *footprint* covers twenty thousand square kilometers, where more than a quarter of a million people live. I believe the area is much bigger."

A nearby huddle of smokers regarded us curiously, their attention drawn by the intensity of her voice and the stiffness of her posture. She gripped my bicep fiercely and shook my arm.

"One village was hit harder than all the others. Twelve hundred inhabitants. Most of the ethnic Russians were evacuated, but not the Tatars. Nobody cared about them. The story is there, in the village. Metlino. A tiny bit of humanity on the banks of the Techa River."

The smokers ground their butts on the sidewalk and dispersed. Crowds swirled around us on the sidewalk. Steam bellowed out of a nearby grate and mixed with cigarette fumes and smoke from the grill. Kato released my arm, but she didn't move away. Her breath smelled like beets.

"If I were to get into trouble, you would help me, right? That's what you do, isn't it—find people?"

The General once put it differently. He and I stood on a ridge overlooking the village of Tsotsan-Yurt on a moonless night.

Cold air washing down the mountain behind us, breaking in the valley below on the blackened timbers of a mosque, still burning two hours after we took our revenge after losing five men in a firefight, tracers lancing through our ranks like green swords.

"Put your nose to the bloody ground and follow their spoor, Volk," he'd said with unmasked fury. "Take the fight to them. Slaughter them like pigs."

Kato regarded me silently, waiting for an answer.

I nodded. "I promise. If you are in trouble, I'll find you, and I'll help you. No matter what."

For the second time she gave me a spiral-bound notepad, although this time she put it into my hands. Red cover, scratched and dog-eared at the corners, five pages inside filled with writing and a sixth page covered with a strange drawing of a salamander.

"What am I supposed to do with this?"

"Nothing unless I disappear. Then read it. Follow the trail. You're the best I know at that. You'll know what to do."

PART II

The river where you set your foot just now is gone,
Those waters giving way to this, now this…

—Heraclitus of Ephesus

Chapter Seven

Two years after I met Kato, Valya bloomed into my life like a white rose sprouting from the black mud of Chechnya.

Magical.

Deadly.

Turned out that she had burrowed into a depression at the bottom of a ravine. She emerged from the muck seconds after three Russian contract soldiers passed within a meter of where she was hidden. They were dressed like the mercenary pirates they were. Camo pants, long underwear with the sleeves ripped off to show steroid-pumped muscles, slung bandoliers, wrap-around shades with chrome reflective lenses, AK-47s dangling by the straps.

Careless.

Overconfident.

Before I could save them Valya brought her Kalashnikov to bear and fired in controlled bursts that cut them down like wheat before a sickle. I learned later they were part of a group that had held her and several others at the filtration point near Achkhoi-Martan. Although the word *held* doesn't do justice to the things that were done there and elsewhere at other filtration points. Valya was taking a small measure of revenge that long-ago day.

Enormous gray eyes fired like storm clouds filled with lightning—they were the first thing that registered as she wheeled to face me when my boot made a sucking sound in the mud. After

that all I saw was the smoking barrel of her Kalashnikov swinging toward me in the second I needed to cover the three meters
between us and take her down in a clawing, biting, kicking heap.

Those same eyes are staring at me now, but they're no longer
lit with fury. They're filled with questions.

"You never told me you knew Kato."

"Everybody knew Kato."

"Not personally."

I don't respond immediately. Instead I walk to the open
kitchen of the loft Valya and I share, the sixth floor of a mostly
abandoned industrial building near Kitay-Gorod. High ceilings,
exposed ductwork painted brick red, concrete floor covered
with Asian throw rugs. Partitioned kitchen with brushed steel
appliances and burled walnut cabinets and granite countertops.
The domes of the Kremlin towers and cathedrals visible through
the east window.

I crack a can of Red Bull and chug the contents without
tasting it. Kato came into my life at random moments. At least
they seemed random at the time. Looking back I realize that
she always had a purpose behind her visits, however unplanned
they might have appeared.

"I helped her once in Chechnya."

"And?"

"She was a presence. Touched by greatness. Most other
people paled in comparison. I saw her after Chechnya and here
in Moscow, but not very often."

"What does that mean, you *saw* her?"

"We had lunch, sometimes dinner. She asked lots of questions. It was her nature to ask questions. I answered the ones I
could."

"Nothing more?"

"Nothing more."

"I've seen pictures of her, Alexei," Valya says dryly, but with
a hint of something deeper.

If I didn't know her so well I might have misconstrued her
meaning. I might have mistaken the emotion in her tone. But

I know her inside and out. The throatiness of her voice tells me all I need to know.

Right now she's not angry. She's not jealous. At least not yet.

I slip out of my shoulder holster. Strip off my shirt and toss it toward the utility room. Unfasten my belt and slide it free of the loops as I close the distance between us. She presses her hand against my bare chest, looking up so that I have no choice but to fall into those big, big eyes. I lower my face until they're all I can see, gray and roiled.

"Kato was beautiful, wasn't she?" I say.

"Yes," Valya whispers huskily. "Amazing and mysterious and so brave to write the things she wrote."

She lets me push her back onto the couch. Her white hair fans around her face like the petals of some exotic flower. Lips parted, eyes hooded, she arches her back to pull her sweater off. I slide my hand over the softness of her belly, feeling the heat of her arousal, the rise and fall of her breast, the urgent flutter of her heart.

"Then let's pretend she's here with us tonight."

Valya falls asleep after our lovemaking.

I don't.

Sleep eludes me. Pills work sometimes, but I don't use them often. Despite the elaborate security protecting the loft, I don't like the idea that I won't be able to spring to my feet fully aware at the first sound.

I slide one arm under my head and contemplate a photo hanging on the long wall opposite the windows. It shows the tilted hulk of the Pripyat Ferris wheel as seen through the window of an abandoned apartment after the Chernobyl reactor blew. Iconic black and white, used in the artwork for the movie poster of a film called *Living in the Zone*. Signed at the bottom by the director of the film. Sasha Tovar. Her signature flows over the cracked concrete beneath the Ferris wheel in smooth lines and confident curves, a metaphorical representation of the woman herself. Sasha Tovar, Prague beauty queen, uniquely talented director, now dead because of my mistakes.

I overpaid for the print and the negative. Purchased them on the website of a London auction house without regard for the cost. They could have tripled the price and I still wouldn't have hesitated.

Sasha captured evil and evoked emotion through the powerful imagery and narrative drive of her films. Kato did it with words. But both of them rendered their art and lived their lives in absolutes, drawing stark contrasts between good and evil. No retreat, no surrender, no fear.

Or maybe that's unfair, at least to Kato. She must have lived her life in constant fear. How many death threats did she receive every day? How many times did the Kremlin denounce her as a demagogue and a fanatic, an enemy of Russia and a friend to terrorists?

Consider what happened to others singled out by the Kremlin. Eduard Markevich. Aleksei Sidorov. Yuri Shchekochikhin. Dmitry Shvets. Vadim Kuznetsov. Vaghif Kochetkov. Anatoly Voronin. Anastasia Baburova. Magomed Yevloyev. And many others, including Anna Politkovskaya, Kato's even more famous sister-in-arms, and Natalya Estemirova, a representative of the international civil rights group Memorial.

Kato knew that grisly roster better than anybody.

Kato reported her stories in spite of her fear.

"You're awake?" Valya says, snuggling against me, her eyes half closed and heavy with sleep.

Moonlight filters in through the latticework in the windows, painting the loft with a glaze of chromium that reminds me of the mirrored glass that covered the soldiers' eyes when she killed them. She draws up her left leg, then covers it quickly with the blanket, still ashamed of the stump and the scars that mar what remains below the hinge of her knee. The prison doctor in Prague failed to smooth the rough edges of bone properly, so her prosthesis hurts her even more than mine does me.

"Like ice picks stabbing bone," she once described it.

Phantom pain still haunts me, too, but I've learned to live with it.

Valya hasn't. Not yet, anyway. She keeps a bottle of white pills hidden in a zippered compartment of her shoulder bag. They offer sweet release and a wicked high. Sensations that become all too familiar all too quickly, I know from personal experience. But Valya is not one to appreciate a lecture about the evil hook of pain pills.

I stroke the scar tissue on her leg. She stiffens, but I don't stop my caress.

"I'm going to follow Kato's path."

She nods, her head pitched down against my chest so that all I can see of her face is the curve of her cheekbone through a veil of white hair.

"What's going on with your safe house?" I say, trying to change the subject.

"Only seven there now. More next week, I think."

Seven women among scores that Valya has siphoned from the stream of human cargo trafficked through Moscow to all points of the globe. Located near the Moscow-Yaroslavl train station in Mytishchi among looming factories and smokestacks and power lines. Valya spent months finding the perfect place, supervising the demolition of three adjacent apartment units and building her safe house in their place. It has a common area for socializing, a communal kitchen, and a bathroom, all ringed by ten tiny cubicles, each one furnished with a dresser and a bunk bed. All told, room for two staff and eighteen refugees.

She built it in secret, using money from my now defunct porn and identity-theft operation. Operates it with the help of one staffer and her contacts with the Red Crescent in places like Georgia, Chechnya, and Ingushetia.

Valya lifts her head and looks at me. Her frown makes me think of the dead soldiers in the black mud.

"Alexei?"

"Hmm?"

"Did you sleep with Kato after we met?"

Valya has no right to ask that question. A year ago her affair with a stunning woman named Yelena Posnova caused both of us too much grief to measure. But that was different. I know it, and Valya will know it, too.

"No," I say.

She gazes into my eyes. "I know I'm not...I know what I did, Alexei. It's not fair, things just aren't fair, right? I just need to know that one thing."

All I can think about is her foot. Losing it changed her. Robbed her of a protective layer, of her bold, devil-be-damned charisma.

"No," I say again.

She nestles against me and pitches her head into the crook of my arm.

"I didn't think you would do something like that."

I stare at the picture of the Pripyat Ferris wheel. A symbol of a country abandoning her people, exposing them to danger by virtue of small lies that grew into something terrible.

Small lies. Sometimes small lies are meant to save something, not destroy it.

At least that's what I tell myself.

Chapter Eight

The next morning I climb out of bed while Valya is still asleep. Hop on one foot out of the bedroom and across the loft to the movie poster for *Living in the Zone*. Propped with one hand on the wall, I remove the framed poster and set it gently on the maple floor. Behind the poster is a wall safe. I open it and retrieve the notepad Kato gave me that day in the open-air market.

Something tingles my spine, a familiar sensation of being watched, and I turn to find Valya standing in the doorway to the bedroom, wearing my shirt, with all the buttons undone. She approaches and stands at my shoulder. Her hand grazes mine as she drags her thumb over the red cover of the little spiral-bound book.

"What's that?"

"Couldn't sleep?"

She shakes her head. "Neither of us. So what is this?"

"Kato's notepad. One of them, at least. I'm sure she had many. She gave it to me three months ago."

"Oh."

Then silence. I can't read the emotion on Valya's face. She taps the cover of the notepad with a chewed fingernail.

"What does it say?"

I flip the cover. At the top, a dateline: *29 September 2009, Mayak, 52 years later*. Beneath that, neat lines of writing, unadorned and businesslike. Valya reads it with me over my shoulder.

A woman stands with her daughter and grandson beneath a wooden alarm bell hanging like a man from a gallows on the banks of the Techa River. The bell tolls in memory of those who perished in the 1957 nuclear explosion at the Mayak Chemical Combine.

The faces of the two women are lined and worn, so haggard their age is impossible to determine. Mother and daughter, but they appear to be careworn sisters.

The boy's face looks like dough pounded into a misshapen mass. A disfigured lump of flesh with a yellow smear of teeth sandwiched between the mound of his chin and the hollow where his nose should be. He is smiling, I realize as I write this. The boy is smiling for the camera. But the combination of atrophied muscles and melted skin turn his smile into an awful grimace.

The story of this family begins in 1946 at a place called Arzamas-75, a "closed town" located 75 kilometers east of Arzamas. The birthplace of Russia's nuclear weapons program...

I flip more pages, looking for something that stands out from the rest. Stop at the drawing of a salamander.

"What is this?" Valya says.

"No idea."

I page back and we read the text more carefully.

Five pages tell the story of one family's collision with history. Three people, representing three generations, one family among the thousands of people living along the banks of the Techa River when a reservoir filled with a bubbling stew of highly-active liquid radioactive waste exploded.

She finishes reading the story before I do. When I'm done I turn back to the first page. Valya points to a blotch at the top where something had been written and erased. She holds the page to the light. I can make out only one word.

Epilogue.

"Her publisher."

She nods. "Right here in Moscow."

"I'll start there."

Chapter Nine

Delveccio squealed like a pig under the blade. After the first two cuts, the threat alone might have been enough, but Stone left nothing to chance. He wrung every possible drop of information from Delveccio's corpulent body.

The fat bastard talked so much that the FBI would be able to follow his roadmap from Vegas to Philly, Brooklyn, and Chicago. With Delveccio off the board, the rest of the dominos would fall one by one. The Bureau was thrilled.

Stone thinks otherwise.

Delveccio didn't have the answers Stone wants. Money laundering, million-dollar kickbacks on massive construction projects, drug deals with the cartels—none of that means shit to Stone.

He wants the trail that leads to Moscow.

And now he's just wasted two weeks of planning. Because Delveccio couldn't tell him jack shit about the two Russians that he didn't already know. Shakalov sent them across the border. So what. Everyone knew that. Who else could it be? Shakalov eliminated most of the competition years ago when he fled Russia and hit the ground running in Mexico City.

Delveccio had only one contact in Russia. A man he called Solo.

Delveccio had shrieked, wept, moaned. But he had nothing to give except for that one name.

Solo.

Just that, nothing more. No last name, no contact information, no description.

"The fucker talked to me on the phone," Delveccio said between tearful sobs and hiccups. "I tried to find out what I could. All I got was a shadow, man, I swear to God."

Stone questioned him longer and harder than he intended. The basement looked like a minor-league version of one of the torture chambers Stone and his group discovered in Baquoba, Iraq. That one had drills, blowtorches, electrified metal beds, and chains hanging from the ceiling. Not to mention so much dried blood the floors and walls appeared to have rusted. All of Delveccio's cuts were superficial. Two-inch-long flesh wounds. It looked like a lot of blood spilled, but only because Delveccio turned out to be a bleeder.

Now Stone uses a laptop in the master bedroom of the Summerlin house to research NSA files about a Russian named Solo.

Nada. Zilch. Nothing.

Next he plugs into the global network of computers known as ECHELON, an automated interception and relay system operated by the NSA and several U.S. allies. Satellite and Internet transmissions, cable and fiber-optic communication—all the data captured, crunched and rearranged into a semblance of coherence, then analyzed. He inputs the search terms *Solo, Russia, heroin, Mexico, United States*. Hits the Return key.

Waits.

The heat from the morning sun beats through the window blinds. Fucking January, and Vegas is still hot. He loosens his collar.

Watching the cursor blink on the screen, all he can think about is how screwed he is to be sitting in the middle of the goddamn desert jerking off with people like Delveccio. Vegas is the right place to set up a corporate office for a man in his business. And it gets its share of Afghan heroin and Mexican flesh-trading and al-Qaeda terrorist threats. But no matter how much money flows through it and how many bells and whistles they add, it's still a jerkwater town as far as Stone is concerned.

Last month was worse, though.

Three days in the steppe. Ass-deep in mud and irradiated water. Digging like a madman. Burying the fresh bodies with the old one. Then an hour later, two clicks away from the gravesite, burying the evidence: blood-splattered parka, untraceable 9 millimeter, soiled condom.

And all of that because of one fuck-up in Iraq.

Goddamn Iraq. Fucking sandbox.

Talk about *heat*. Bagdad heat beat the hell out of Vegas heat.

Sweltering all the time, no relief even in the shade. Loaded down with gear, feeling the squish of sweat in your boots with each step. Eaten alive by mosquitoes. Coated with a fine layer of sand and dirt before you can dry yourself off after a sixty-second shower. Barrel of your M16 too hot to touch without gloves.

Even hotter after the firefight began. A cluster fuck that started with one shot from a sniper. Location unknown. You hear the crack of a shot, you *move*.

Drop to the asphalt. Pedal your legs to push yourself on your back toward the safety of a wall. Try to disappear into a crack too small to trip over.

Think. Assess.

He was uninjured. Out of the immediate line of fire because Lieutenant Daly hadn't appreciated being saddled with "some D.C. prick," an attitude that initially pissed Stone off. "Privileges go with the territory," Stone had told him. Stone was still on the government payroll then. Officially described as "unattached," although "untouchable" would have been more accurate, at least until the day of the firefight.

Lieutenant Daly's hostility turned out to be a lucky break, because it meant Stone was a hundred meters from the rest of the platoon when the sniper cut loose and the shit hit the fan.

"Man down!"

"Where's the fucking shooter?"

Voices over the radio and from across the street. Screaming. Shouting.

Several more gunshots came from Stone's side of the street. A plume of smoke blew from a window cut into a building made of crumbling brick—only twenty meters up the road from Stone at the end of the same brick wall giving him cover. More men screaming across the road, another man hit.

Stone edged toward the window, his back to the wall.

Four meters away. At least two men chattering in Arabic.

A baby wailed.

Per the O-6 colonel at the morning briefing: *Fuckers use human shields all the time.*

The first man down—Ruiz, that was his name, Ruiz from San Antonio. The guys in his unit called him Rico. He was screaming like a banshee about his leg, his fucking leg. "Oh, please, God, help me!"

"Hold fire!" the lieutenant hollered into a radio. "Where the fuck is the cavalry?" he yelled, calling in air support.

Everyone shouting. But nobody firing on the American side. They obeyed the lieutenant's command. They didn't know where to aim. They were afraid of killing civilians.

"Stay down!" the lieutenant yelled. "Wait for help!"

"Gotta help Rico, man!"

"Where are those fuckers?"

Stone knew the answer to the last question.

Right above me, that's where. Fuck this.

Stone shed his pack. Took a deep breath. Slid the rest of the way along the rough brick, M16 on rock and roll. More shots fired. Above him, the ugly barrel of an AK-47 poked from the window, belching fire and smoke. When the AK withdrew, Stone leapt up and stuck his M16 through the opening and cut loose.

Emptied a magazine.

Dropped with his back to the wall. Ejected the magazine and slapped in another, hands shaking. Everything seemed to be happening in slow motion. All he heard was the dull roar of blood in his ears.

He popped back up, fired a burst through the window, dived in behind it, rolled, came up firing.

Dead guy in the doorway. Shot to rags. The walls on either side of him riddled with holes.

Another dead guy off to one side. He had caught a round in the face, a rose shot, his skull opened up like a flower. AK-47 on the floor, smoke leaking from the barrel.

Stone got to his feet. Drew a deep breath. Let it out slowly.

The lieutenant appeared at the window. He shouted something that Stone didn't catch. He motioned, and one of his men rolled through the window, immediately followed by another.

They flanked the doorway on the far side of the room. *Vertical coffins*. That's what one of the CIA specialists who was an LAPD officer before the war called doorways. Go through them and you die. The men communicated with practiced hand signals.

Go!

One of them was back in less than ten seconds. Richie Bellows, another Texan, always played shit-awful country music in camp.

Stone could hear again. More shots. More screams and shouts. From above, the *wump-wump-wump* of a hovering helicopter.

"It's bad, Loot," Richie said.

A woman was crying. Wailing, really. No mistaking the sound coming from the other side of the door.

Stone followed the LT through the door into a hallway. The far wall was ventilated with the same holes as the first one. Nothing to them, these walls. Like tissue paper stretched over Popsicle sticks. Across from the first door, another door. In the room on the other side, a woman.

She was huddled in a corner, rocking back and forth, making a sound that made Stone's skin crawl. A low moan that climbed in pitch to a keening wail, then subsided before starting up again. She wore a black burka and cradled a small bundle in her arms, captured as if in a cage behind the golden bars of sunlight beaming through bullet holes in the wall.

The lieutenant gently pulled away her sleeve to reveal her burden.

A baby swathed in a bloody blanket. A silent baby.

The mother wailed, a piercing cry of pain that shredded the dusty air.

Daly and the two soldiers stared down at her, looking dumb-founded. Stone's guts frosted, squeezing him like a fist made of ice. Lieutenant Daly stood transfixed for a long time, then wheeled on Stone and aimed a grease-blackened finger at his face.

"You disobeyed a direct order! You're going to fry for this, you bastard!"

The laptop in front of Stone makes a beeping sound. He startles out of his trance and stares at the screen.

ECHELON has generated more than a hundred hits. He scrolls through the list, culling those that obviously have no relevance. That leaves a dozen. One name appears in several of them.

Lazar Solovie.

Stone clicks on the bio. Reads for several minutes.

"Shit."

"What did you say?"

Daphne Graham stands in the doorway, giving him a quiz-zical look. Stone hits the Escape key.

"Nothing."

He clicks through a few screens and boxes to remove the cookies and then erases the search history. ECHELON will know. It keeps records of everything. But he doubts anyone from the NSA's SIGINT unit will care to look. Not now, and maybe not ever.

Graham moves from the doorway to stand as close as she can get, one hip brushing the other side of the table. She points down, toward the basement.

"That was a waste of time," she says.

"Delveccio? No good for us, but not so bad for the FBI. And they can go to work on Jimmy D, too."

"I wonder."

Stone opens a secure link to check his email. Nothing he cares about.

"You wonder what?"

"Why did you go out on such a long limb over Delveccio? Some bullshit job, that's all this is. Why would you do that?"

Because I fucked up in Iraq and now the goddamn French own my ass. And the French have lots to hide from the international community they claim to adore.

"The money, Graham. Remember that. It's always about the money."

She shakes her head. "I don't think so. The feds would have paid whether you sliced and diced Delveccio or not. Why would we do work that dirty for them?"

Her voice is shaking. It sounds like a combination of fear and barely controlled rage. Stone shuts down his laptop.

"You mean *I* did the dirty work."

"Glad to hear you say it. Because that's exactly how I'm going to put it in my report."

"I'm the guy who reads your reports."

"The government hires us, Grayson. The NSA sees our reports. And if they want, Congress sees them, too."

"They see *my* reports. *My* summaries. Get it? Don't worry, I'll cover your ass the way I always do."

Her eyes flash. "This time I'll make sure they read my version."

Stone closes the laptop. Packs it into the shoulder case. Leans over the table until his face hovers inches from hers.

"You're fired. Go play with dolls."

"Fuck you, Stone! I'm blowing the whistle."

"Whatever blows your skirt up," he says. He grabs his bag and marches from the room.

Chapter Ten

I leave the loft before first light, on my way to visit the offices of Kato's publisher, Epilogue. Decide to walk, to take my time. An hour later I find myself several kilometers out of my way, passing Kato's building on the other side of the street.

She lived in a refurbished Stalin-era mid-rise in central Moscow. White limestone, the first two floors blackened by soot, a crooked awning over the door. Nondescript. Ordinary.

But not today. Brightly colored flowers piled everywhere add color and life to the drab exterior today.

Everybody knows now: Kato is dead.

And so this spontaneous memorial.

The mounded flowers paint a rainbow of floral colors: pinks, reds, whites, and purples. Blooming among the flowers are homemade signs expressing condolences, messages written on scraps of paper, yellow ribbons. Flickering candles in glass jars or melted onto the concrete sidewalk, pinpoints of yellow light in the gray morning.

All surrounded by a swirling jumble of people: a mother carrying her child in a sling in front of her body; an aged veteran wearing a red beret; a gaggle of students from Moscow University hoisting a placard that reads, "Justice"; enterprising street vendors selling fruit drinks, candles, and trinkets; protesters waving signs denouncing the government. Street performers have taken up residence next to uniformed policemen, who hold themselves stiffly, moving only their eyes, alert for an outbreak of violence.

I think Kato would have enjoyed the spectacle.

We met here once, more than a year ago, after I told her I could get in and out without alerting the doorman. She maintained her flat in a spare style. A few sticks of furniture, some framed photographs taken by a photojournalist she knew and liked, everything neat and in its place. Functional. "A place to work and sleep," she called it.

I don't know whether she had an office anywhere else, but I doubt she did. I always pictured her writing in the field. Riding on the back of a tank in south Georgia, covering a street demonstration in Petersburg, sailing with Greenpeace in the wake of a freighter carrying nuclear waste to Siberia. Always scribbling on a pad like the one she gave me that night in Chechnya and at the open-air market.

So I don't know whether I'll be able to learn anything useful from her book publisher. But I figure I may as well try.

Epilogue's offices are located several kilometers south of Kato's building. I could walk there if I wished. Instead, I stand at the curb and signal for a gypsy cab, motioning with my hand held low. A middle-aged man in a fifteen-year-old Lada pulls over. I tell him where I need to go, and he quotes an acceptable price. I get in, and he pulls into traffic. We travel in silence. I spend the time considering what I know about Kato's publisher from what Valya culled from its website.

Not much.

One Joseph Mitlov established Epilogue in 1993. The company grew to eight full-time staffers by 1999, when it expanded to include a weekly newspaper. Two years later the newspaper lost its charter. No reason given, but Putin's rise to power brought the demise of many alternative newspapers. Most of those that didn't fail were bought. Kremlin-owned businesses purchased news outlets like baubles, paying a "free-market price" in a market as free as a camp ringed by concertina wire and guard towers.

Epilogue published two of Kato's books. Both of them short, concise, and crammed with the kind of details one can only see and learn by being on the ground.

Hard ground.

Places like the ravaged Chechen village near Shali where Russian troops executed their *zachistka* in the days before Kato and I first met. Or a mountain cave with the terrorist Basaev a month after he orchestrated the Beslan School massacre. Or on location in Dagestan when OMAN troops ordered the name of a duly-nominated candidate stricken from the ballot and purchased an extra hundred thousand ballot papers from the printer to ensure that their candidate won.

Hard stories.

The kind of stories only someone with many sources from all sides of a conflict can write. An insider's portrayal of the Dubrovka theater siege. Tales from the streets of Nazran on the night when two hundred rebel fighters took control of the city and killed scores of militiamen and civilians. The eyewitness account of a woman and her daughter who watched as a villager was beaten to pulp by six soldiers who leaped from an armored personnel carrier and pounded him into the ground with rifle butts before one of them put a bullet into him.

Hard ground, hard stories, and hard books to publish, too. Somebody at Epilogue has a great deal of courage.

"They shouldn't have killed her," the driver says, startling me. He wears horn-rimmed glasses over sharp features. Eyes set close together, lips pursed.

"Who?"

"Kato."

"I mean who killed her?"

He glances over his shoulder before changing lanes, then looks at me with surprise on his face.

"How should I know? But if they wanted to silence her, they failed. The things she wrote will ring louder now."

I can't tell whether he believes that is good or bad.

He double-parks and watches me count the money into his palm. I step out of the Lada, then lean in through the open door and capture his gaze.

"For the moment, the eyes of the world are on Kato and the things she wrote. That won't last more than a few days. And then? No more stories."

"There's that," he says, nodding, answering my unspoken question.

He is one of those who believe Kato was a rabble-rousing troublemaker. The fact that he offered his opinion so freely probably means he thinks I'm a government agent. That's a sensible assumption. He picked me up near the memorial, which someone like him would view as a demonstration in need of watching by the Kremlin. And my bearing suggests that I would be the kind of person assigned to do the watching.

I close the door and pound my open palm on the roof. He rattles away in a wash of exhaust fumes.

I move off the street. Stand among the pedestrians, lost in thought, hearing the echo of Kato's voice from that night in the mountains.

Who do you think you're protecting Mother Russia from? And who are you protecting her for?

Who indeed?

Chapter Eleven

The address for Epilogue leads me to a six-story building made of Soviet cinder block. No security in the lobby. Dirty marble floors, walls and pilasters covered with cracked plaster, tiny elevator groaning away in one of the upper floors. A wall-mounted board lists the building's tenants in moveable white letters. Epilogue is one of several tenants on the fifth floor.

The elevator sounds as if it will take forever to come down. I take the stairs.

The fifth floor stairwell opens onto an empty hallway lined with doors on both sides. Faded rectangles of paint mark where signs used to be. Epilogue appears to be the only tenant left. Its sign is made of plastic screwed into the plaster wall. The door next to the sign is made of wood with a pane of opaque glass in the upper half.

Inside I find a reception desk, but no receptionist.

The phone behind the reception desk rings.

"Epilogue," says a muffled male voice in another room.

I follow the sound to a short hallway, two offices on either side. Lights shine in the office on the left.

"We're not accepting manuscripts at this time."

I peer inside. The weary tone of voice matches the slump-shouldered figure seated at a desk facing a window with his back to me. The window frames a view of the soot-blackened brick of the tenement next door and a slice of gloomy sky.

He hangs up and swivels his chair to face me. We study each other.

He's balding. Dark circles under his eyes, drooping cheeks, like a balloon with most of the air let out. Brown polyester suit.

"Mitlov?"

"That's me."

"I'm Volk. I called earlier."

"You got identification?"

"Nothing official."

He strokes the strands of black hair on his oversized pate, moving his head beneath his hands, like a wasp cleaning itself.

"The worst kind, those that aren't official. Kato told me that once. She said those are the ones to fear the most."

The top of his gunmetal desk is crowded with loose papers, a coffee mug, and a bound manuscript stained with brown rings made by the mug. A picture of Lenin resides in a simple red frame on the credenza behind him. Stacks of books cover the floor. He finishes his assessment of me and turns his chair to stare out the window.

"So what do you want?"

"Kato was my friend."

"Many people called her their friend. She called them sources."

"What did she call the person who murdered her?"

The back of his neck colors. He starts to say something, then taps the return on his keyboard to light the screen. A document appears. He gestures toward it.

"In the story I'm working on right now, I call him a murderer. Probably a government agent. Faceless, soulless—a reptile." He glances at me. "Sound familiar?"

I don't respond. He sighs.

"The real question is what do you call the person who *ordered* her killed?"

He loads the question with contempt and stares at me for a long time after he asks it. I refuse to be baited.

"How much do you know about her death?"

He snorts. "Next to nothing. The local paper reported the discovery of four bodies. Found buried in the mud on the banks of the Techa River. Shot in the head. It wasn't until late last night that one of them was identified as Kato."

"How did you learn about it?"

"I received an email from a journalist in Chelyabinsk. Well, I suppose we can call him a journalist. Is there such a thing anymore? He is a blogger, really, one of those people who write because they seem to have no choice. He sends me stories all the time. 'Dispatches,' he likes to call them."

"Let me see the email."

He strokes his pate some more, making the same wasplike movements. "So you can cover it up? Hide the tracks the same way you did with Anna and all the others?"

"I told you. I was Kato's friend."

"And I already told you, she didn't have any friends."

In the past I may have forced answers out of him. From the tense way he's holding himself, Mitlov seems to sense as much. But he doesn't look like a man who's ready to back down.

"Did she give you any of her notes about the story she was working on?"

"Only a working title and an outline. More of a sketch, really. A month ago. I heard nothing from her after that." He goes back to staring out the window. "Now this."

"Was a month a long time between updates?"

"What are you suggesting?"

"Was it?"

He doesn't answer for a long time. "She used to email once a week," he says finally. "I started to worry about her a couple of weeks ago. I tried her cell phone, but it went straight to voicemail. I sent more than a dozen emails and texts that went unanswered."

"Which means what?"

His slump becomes more pronounced. It makes him look smaller. "They won't release any information about the state of her body. Only that she and the others had been shot in the head."

"Nothing about *when* it happened?"

"No, but the students who were killed with her had only been missing for four days."

"How do you know they were all killed at the same time?"

He scowls. "How do we know anything? We know what we're told. That's it. How are we supposed to investigate something that happened so far away? Something that the Kremlin wants to hush up as soon as possible? Today, tomorrow, maybe for a week the people will remember. They'll talk, they'll demonstrate. A few of them will write letters demanding answers. If the story refuses to die, some thug will be arrested and charged. But not convicted. They're never convicted."

"Maybe this time will be different."

"Uh-huh. Are we done here?"

"I want copies of Kato's outline and emails."

"Suppose I refuse."

"Then I'll have to insist."

"A man walks into my office out of the blue. He looks like a criminal, or a government agent, assuming there's a difference. He claims to be a friend of a murdered journalist and demands to see her notes and my private files."

He pooches his lower lip while he considers his own rhetoric. Then he reaches beneath his desk, fumbling a bit. I lunge toward him, but I'm too late. He hits the button to turn off his computer.

"I don't think so," he says.

Keeping my body between him and the door, I reach beneath his desk and hit the power button. The hard drive whines. A cursor blinks in the middle of the screen, then the screen lights up. His user name is J. Mitlov. The password line is blank.

"What's the password?"

He stares out the window.

I draw my SIG from beneath my left arm. Dangle it next to my thigh. Turn him in his chair so that he faces me.

"The password?"

He doesn't say anything. His eyes take on a distant look.

Who would have believed that the heart of a lion would beat so strongly in such an unlikely man? More men like him, and Russia could be saved.

I turn the computer tower around with my foot. Use the screwdriver attachment to my pocketknife to unscrew the panel and remove the hard drive. A man Valya knows will be able to retrieve its contents.

I put the drive in my pocket and holster the SIG. Write the number for my cell phone on a yellow sticky note next to his keyboard. Step away.

He tracks me with his gaze. "What now?"

"I'll take what I need. My friend will return the drive to you when I'm finished."

"That's not what I meant."

"I'm not going to hurt you. But the next person through the door might. Especially if they think you're hiding something. Are you?"

His face goes blank again. I turn away.

"I'm going to Mayak. Call me if you want to talk. Or if you really want to learn what happened to Kato."

Chapter Twelve

Several hours after my meeting with Mitlov I'm gunning a red Ducati motorcycle through the streets around the Kremlin, bent forward into the rush of wind, chewing fumes, my chest thrumming with the vibrations of the powerful machine. Valya straddles the seat behind me, hugging me tightly. Her silky hair tickles my neck. To our left the Moscow River flows like liquid slate in the light of a gray afternoon. The high wall of the Kremlin blurs reddish-blue on our right.

"I'll drop you at the Garden," I shout over my shoulder, then lean into the turn north toward Alexander Garden.

I'm glad my back is to her. Before we left the loft I caught her staring curiously at me, seeming to sense that I am drifting in some subtle way she doesn't yet have a handle on.

I power the Ducati over the curb and onto the sidewalk outside the Okhotny Ryad shopping mall.

"I'll wait in the gardens," Valya says, her breath warm in my ear. She bites my earlobe, then hops off the bike.

I blat the engine, watching her wade through the crowds toward the circle of flowers in the garden. A tourist bumps her, says something she doesn't acknowledge. I don't need to see his face to know that he has the same gaping expression many men and some women display when they see her for the first time. She's a silent thief, stealing hearts without trying.

I roar off, threading through the tourists outside GUM and St. Basil's Cathedral. Cross the river and make a right toward a mansion that used to house the British embassy. Pull into an alley, park, and chain the Ducati to a lamppost. Push my way through a row of high hedges to a low structure that looks like a concrete pillbox. Bang on the metal door.

One. One, two, three. One.

I wait. Two minutes pass. The old British embassy looms to my right and behind me, all of its lower levels hidden behind the hedges all around me. The top of the Kremlin's Tainitskaya Tower rises on the far bank of the river. A barge churns along the river, invisible from where I am, only the thrum of its engines and the rolling hiss of its wake marking its passage.

A metallic scraping carries through the door as the bolt slides free. Somebody on the other side swings the door open on oiled hinges to reveal two green-uniformed soldiers standing at the top of a flight of rough-hewn steps. One of them checks my identification. Nods and stands aside to allow me to pass, then follows as his partner leads the way down two flights to a long tunnel beneath the river. The tunnel ends at a security checkpoint beneath the Tainitskaya Tower.

The lead soldier takes my SIG. Makes me remove my prosthesis and pass it through the metal detector on a conveyor belt. Once it's safely through the scanner, I hop on one leg through the portal without setting off any alarms, where he gives me a chair so I can reattach my foot.

A different soldier leads me away. Ramrod straight, moving in concert with two other soldiers behind me. These men are part of the General's cadre of personal bodyguards. They are poles apart from the men stationed on the other side of the river. Dobermans compared to poodles.

Smooth tile gives way to worn stone steps as we go lower. The granite walls glisten with slow-weeping river water. We follow a series of curves, then one last checkpoint, where another set of guards check my identification again. Finally, we reach the gnarled oak door to the General's quarters. The door swings open with an electronic hum.

I step inside.

Darkness fills most of the rectangular room, broken only by a cone of light shining in the far corner, where the General sits behind a wooden desk surrounded by computer monitors. Stone floor and dripping walls. Thick, sagging beams overhead.

The door whirs closed behind me and seals itself with a hydraulic hiss. The General motions me closer. He regards me over the top of black-framed reading glasses.

"When are you planning to come back to work?"

"Soon."

The truth is that I don't know. His definition of *work* includes many things. Running his illegal empire—extorting legitimate and illegitimate businesses, peddling illegal or untaxed goods, selling secrets and lies. International travel as a "special envoy" to set the stage for one of his other agents or to clean up behind him, known in the trade as *mokriye dela*: wet work. Before that, two years of intense training followed by five years marinating in the simmering conflict in Chechnya and the surrounding republics.

The General pours two shots of vodka from an unlabeled bottle. Pushes one toward me. Raises his glass to mine.

"Here's to today. Today is a good day."

Whether I'm suffering from fatigue or whether my malaise originated with the nature of my last trip to America, I can't say. But the reason hardly matters. The simple fact is that for the past few weeks I've been incommunicado. Ever since I returned from Los Angeles I've been content to stay in the loft with Valya. That ended when Ilya said the name *Kato*. But now it appears I won't have the luxury of time to investigate her murder. I straighten.

"Yes, sir."

He flips through an open file on his desk. Some of the pages appear to be made of flimsy onionskin, probably old carbon copies. Which tells me they are second- or third-hand, not original documents created by operatives within his sphere of activities, as wide-ranging as those tend to be. They're either stolen or passed on by one of his many contacts in politics, the military, or intelligence.

"I'm sure you heard," he says. "The body of a famous journalist was discovered a few days ago. Katarina Mironova. She went by the name Kato." He fixes his icy stare on me. "Did you know this woman?"

"I met her in Chechnya. She'd caught on with a column of armor twenty klicks outside the village of Shatoi."

The General turns a page in the file, nodding. I keep my expression flat while I mentally race through all my other meetings with Kato that might have been recorded or noted by prying eyes.

"I saw her again near Khalkiloi."

That's where a ten-year-old girl stepped on a "petal," a wicked land mine that tears off toes and chunks of feet. Kato and I rode with her on a transport to a base with a helicopter. I pressed bandages to her mangled stump while we bounced over the rough ground. Kato pillowed the girl's head in her lap, wiping the tears and sweat away from her cheeks. The white bandages changed color like leaves in the fall: first bright crimson, then burnt rust as her heartbeat weakened. Somewhere in a valley that looked like the bottom of a scorched bowl the girl opened her eyes wide, stared up into Kato's face, and said, "Mama?"

The girl died before we reached the helicopter, but there would be a record somewhere that I had requested an airlift. That record might refer to Kato.

Sure enough, the General runs his stubbed forefinger along another onion-skinned page of the file and grunts.

"March of 2001, it says here. Why did you need a helicopter?"

"I had information about a force of rebels on the move outside Khalkiloi. Turned out to be false."

"Why was she with you?"

"I needed to quarantine her to make sure she didn't reveal what we knew. What we thought we knew."

He turns to another page. I stand perfectly still.

"I saw her another time in the mountains on the Dagestan border. I didn't talk to her there." I wait for a reaction without getting one. "She seemed to follow the most intense fighting." It goes without saying that I would have been at those places.

All of that should be broad enough to cover references to Kato and me in the wartime files the General has obtained. I think back on other meetings in the past several years, during my undercover work as a crime boss.

"She approached me a few times in Moscow, hoping to work me for information."

I stop there. I don't know everything his file contains, but I hope that what I've said so far calms any suspicion he might have upon seeing so many references to the two of us together.

He pushes the onionskin pages away. "She didn't get much, I'm sure."

The General's voice is tinged with pride. The pride only a father—or one who has acted like a father—can feel. All those years now since he plucked me from general population of Isolator Five, a maximum security prison in Moscow. I was shivering from the cold, hungry, bruised from fighting to protect myself from the other inmates, all of them older than I was. He saw something in me that day, something that caused him to finance my education and training and turn me into…what?

It is a good question. His enforcer, agent, envoy? All of those things and more, including scout, sniper, shock trooper, assassin, spy. I've played many roles over the years. The General knows that loyalty and predisposition carry a person only so far, however. "Trust nothing entirely," he once advised me.

He should heed his own advice, especially now.

"What does a dead journalist have to do with us?" I say.

"One of the men I commanded in Chechnya is accused of murdering her, along with three students from Moscow University. You remember Rhino?"

Rhino. Everybody knew Rhino, even if they didn't know his real name.

He looked like his namesake. Grayish coloring, stolid, so strong I always figured his muscles and ligaments attached differently from those of normal people. The men in his battalion used to fight him in a circle of stones lit by firelight, wagering everything they owned that he could whip all comers. I once saw him beat an overmatched opponent nearly to death, but he was far from a cold-blooded killer.

"Did he?"

The General stares at me. "Does it matter?"

"I suppose not. Unless…"

"Right. Unless somebody needs to find out the truth."

"Who?"

"Somebody in the Kremlin. Somebody important who doesn't want the international press making unfounded accusations."

He glowers at me for a moment. Pours himself another shot, downs it. Sets aside the glass and steeples his stubby fingers. Always thinking, the General, the depth of his intellect more than enough to outweigh the handicap of dwarfish limbs.

"That's enough for now," he says. "Go to the hospital in Chelyabinsk. They have the body in cold storage. Talk to the coroner. After that, go to Prison Colony No. 1 in Kopeysk and talk to Rhino. Get his side of the story. Then go to Mayak, where Kato was killed. Learn the truth."

He adjusts the papers on his desk while I stare over his shoulder.

"It's nothing for us," he says. Meaning no profit. No valuables to steal, no enemy to hunt down and kill, no secret to expose to blackmail or destroy an enemy.

I don't believe him.

The General commanded the 58th Army during the worst years of both Chechen wars. He leveraged that position into an empire that sucks cash from every aspect of the Russian economy. If something makes money, the General probably has a hand in it. So many of the things I've seen and heard and done on his behalf prowl the recesses of my mind, waiting for a spark of recognition or an association.

One of those memories returns to me now. Over his shoulder, mounted on a wall made of river rock, is a steel shelf bisected vertically by a round steel pillar. That's what triggers the memory. The shelf calls to mind a homemade gibbet I once saw. Two soldiers with their hands tied behind their back, a rope attached to them to hoist them off the ground, all their weight on their dislocated shoulders. New recruits, I thought, when I found them—victims of *dedovshchina*, violent bullying entrenched in the culture of the army. Called spirits, stomachs, starvers, faint-ers, or goblins by the men who'd been in country more than six months. They had been beaten until the skin split. After I cut them down I discovered they weren't new recruits after all. Their comrades had left them there to die for a different reason.

The skin around the General's eyes tightens.

"You remember the piece Kato did about the sweep in the village near Shali? Lieutenant Colonel Baburka lost his commis-sion and damn near went to prison because of it."

Baburka the rapist and murderer, the sordid tale told so pow-erfully in Kato's blue notepad, the story I sent to Kato's Moscow editor a week after our first meeting.

"So, you go." The General waves his hand dismissively and hits the button to alert the guards to come for me. "Find out about Rhino. And along the way, find out what you can about that woman's sources."

The irony of the moment isn't lost on me. This is precisely why I came to the General, to enlist his help tracking down Kato's murderer, although I could never have told him that. I'd planned to use misdirection to arrange travel and entry into the Mayak nuclear facility. Now, not only do I have the General's backing while I search for Kato's murderer, I'm being sent to search for her key informant.

I'm being sent to search for myself.

Chapter Thirteen

Aeroflot flies nonstop from Moscow to Chelyabinsk. Two and a half hours through a thunderstorm. Stewardesses remain strapped in their seats for all but a few minutes. We slap down in heavy rain and taxi toward a low-slung terminal that appears as a blurry row of lights in the darkness.

Local time is 7:30 P.M. Early in the night shift for people in the medical and policing professions, I hope. I don't want to wait until morning to get to work.

This is my first visit to Chelyabinsk. A small city turned industrial powerhouse during World War II when Stalin moved large factories away from the advancing German armies. Home of the Chelyabinsk Tractor Plant, the Chelyabinsk Metallurgical Plant, and several sprawling facilities for the production of T-34 tanks and Katyusha rocket launchers. Known for a time as Tankograd. Tank City.

The Chelyabinsk region is also home to several nuclear weapons labs, similar to Los Alamos and Livermore in the United States.

The Mayak nuclear fuel reprocessing plant lies a hundred and fifty kilometers to the northwest of the city, according to the maps and files Valya printed for me before I left Moscow. It sits only six kilometers from Lake Karachay, a dumping site for its radioactive waste. A picture Valya printed off the Internet shows the bruised surface of the lake, with three smokestacks in the distance.

The jet engines change pitch as the plane arrives at the gate. I get off, sling my duffel over my shoulder, and head toward the signs for ground transportation. As soon as I turn on my phone it buzzes to signal I have a voicemail.

"It's me." The sound of music flows around Valya's voice. She likes to listen to a wide variety of artists with the volume cranked up. "Mitlov's files were encrypted, but Griga was able to open them."

Grigorii Tvertin. One of her friends from Moscow University, a hacker who used to work in our identity-theft operation. Last I heard he'd been hospitalized after the police beat him while "dispersing" a gay rights parade.

"He found a folder that contained Kato's outline for her book about our nuclear program and a few emailed notes. The last note was dated a bit over a month ago. Two words and a question mark: 'Chemical Osaka?' Do you know what that is?"

I pass through the baggage claim area. *Chemical Osaka.* I don't know what those two words mean.

"So call me, okay?" Valya's voice fades away, replaced for a few seconds by a driving bass line. "Maybe Griga will take me to one of his parties." She laughs and hangs up.

I step outside the terminal. The rain drums a staccato beat on the overhang above a line of three taxis. I climb into the first one and tell the driver where I need to go.

He stubs out the butt of his cigarette and grinds his ancient Volvo into gear. Regards me in the mirror as he lights another cigarette from a pack labeled with the Jin Ling brand. Made by the Baltic Tobacco Company in massive quantities, then smuggled into the European Union. The brand is a large part of a growing problem in the illegal tobacco trade. The General used to take a cut of the profits of BTC. I don't know whether he still does.

"Why *that* hospital?" the driver says. "Mostly military there."

We pass shops, restaurants, parks. The city lights smear color on the wet windshield and illuminate the interior of the Volvo in reds, greens, and blues.

The driver stops at a traffic light. The tip of his cigarette glows burnt orange. He glances into the mirror. He wants to ask another question, but the look of me silences him. The memory of the KGB and its heirs weighs too heavily, here and everywhere else in the former Soviet territories. Better to swallow questions before they take unpredictable flight.

He drops me on the street and points to a well-lit building across the square. I pay the fare, walk the rest of the way in the rain, and step into the antiseptic lobby of the hospital. Lots of people milling about, including a flock of nurses heading out for lunch or dinner, depending on their shift.

I check the directory, then ride the elevator down to the morgue.

The doors open onto a long corridor lit by exposed fluorescent tubes. Closed doors on both sides, closed double doors at the end. The smell of formaldehyde is pronounced here, joined by the dank scent of mold and musty air that doesn't get circulated often enough. The pungent combination wrinkles my nose.

I start down the hall. My boot heels rap like drumbeats against the tile floor. The closer I get to the end of the corridor, the more powerful the smell becomes.

A door opens behind me.

"Hey! What are you doing down here?"

A chubby man with a reddish beard stands in the open doorway. He's wearing a yellow-and-orange Hawaiian shirt and striped Bermuda shorts under a stained lab coat. Unlaced Doc Martens on his feet.

I remove my ID from the inside pocket of my coat. Flip it open to the photo.

"Colonel Alexei Volkovoy," I say. "Here to meet the medical examiner."

He studies the photo without taking it from my hands. The stains on his lab coat look like brown Rorschach blotches. One of them shows the trail of a finger and ends in a smear of some gooey substance.

"Colonel, huh? Think that impresses me? You all look alike on the table."

The top of his head reaches to my chin. He stares up at me with watery blue eyes.

"You a black?"

Meaning a soldier who fought in Chechnya. When a person with dark skin is asked the question, it means are you Chechen. He says the word without the same rancor that the Nashi Youth used on the train.

"Five years," I say.

He scratches his beard. Motions for me to follow him down the hall.

"Then perhaps this won't bother you too much."

He leads me to the end of the hall and through the double doors, which swing closed behind us. The lights are even brighter here, the smell worse. Four tables line the far wall. Naked bodies on two of them. One a woman. Hard to tell her age. Her body seems to have melted onto the table, her flesh swollen around the straps holding her in place.

"My name's Otari," the M.E. says.

The second cadaver is a man. Missing the top of his head. Ragged on one side. The smooth edges on the other side tell me Otari sawed off whatever was left of the top of the dead man's skull to examine what was inside. Otari's gaze follows mine.

"Local man," he says. "Ran a gambling parlor. Didn't want to give the boys their cut. Took a round in the temple, two hundred meters, according to the police. Good work, eh?"

He licks the ends of his middle finger and thumb and uses them to flatten his eyebrows. He starts with his finger and thumb together over the bridge of his nose and spreads them apart. Then he drags his palm down his face and over his beard in a tired gesture.

"Fucking head hurts all time. The chemicals will kill me. You think anyone in Moscow will care?"

"Do you have an assistant?"

"Why?"

"Maybe he'll slice you open and take a look inside when you're dead. File a report about the dangers of the chemicals in the morgue."

He stares at me. "Funny guy."

"I'm here to see the bodies from Metlino."

"Uh-huh."

He walks to a wall of numbered drawers. Pats his fingers on his lips, considering. Slides one open to reveal the bony white body of an old man. Translucent skin. Black hair dulled in death, but still full. Maybe not as old as I first thought. I step closer before Otari can close the drawer.

"How old was he?"

Otari checks the red toe tag. "Twenty-four. Why?"

"How did he die?"

"Boring. Cancer."

"So young?"

"Are you fucking kidding me?"

I don't respond. Just wait him out.

"You know the half life of plutonium-239?"

"No."

"Twenty-four thousand years. How about U-235?"

I shake my head.

"Seven hundred million years."

"So?"

"Some of those people over there," he gestures vaguely toward the northwest, in the direction of Mayak and Lake Karachay. "Some of those dumb fucks grub around in the dirt like they're playing in a sandbox. I've seen little kids *eating* the stuff."

Chapter Fourteen

I walk over to the twenty-four-year-old cancer victim laid out in the drawer. Oteri watches me, scratching at his beard with his fingernails, like a dog with fleas.

Now that I'm closer, the dead man looks more his actual age. Skin the color of ash, puckered as if he'd been shrink-wrapped in plastic and left in the sun for a few days. On his thorax a Y-shaped stitching of black thread, marking where Oteri made his cuts.

"So he died of radiation poisoning?"

"What else? You want to know how many 'cancer' victims I get every week?" Oteri uses his fingers to put quotes around the word *cancer*. "When a fucking lake blows radiation over a few thousand square kilometers, people die. Fifty years don't mean shit. People will keep dying for another hundred years. Longer. There isn't enough time in the day to look too closely at all of them."

I back away from the body. Nod to tell Otari to close the drawer. While he busies himself with that, I look around.

The brass handles on the drawers reflect a dull gleam under the harsh lights. They've been worn to lusterless silver by so much handling over the years. The three tables along the side wall have a similar look to them, worn through the porcelain finish to reveal the leaden layer below. Dark stains of grime and spilled fluids on the tile floor prove that nobody around here cares enough to mop very well. I must have become accustomed to the smell, because now it is the sight of the place that's making me dizzy.

"Show me the bodies from Metlino."

Otari shrinks back. The words must have come out harsher than I intended.

"Yeah, sure," he says. "Relax."

He walks across the room, opens a small file drawer, and flips through several cards inside.

"Four bodies," he says over his shoulder. "All together in a pit. Not very deep, less than a meter, then covered with dirt and brush. Near a bend in the Techa River."

He slides the file closed and returns to the wall of drawers. Reaches for the handle of a drawer, then pauses like a magician about to perform a trick. Pulls it open.

I close my eyes.

I can't bear to look.

I think my problem is that I don't want to remember Kato this way. Cold on a slab in this squalid room, sliced open and examined by this jaded man with his wet blue eyes.

I open my eyes.

The body is not Kato's. It's a young woman, hardly more than a girl. Tangled brown hair. Delicate features. Long lashes against the pale flesh.

Oteri gives me a curious look, but doesn't comment.

I check the toe tag.

Anne-Laure Raux. French. A name I recognize. She was one of the students who were murdered with Kato. From the University of Lyon, attending Moscow University for a semester, according to the newspapers.

"How?"

Oteri puts his hands on either side of her head and turns it. The back of her head is shaved. Stitching shows where her skullcap was replaced and the skin sewn back again. Just above the line of stitches, a neat, round hole. Must have been made by a small bullet, because it made a hole no bigger than a pencil eraser, and it pinged around inside her skull without making an exit wound.

"Twenty-two caliber," Oteri says helpfully. "The gun was placed directly against her head." He purses his lips and gives a disapproving shake of his head. "No art in that."

"Next."

He closes the drawer on Anne-Laure and opens another.

I close my eyes again.

Open them. Ignore Oteri's curious gaze.

A boy this time. Hairless chest, white as snow. Lanky, shoulder-length hair dyed blue, black at the roots. Small hole in the back of his head, larger exit wound just above his left eye. I check the toe tag. Mikhail Makashev. A student from Moscow University.

"Same thing," Oteri says. "Muzzle right up against the skull. Different angle, so this time the bullet went all the way through."

"Did they recover the bullet?"

"No."

"So you can't tell whether it's the same gun?"

"No."

I nod. He goes through his same routine while I go through mine. He closes one drawer and slides open another. I close my eyes, then pop them open.

A woman, but not Kato.

Lena Sokolova, according to the tag. Young in years, maybe, but not youthful in appearance. Stringy, dishwater-blond hair. Thin to the point of emaciation. Needle tracks on both arms, some scabbed over, a few of them fresher. A map of blue veins that looks like small pipes under her skin. No sign of trauma on her face or the part of her head that's visible to me.

"A drug addict?"

Oteri nods. "She didn't feel a thing. She was loaded on heroin when she died."

"How was she killed?"

He nudges her head with the back of his bare hand. It lolls drunkenly to one side. "Somebody snapped her neck like a celery stick." He looks pleased. "Not so pedestrian as a bullet in the back of the head."

"The newspapers said all three students had been shot."

He scratches at his beard again. *Shick, shick, shick.* "How often do the newspapers get everything right?"

"Okay. Go."

He closes the drawer on Lena's pockmarked body. Marches to another bank of drawers, the magician on his stage. With a theatrical flourish, he pulls one open.

I look away. My stomach hurts. The lights are so bright I can see the veins in my translucent eyelids. Oteri clears is throat.

"Are you all right?"

"I need water."

"I'll have to go get it."

"Then go!"

I hear him walk away. I open my eyes with my back to the drawer. Turn all at once, as though I can surprise myself.

I was right.

The first flash of her body, like a single frame suddenly appearing on a reel of blank film, is more than I can bear. I turn away. Close my eyes, then open them again as wide as I can, stretching the lids.

The fluorescent lights buzz like a swarm of bees. The glare waters my eyes. I put a hand on one of the dulled brass handles to steady myself.

"Are you sick?"

Oteri's voice echoes in my head. It seems to have traveled a great distance to reach me. He hands me a Styrofoam cup half-filled with water. I chug it. It leaves a metallic taste in the back of my throat.

"How long?" I say.

"How long what?"

"How long was she in the fucking dirt before somebody found her?"

"You don't have to shout at me. What's the matter with you?"

He moves to the side of the drawer. I can't face him. If I did, I would have to look again at Kato's body, and I can't do that. Not now, not ever.

"Her body is not like the others," I say. "She's…decomposed."

"That's right."

"Shut the drawer!"

"Yes, yes, of course."

Metal grates over metal as he rolls it closed, the sound like a dull blade sawing through sheet metal. How long since the wheels or the rails have been cleaned, if ever? When I turn to face him, Oteri is staring at me with a combination of fear and curiosity.

"I thought you said you served five years in Chechnya? You act like you've never seen a dead body before."

"The next time I have to ask this question, I'll do it with my fist down your throat. Answer me! How long after she died did they find the body?"

"Four to six weeks."

"Those others. How long for them?"

"Between three days and five. The heroin addict was dead the longest."

Lena. Doped to the gills, easy prey. Killed and dumped on top of Kato to confuse the scene. Joined later by the other two.

"Katarina Mironova. Kato. Was her neck broken?"

"No." He drags out the word, shaking his head slowly. "You couldn't see?"

"I didn't look closely."

"Oh."

He scratches at his beard some more. *Shick, shick, shick.* The sound sets my teeth on edge.

"Maybe you should look more closely," he says. "They're taking her away tomorrow."

"Who's taking her away?"

He arches an eyebrow. "Your people from Moscow. Didn't you know that? Now that she's been identified they want to do a *proper* autopsy."

No they don't. They want to cover up. I don't say a word, just look at him.

"Well," he says finally. "Kato, she was shot in the head the same way as the other two. But the slug that killed her came from a large-caliber handgun against her forehead."

After he dumped Lena, the drug addict, the killer refined his plan. Decided to make the other two look more like Kato's murder. Then somehow managed to have the story made public, saying that Kato and three students had been killed together in the same way. Why? And who was likely to have enough clout to get the story reported the way he, or they, wanted it reported?

Oteri's not stupid. I believe he's already made the same connections I have. And probably one other. I look into his watery blue eyes.

"Different MO, different killer?"

He shrugs. "Maybe."

He looks away. Nothing over there except the wasted body of the radiation victim. Then he looks at me again.

"Yes," he says. "I'd stake my life on it. You're looking for two different killers, one killed the reporter, someone else killed the other three. That's why you're here, right?"

Chapter Fifteen

Grayson Stone logs back onto ECHELON. Sits staring out the window of his room in the Comfort Suites on Tropicana, watching a Southwest Airlines jet lift off from McCarran while he waits for the program to boot up.

Lazar Solovie.

A cipher, nothing more than a few dates on the screen. Not much of anything unusual about the man, in ECHELON or elsewhere, for that matter. Which serves only to make Stone more suspicious.

Solovie's bio: DOB, October 17, 1969. Born in Kazan. Stone went there once during the nineties to deliver a bag stuffed with American dollars to a Tatar warlord whose separatist tendencies were being nurtured by the CIA. A city of more than a million spilled along a curve of the Volga River at the confluence of the Kazanka River. Solovie attended Kazan University, showed a talent for physics, transferred to the Russian Academy of Sciences, graduated from there and later from the Moscow Institute of Physics and Technology, attended MIT and Cambridge on academic scholarships. Never married. No children.

So the fuck what?

Stone digs deeper. Learns that Solovie's stint at Cambridge was arranged by nuclear scientist Vladimir Nechai, then the director of the top-secret Chelyabinsk-65 nuclear complex. A facility located in the shadow of the Mayak nuclear processing plant.

Less than fifty kilometers from where the body was buried. No way could *that* be a coincidence.

Okay. One connection made. Any others?

Stone cross-references the name *Vladimir Nechai*. Navigates to the NSA's file. Finds more than 500 pages of data. Clicks through to the last entries, where the most recent information would appear. Locates a *New York Times* article dated November 1, 1996.

Vladimir Nechai killed himself in 1996. His suicide shocked the nation and came to symbolize the decline of Russian science after the fall of the Soviet Union. According to the official story, Nechai was despondent over the financial problems at Chelyabinsk-65. Depressed by a situation that seemed destined never to improve.

"Bullshit," Stone says under his breath.

Sure enough, a CIA analyst's note appended to the *Times* article suggested foul play. Nechai didn't have a history of depression, no more so than many other Russian scientists at the time, most of whom felt trapped in a hopeless future. The analyst claimed that his sources in the KGB believed that the suicide note—later "lost" by the local police—looked suspicious.

Stone returns to Solovie's file.

Rereads it.

Finds jack shit.

He pulls out the blade of his pocketknife. Tests the tip with the ball of his thumb. Slides the razor-sharp blade along the heel of his palm, where it sinks into a patch of callous. Skin at least an eighth of an inch thick, the layers of scar tissue from countless cuts. Stone presses harder until the blade slides deep enough to draw blood.

Fuck it. Better to know than stay in the dark.

He grabs the phone. Enters eleven digits from memory. Waits for a buzz, then hits seven more.

A series of clicks before a disembodied voice says, "Please identify yourself."

"Grayson Stone," he says, then mutters, "Fucking spooks."

"Please repeat the name."

Shit.

"Grayson Stone," he says, louder this time. "Calling for Brock Matthews."

Another series of clicks, followed by several minutes of silence.

"What's up, Stone?"

Brock Matthews' voice is clipped, impatient. Back in the days when they served on the Russia desk together Matthews was a hard-charger who thought he was smarter than everybody else. Turned out he was right. Matthews rocketed to the top, and Stone ended up with the short straw doing dirty work in every Third World shithole with a problem. All of which changed when Graystone Security came into being.

"I got a name I need you to run."

"I don't do favors for contractors."

"Uh-huh. Listen, I got nothing to trade right now, Matthews, but it won't kill you to put a little in the bank. Maybe someday you'll come in from the cold."

"I doubt it. And if I ever do, a guy like you won't do me any good, anyway."

Stone clenches his jaw to keep from saying anything. Waits out the silence.

"All right," Matthews says. "Give me the name."

"Lazar Solovie. Russian nuclear scientist."

"Why him?"

Stone detects a hitch in Matthews' voice. The barest hint of hesitation. Stone would have missed it if he hadn't been concentrating so hard. Matthews is good enough that most people wouldn't have noticed it, but Stone lives for signs like that. This one tells him that Matthews either knows or knows of Solovie.

"I ran across the name on a project for MI6. Apparently the guy might have had sticky paws while he studied at Cambridge."

"Which project?"

Now Matthews is the one fishing. Stone likes the power shift.

"MI6 called the shots on this one. Ask them."

Matthews won't go directly to MI6, Stone knows. Not yet. He'll wait. Circle like a vulture, pick at the edges, try to find an angle that suits his needs. That should give Stone enough time to take care of business.

"I'll check it out," Matthews says. "If I find anything I can share with you, I'll have it couriered. You going to be in Vegas for a few more hours?"

"Unfortunately." Stone gives him the address of the Comfort Suites, even though he knows Matthews probably doesn't need it. A call to this number on a landline would have been traced before Matthews picked up the phone.

"Why are you there and not in your office?" Matthews says.

"I don't want the distractions."

Stone figures Matthews already knows about Delveccio and the Russians carved up in the desert. Matthews works Russia 24/7. Meaning his question is designed to lead to more questions, so that Matthews can satisfy his curiosity about why Stone is interested in Lazar Solovie.

"So don't be one," Stone adds, and disconnects.

He contemplates the view from his window some more, wishing he had more time. But the world doesn't work that way.

"No," he says aloud, recalling the past. "It sure the fuck doesn't."

Remembering Iraq. Remembering the day everything changed.

Chapter Sixteen

Four people witnessed Stone's handiwork that scorching day in the Iraq desert. Lieutenant Daly. The first two soldiers through the window—Richie Bellows and a kid from upstate New York named Bachner. And, of course, the mother of the dead baby.

Lieutenant Daly: "You're going to fry for this, you bastard."

Stone didn't answer. Made no attempt to justify, to rationalize, to explain. Simply watched in silence while Daly ordered Bellows and Bachner to secure the area. Watched them flank the next doorway and plunge through. Watched Daly squat beside the mother.

Outside, the world exploded as the firefight became a full-scale assault by American and coalition forces. How were they supposed to know that the battle was over? That it had begun and ended right here in this room?

The mother rocked her dead baby. Daly shifted from a squat to a kneel. He spoke quietly, apparently doing his best to comfort her.

Stone returned to the first room and picked up the AK. Carried it with him back into the room where Daly was still mumbling to the mother.

Her eyes widened when she saw him approaching. Daly must have seen the expression on her face, because he looked over his shoulder just as Stone pulled the trigger and burst his head like a dropped watermelon.

His body collapsed onto her. The mother opened her mouth to scream.

Stone shot her twice in the chest.

He walked farther into the building, following the path that Bellows and Bachner had taken. The door they went through opened onto a long hallway with rooms on both sides. All empty. He could hear them clearing another part of the building.

He went back and waited outside the door of the blood-splattered room until Bellows and Bachner completed their search and returned. They walked past him without a word, backs straight, both their faces set in an accusatory glare. They didn't notice that he was carrying the AK instead of his M16. They stopped dead when they saw the carnage on the other side of the door.

Stone killed Bellows first. Dropped him with a single bullet to the base of his skull.

Bachner hit the ground, twisting to swing his rifle to bear. Stone's first round struck his body armor mid-chest, knocked him onto his back. The next one took off his hand. Stone finished him with a final bullet through the faceplate of his helmet.

He dropped the AK. Drew a deep breath.

Done with that part. Now for the cover-up.

"Don't move, please."

Despite the warning, Stone pivoted, reaching for his side-arm—and found himself staring down the bore of a FAMAS G2 assault rifle.

The man holding the rifle leaned negligently against the jamb. Drab CCE camouflage pattern on his FÉLIN combat suit. Light-brown hair pasted to his head by the heat and weight of a helmet that he must have just removed. Brown eyes crinkled at the corners, matching the oily smile and the pleasant expression he wore like a mask.

"Well, this is quite a big problem, no?"

French accent. Rock-steady grip on the FAMAS. No identifying marks or insignia on his suit. Which might mean nothing, but could mean that he was Stone's counterpart among the coalition forces.

Stone mirrored the Frenchman's smile. "I was just trying to figure out what happened here myself."

The Frenchman threw back his head and laughed.

"Yes! Of course. How about if we *figure out* together, eh? Two heads are better than one, don't you think?"

He cocked his head, listening to the staccato crash of the battle outside. The rifle never wavered. After a moment he seemed to remember that Stone was there.

"*Vogue la galère*. Let's keep on, shall we? We should hurry, yes? In a few minutes they're going to realize they're shooting at bricks and, ah…" He dropped his gaze to the dead mother and her baby and pouted his lips. "And innocent Iraqis."

He offered Stone another liquid smile.

"*Associés?* Partners? What do you say?"

Chapter Seventeen

I leave Oteri surrounded by the dead in his wretched morgue.

Time to see Rhino. To hear his story and decide like a one-man jury whether he's guilty or innocent of killing Kato.

A nurse in the hospital lobby directs me to a train station. The downpour has turned into a misty drizzle. Icy drops slide down my spine, routed there from gutters, overhanging ledges, and the awnings in front of the closed shops along the way to the station. Like a city shaking off the cold sweats.

The trip takes me fifteen minutes, walking fast, preoccupied.

I decide that Oteri will soon join his charges on a slab. The men who come from Moscow to pick up Kato's body will have their orders, one of which will be to rid the world of those who know too much. I think that Rhino is guilty of many things, but one of them is not the murder of Kato.

I'll soon know the answer to the last question.

When I arrive at the train station I catch another cab and ride it to Prison Colony No. 1, located in the town of Kopeysk less than fifteen kilometers to the east. The driver drops me in front of a stolid concrete edifice designed by Soviet architects with unimaginative efficiency.

Two security checks later, one of the guards leads me through the final sally port. When the last set of sliding doors clangs shut behind us, we're at the head of a long row of cells. They're little more than concrete cages for men dressed in rags, some asleep, some staring listlessly through the bars as we pass, the sound of our boots echoing against stone and steel.

Two years ago the warders beat four men to death here. The Federal Corrections Service said that the prisoners attacked first, armed with shivs. Inmates claimed that the guards provoked the fight with beatings and constant harassment.

Kato covered the investigation conducted by one of the better-known human rights groups. The group confirmed that eight other prisoners suffered serious injuries on the night the four died. They called the beatings "standard procedure" and labeled Prison Colony No. 1 a "torture colony." Kato quoted one of the investigators that, "Whenever a new batch of prisoners arrives—twenty to thirty people—they are led into a corridor, stripped naked, made to stand along the walls and then beaten with varying degrees of ferocity."

I peer into each cell as we pass. Beaten or not, these prisoners all appear to have reached a state of cowed submission.

Including Rhino.

His cell looks like a shrunken version of the others. No bed, no toilet, no sink, just steel bars across the front of a concrete box. I once found the body of a man buried in an open sewage pit. Rhino smells better than that, but not by much.

He sits with his back against the wall, his legs stretched in front of him, one of them at an odd angle, his chin on his chest. He raises his head when our footsteps stop outside his cell. His eyes gleam in the murky darkness. Then he straightens his shoulders as recognition dawns.

"Captain?"

When he knew me my rank was captain. Now I'm a colonel, my last two promotions payback by the General for six months in a mud pit in the mountains of Chechnya.

"Can you stand?"

He starts to rise. Winces. Puts his hands under his knee and tries to straighten the crooked leg. Groans.

"Stop," I tell him.

I gesture for the guard to open the cell door. He reaches for the key, hesitates, then draws a truncheon from a loop attached to his belt and holds it in his right hand while he unlocks the door and steps back.

"The man's an animal. We can't protect you in there."

I step into the cell. "Leave us."

"I have to lock the door."

"So do it."

He bangs the door closed, makes a show of locking it, and stalks back the way we came down the long row of cages.

Bruises color Rhino's face eggplant purple. Split lips, a gash above one eye, and blood seeping from his right ear. He gazes at me through the twin slits left by the swelling around his eyes.

"My leg hurts the most. I'm afraid I'm going to lose it, captain. Like yours."

I find a hole in the knee of his pant leg and tear it wider. He clenches his jaw as the movement jostles him. Sweat pops on his forehead. He doesn't look down.

"How bad is it?"

I can't see the broken bone, but I can see one end of it poking like a tent pole beneath his skin a few centimeters below the knee. Red lines of infection radiate from a swollen bruise that looks like a lump of coal.

"Bad."

I rearrange the ripped trousers to cover the spot. I can't tell whether the moisture around his eyes is sweat or tears.

"They say you killed the journalist, Kato."

He grimaces. "Yeah, that's what I hear."

I settle next to him, leaning back against the cold concrete wall with our shoulders touching. He relaxes into me and closes his eyes.

"My leg's the least of my worries, isn't it, captain?"

"Did you know Kato?"

"No. Well, I saw pictures, you know, like everybody. Never met her in my life. Now they say they have evidence I popped her."

"What evidence?"

"They showed me an HK .45. Beautiful weapon. New. Way out of my price range. And you know I don't go for anything that big."

"That's it?"

"They say it's got my prints all over it."

Once Rhino was in custody, anybody could have placed the pistol in his hand and pressed his fingertips onto the grip and the slide while he was unconscious.

I once saw Rhino tethered to a contract soldier with a two-meter length of chain linked to them with two sets of handcuffs, each one attached to their left wrist. Both men stripped to the waist. The contract soldier corded with muscle, built with thick thighs and a powerful belly. Rhino gleaming whitely, lathered up, meaty slabs of muscle bulging like armor. They walked into a circle of three hundred men all shouting their bets and clamoring for a better view. Rhino dismantled his opponent in less than a minute that day, pounding him into the ground, then methodically, brutally, smashing a fist into his face until four men dragged him off.

Now I feel a shudder pass through his body. I feel his forehead. It's burning with fever. I'm probably too late to save him. Besides, why save a man destined for the gallows?

But still…

"I'll try to get a doctor, Rhino. Medicine, food, water, and a bed."

Now I can see for sure. The moisture on his broad face isn't sweat.

"I'm fucked, captain. I've seen it happen too many times. It's my turn in the box."

"What were you doing in Chelyabinsk?"

"Working. Or trying to work. Some guy hired me for protection. Good pay, steady job, he said. It's been a long time since I got good work."

"Who?"

"Don't know the client, captain. They sent me a ticket. I landed at the airport, met my contact, went to a dacha north of the city. Waited for two days, woke up one morning with a gun in my face and five policemen in my room."

"Who was your contact?"

"Some French fuck. Never said his name. Always had a smile on his face that made me want to wash myself."

"French?"

He nods. "Heard him talking one night in English, though. Don't know what he said."

"Talking to who?"

"Never heard a name. Sorry, captain."

He rests his head on my shoulder. Sighs.

The French have their fingers in many Russian pies. Among other things, they have a long association with Russia's nuclear program, one that includes the on-going disposal of French nuclear waste, I know from my talk with Kato at the open-air market. The conversation Rhino overheard in English could mean the Brits or the Americans are involved in something with the French, or it might be that the Frenchman and the person he was talking to shared only that language.

I listen to the ugly sounds of a prison at night. The low murmur of conversation, punctuated by jeers and threats shouted between cells; coughs, farts, the sound of someone defecating; and, from the cell across from Rhino's, a man weeping so quietly I can tell only by the hushed sound of his sobs.

Just when I think Rhino has fallen asleep he shifts his weight. "Captain?"

I nod to say I'm listening.

"Did you know the men used to argue about who would win in the pit? Me or you. What do you think?"

I think we both would have been badly hurt.

"You," I say.

I feel the shape of his smile against my shoulder. "I was the best, wasn't I?"

"You were the best, Rhino."

Chapter Eighteen

After leaving Rhino I check into a Chelyabinsk hotel. Use the business center to send an email update to the General.

Two workers. One mechanic, one cleaner. Not Rhino. Off to the park in the morning.

The General will get the gist of it. Two killers. One killed Kato, the other found three innocents, murdered them, and used their bodies to "clean" the murder scene by adding to the confusion. At the same time, someone lured Rhino to Chelyabinsk to take the fall. That person probably got paid a few thousand rubles to set the trap with the offer of a job. I can't prove as much in court, maybe, but the tracks of what happened are obvious to someone who knows how to read the sign.

The politics of what happened are not as clear, but this much I know. As bad at their job as men like Oteri and the local police are likely to be, they must have reached some of the same conclusions as mine. Yet the press still reported the story wrong. That could happen only with help from on high. Someone powerful enough to demand prior review, connected enough to ensure stories get printed the way he wants them to be. Someone capable of manipulating the facts about the three "students" and the timing of their death.

All of which raises the question. *Why?*

I log off the computer. Haul my duffel up three flights to a room with concrete floors, white plastic panel walls with thin strips of plastic to hide the seams where the panels met, clean sheets over a mattress dotted with specks of blood. A sure sign of bedbugs.

I spread my coat on the floor and use my duffel for a pillow. Stare up at the ceiling with my fingers laced behind my head, thinking about that question.

Why?

Trying to see past the obvious, the many people Kato exposed and offended with her stories. Careers derailed, reputations ruined, lives destroyed by her revelations.

I read one of Kato's stories in an old newspaper I found near the Chechen village of Khalkiloi while searching for a missing soldier. I discovered the soldier's body in a wattle and daub shepherd's hut with a window made with a piece of windshield glass. He'd been dead for many days. His thorax split open like a can of tinned fruit, the black flesh curled back to reveal a seething mass of maggots.

Somebody had covered his face with brittle pages from a Moscow newspaper. Banner headlines blared Kato's story on the front page. I read it by the light of a dying sun outside the shepherd's hut, looking down into a valley, cool and blue in the shadows like a lake, surrounded by mountains glazed with the sun's fire rearing into a blood-red sky.

The story was one in a series about a Dagestan politician who grew rich trading weapons to Chechen separatists. Weapons used to kill Russian soldiers. His trial lasted a day. The judge sentenced him to twenty years of hard labor. The judge had no other choice, no matter how much he was offered in bribes. Kato's stories had touched too many mothers and fathers and sisters and brothers.

I remember thinking that day that the politician fared better than common soldiers caught trading with the rebels. The two soldiers hung from the gibbet by their hands tied behind their backs, beaten until their bones shattered, faces so swollen that none of their features remained. Their crime: selling stolen tubs of butter to local villagers.

One sold guns; the others sold butter. The gunrunner was punished only because a journalist had the brains and guts to find the story and report it, although the Kremlin commuted his sentence two years later, after the furor died down. The butter traders suffered immediate retribution from their own comrades.

Guns and butter, but such different outcomes.

I learned later that Kato didn't stop digging after exposing that first politician. She connected him to others. In the end, the story I read that day in Khalkiloi reached all the way to some of the men in the Duma.

Plenty of candidates for her murderer, in other words.

But why here in this part of the world? Why now?

Why?

I think the answer lies buried in the mud on the banks of the Techa River. Maybe in the form of a spiral-bound notepad with a story inside that someone didn't want the world to know.

PART III

"At this point, all the government has to do
is wait for the victims to die."

—Mary Dickson, a Utah resident who lived downwind
from the fallout from the Nevada nuclear test sites

Chapter Nineteen

The next morning I wait outside the hotel for a car the General had arranged. Per his instructions, I look for a black Volga driven by a man named Jonas Kepler, a former staff officer attached to the 58th Army. I hadn't asked the General whether Kepler could be trusted. The General would have told me yes—his staff officers endure extensive background checks and frequent vetting—and he probably would have viewed the question as an insult.

But I know the truth. The truth is that people change. And those who live their life in the shadows, as men who work for the General tend to do, learn how to mask those changes. They discover ways to survive and cope with the things they're asked to do. The man who existed a year ago could be gone now. So the question about whether he can be trusted is one I want to decide for myself.

A dented black Volga turns onto the street in front of the hotel. The driver peers at me through the passenger window as he slows to a stop at the curb. He emerges from the car like an uncoiling snake. Tall, skinny, and sallow-skinned, a mole the size of a marble on the side of his neck. His smile reveals teeth the color of aged ivory.

"Colonel?" he says hesitantly.

"I.D., please."

He hesitates, then reaches into his breast pocket and pulls out a worn leather case. He opens it to show me a work identification card behind clear plastic. The picture matches. The badge identifies him as a salesman for the Chelyabinsk tractor factory. Good cover for a man who probably needs to travel to international destinations on assignments for the General.

I open the back door of the Volga and toss my duffel inside. He winces when I slam the door, then he opens the passenger door and gently closes it behind me after I climb inside.

He checks the mirrors, signals, and drives slowly away. Once we reach the M-5 heading north he glances at me.

"We are going to Mayak?" he says.

"Where's my gun?"

"Of course." His Adam's apple bobs as he aims his chin toward the back seat. "In the gym bag."

A green Adidas bag. It zippers open. Inside is a Chinese-made T30 Tokarev pistol, all the markings on the frame filed off. Silver with a cracked black grip embossed with a stylized Chinese star. Eight-round magazine, but only three rounds inside. No safety.

Kepler watches me from the corner of his eye.

"Not bad, eh? My father brought it back from Afghanistan."

"Why only three rounds in the magazine?"

His eyes widen. "Do you know how hard it was for me to find a gun? Any gun? Now you want to complain about three rounds? How many do you plan to use?"

The Adidas bag holds a square of brown cloth. I spread it on my lap and disassemble the Tokarev. Clean bore, although it looks like it's been fired often. Short coil springs. Flat striking surface. The feed ramp on the frame meshes perfectly with the feed ramp on the barrel.

Kepler whistles tunelessly. He steers with both hands on the wheel, oblivious to all the vehicles rushing past us in the other lane. The mole on the side of his neck looks like a slug. It arrests the eye. The rest of him seems to hide behind it.

He clears his throat, but doesn't say anything for another kilometer. When he finally does, he addresses the windshield, refusing to look at me.

"They tell me, pick up this man. Take him first Mayak, then wherever he tells you. Bring a gun. Where am I supposed to get a gun? He is a colonel, they say. A colonel? Is he old, young, fat, skinny? Nobody knows. You see how this is hard for me?"

"How much longer to Mayak?"

"A couple of hours. Where are we going once we get there?"

"The reprocessing plant."

"What's there?"

I finish reassembling the Tokarev. Slap the magazine into the butt. Put it in my lap, lean back, and close my eyes. Thinking that Kepler—the Mole, as I've come to think of him—asks too many questions. Which means he's either a bad driver or a problem.

Or both.

He puckers his lips and starts again with his tuneless whistling.

Two hours later he signals to exit the M-5. We drive past uncultivated fields and stands of birches and firs. The Mole signals, turns. He seems to know the way. We drive along an empty lane for several kilometers. Turn again.

The foliage thins. Between the bare branches are glimpses of a desolate lakebed the color of burnt umber and ashes. Like an ancient pot left to boil until whatever was inside was reduced to a gooey mush.

"Lake Karachay," the Mole says. "The most polluted spot on earth, according to the scientists who monitor such things."

No road signs warn that we are passing through a radioactive zone, through the heart of one of the most dangerous places on the planet.

A paragraph from Kato's red notepad springs to mind: *A moonscape*, she wrote of Lake Karachay. *A dumping ground for Mayak's radioactive waste, dried and dead, the gray dust blown by the wind over hundreds of square kilometers, exposing hundreds of thousands of unsuspecting innocents to radiation.*

She cited a report by the National Resources Defense Council saying that the radiation level in the region near where Mayak discharged its radioactive effluent into Lake Karachay was sufficient to deliver a lethal dose to a human within an hour.

We travel another kilometer east before the road curves and takes us north for several more kilometers.

Smokestacks rise in the distance. Ahead and to our left, an occasional building marks the outskirts of the closed town of Ozyorsk. *Closed* meaning travel and residency restrictions, mail sent and received using post office boxes in other cities. Nowadays they're most often referred to as "closed administrative-territorial occupations." During the Soviet years, Ozyorsk was known as Chelyabinsk-65 and Chelyabinsk-40.

I recall the drawing in Kato's notepad of a salamander. The meaning became clear to me when I researched this area. Kato drew the coat of arms for the town of Ozyorsk: a flame-colored salamander that represents the 1957 disaster at the nuclear plant.

"How are we supposed to get in?" the Mole says.

I don't answer. He whistles some more.

"This facility reprocesses spent nuclear fuel from our submarines and icebreakers and power plants," he says. "The environmental nuts shout and complain, but what else are we supposed to do?"

"Just *our* spent fuel?"

"Who else's fuel would we reprocess?"

From Kato's notepad: *Mayak's five nuclear reactors were built in the years 1945 through 1948. Their purpose: to make, refine, and machine weapons-grade plutonium. Later the plant began reprocessing plutonium from decommissioned nuclear weapons. Later still, it provided the same service for foreign nuclear reactors, mainly the French ones.*

I recall the curl of Kato's lips when she talked of Europe using Russia as a dumping ground for its nuclear waste. *How convenient for them. How superior they must feel.*

We arrive at a long chain-link fence topped with concertina wire. Dirt berms shield the facility. No warning signs near the fence.

"They're not going to let us through the gate," the Mole says.

I tuck the reassembled Tokarev deep among the springs and framework beneath my seat, thinking of the possible link between Kato's reference to the French and Rhino's story. *Some French fuck.* I motion for the Mole to keep going.

"They'll let us through. We're expected."

Chapter Twenty

The Mole eases the Volga to a stop at a gate built into the fence. The gate is made of doubled chain links with steel wheels mounted on metal rollers. Flanked by a stone guardhouse with a steeply sloped roof.

A guard steps out. No more than a boy. Green uniform, black belt with a pistol in a holster, a clipboard in his hand. He approaches us with a wary expression as the Mole scrolls down the window. He seems surprised to see us.

"No visitors allowed here," he says.

The Mole looks at me. I hand him a sealed envelope, which he stares at for a moment before passing it to the guard.

"Give that to your superior officer," I tell the guard through the window. "He'll need to make a phone call. We'll wait."

I don't know the contents of the envelope. The General gave it to me before I left. For all I know, it carries instructions from Vladimir Putin, although I doubt that, because the General and Putin have been at odds since the beginning of the second Chechen War in 1999. More likely it contains a letter of introduction and authority from Constantine, a longtime Kremlin power broker who works with the General. One of those men who survives transitions of political power as easily as most people cross the street.

The guard stares at the envelope as if it has fallen from the sky.

"Do it now, soldier. Move!"

He scurries back to the guardhouse. Its small window reflects the dull morning light, preventing us from seeing inside. The Mole shifts his weight to put more of his back to me.

"Toward the end of the war our convoy passed a checkpoint built of stone just like this one," he says, talking out the window. "Manned by members of the Chechen militia, men who fought on our side. An officer and two soldiers, one of them wounded, wrapped in bloody bandages from his ankle to his thigh. We were pulling out. They didn't say a word. Just stood there and watched us leave. They would be dead by dawn. We knew it, they knew it."

"You lived."

He turns to face me. "What is that supposed to mean?"

"Some live, some die. I don't know why. I gave up trying to figure that out a long time ago."

He stares at me. Looks away. Runs his hand over the steering wheel like a man trying to coax a genie out of a bottle.

"Everybody was for sale there," he says.

"Here, too. People are for sale everywhere, in times of war or peace. All that matters is the price."

He studies the wheel some more, narrowing his eyes. "What about you? What brings you here? Money? Orders?"

"Some people can't be bought for any price. They do what they think is right, no matter the cost to them."

"You are such a person?"

"No."

"Who is?"

I picture Kato in the mountains of Chechnya, squatting on her haunches, inching closer to my pack in the shadows thrown by the distant firelight, determined to see that her story was published.

"Precious few," I say. "They're worth protecting."

A motor whines, and the gate trundles open, steel wheels rattling along tracks embedded in the asphalt. A moment later the door to the guardhouse swings open. The soldier emerges and walks around the car to my side. Stands saluting while I roll down the window. It sticks halfway down.

"Sir," he says. "Commander Glotser requests your presence in the administrative building E. Go through the gate to the next guard station. They'll take you from there."

When I give him a halfhearted salute in return, he turns on his heel and retreats to the guardhouse.

The Mole shifts the Volga into gear and drives us through the gate, then follows the road between the dirt berms. I don't know what's on the other side of them or what tunnels and underground facilities lurk beneath our wheels. But the point of my conversation with the Mole hasn't been lost on me. He is conflicted—about me, about his role here, about what he has been paid by the General or by another man to do.

He defies easy categorizing, but he's no simpleton. I know that now. Just as I know that I trust him not at all.

Chapter Twenty-one

The package from Matthews arrives in less than three hours. Stone spreads the pages on the bed in his Comfort Suites room and settles over them with four Jack-in-the-Box tacos.

Thirty pages of files from the CIA, the NSA, Interpol, MI6, and the IAEA, the International Atomic Energy Agency of the United Nations.

Stone organizes the pages chronologically. Reads everything through once, quickly, polishing off the tacos before he's through. When he's finished with his second reading, he takes a few minutes to process what he's learned, nibbling on bits of meat, lettuce, and cheese that have fallen onto the bedspread.

Lazar Solovie.

Nuclear scientist.

Maybe a KGB and FSB spy, maybe not. The Americans believe he's straight, the Brits think he's bent. The IAEA keeps assigning him greater responsibility. Iraq, Iran, North Korea—all the nuclear hot spots. Stone thinks the IAEA assignments suggest that Solo must be on an FSB leash, because the Russians and their Third World lackeys control the levers of power in the United Nations.

Buried among the rest of the paperwork Stone finds a copy of the memo he's already seen from ECHELON's files. The memo from the CIA analyst suggesting foul play in the death of Vladimir Nechai, the director of the top-secret nuclear complex located in the shadow of the Mayak nuclear processing plant.

The memo generated a spate of responses, none of them decisive, but all broken down along familiar lines: the Americans didn't buy the story of Lazar Solovie the cold-blooded killer, the Brits weren't so sure. Dark hints about their suspicions during his years at Cambridge, clues that suggested information known only to him and a handful of others was getting into the wrong hands.

None of it conclusive.

But Stone knows a few things the analysts don't. The Delveccio interrogation ties Solo to two dead Russians in the Nevada desert, both connected to a Russian drug dealer named Shakalov. And somehow they all tie to a dead journalist in the wasteland north of Chelyabinsk along the Techa River.

Stone reaches his own conclusions.

Lazar Solovie.

Nuclear scientist.

Soviet and Russian spy.

Murderer.

Or, perhaps more accurately, a man who orders murders to be committed.

Stone makes an overseas call to his contact in the Action Division of the Directorate-General for External Security, the French foreign intelligence agency. The call lasts twenty minutes. Once he has his marching orders, Stone packs the papers from Brock Matthews into a metal briefcase, locks it shut, and heads out to his car, swinging the case by his side.

Glad to be leaving. Glad to have the scent.

And delighted to have the opportunity to turn the tables on the French. Not because of some ill-defined resentment or a jingoistic fuck-the-French attitude. Stone is a political agnostic. No, he's hated working for the French for all these years because they're cheap. Their work took him away from better-paying jobs for the Americans, the Brits, and the Chinese.

Not this time. This time the Action Division is going to have to spread its legs. He doesn't have all the pieces yet. But he has enough to infer that they have something very big and very embarrassing they want buried. And French money spends just as well as any other money.

By the time Stone arrives at McCarran to catch his flight to Kennedy, he's whistling. Looking forward to acquiring the target.

Lazar Solovie.

Murderer.

My kind of guy.

Chapter Twenty-two

As soon as the Mole drives us through the gate and the high berms, another portal appears directly ahead. A long boom flanked by two low-slung buildings and manned by three guards, one each on either side of the boom, and a third waiting on the side of the road.

The third man wears captain's bars on the shoulder of his greatcoat. Hat pulled low over his eyes, his bearing tense. He regards the Volga without expression, then shifts his gaze to the Mole and me. He stiffens when he sees the Mole, but his change of expression is too fleeting for me to put a name to it. Maybe recognition, maybe surprise.

Maybe nothing.

He keys a microphone attached to his lapel and speaks into it. Then he motions for me to roll down my window. The wind blows a cold blast of air in my face. He studies me.

"Papers, please."

I hand him my military identification. He looks from it to me, then back again.

The photo is old. Taken five years ago, during the months when I rehabbed my leg. The pain shows in my clenched jaws and the deep lines in my forehead. The light from the flash caught my eyes just right, capturing the feral glow that always seems to give people pause the first time they meet me.

The captain hands my ID back. Salutes.

"I need to ride with you to Building E, sir," he says.

When I nod, he opens the rear door and climbs in behind me.

"Pull forward, make a left, follow the road."

The Mole gives me a sidelong glance, puts the Volga into gear, and drives under the raised boom.

Ahead of us looms the Mayak nuclear facility.

Domes and smokestacks and low buildings made of tilt-up concrete walls. Heavy trucks, two bulldozers, and a front-end loader smoothing dirt in the distance. Scattered cars and a few military trucks parked near the buildings.

I turn in my seat to see the captain better. His cap is in his lap. Without it, he seems less imposing than he first appeared. Small eyes like a burrowing animal's. Horseshoe-shaped bald spot, black strands of hair plastered to his dome looking like cracks in his skull. A ski-jump nose too big for his face.

"How many people work here?"

"That's classified, sir. Commander Glotser can tell you, if he wishes."

His gaze slides toward the Mole. Once again a strange look clouds his face.

I turn away just as the Mole pulls into a spot near a set of metal double doors outside a concrete building. A sign in the patch of dirt in front identifies it as Building E.

All three of us get out of the car. The Mole stretches his arms above his head and yawns.

"Keep your hands above your head," the captain says.

The tone of his voice causes me to tighten and turn. He's drawn his service pistol and has it aimed at the Mole's narrow back. The Mole freezes. Only his eyes move, rolling as though he's trying to see behind him, then angling toward me.

"What's happening?" he says.

I raise an eyebrow at the captain, who approaches the Mole slowly with both hands holding his pistol out straight.

"Don't move," he says to the Mole, and he cuffs the Mole's right wrist with steel handcuffs and yanks it down behind his back, then does the same with his other hand and crunches the cuffs. He jerks on the chain to make sure they're secure. The Mole's knees buckle, and a sharp cry of pain escapes his lips.

I take a step closer, to within an arm's length, from where I believe I can disarm the captain if need be.

"What are you doing, Captain?"

But it's not the captain who responds.

"Your driver is a known terrorist."

I whirl at the sound of the voice behind me. The man facing me wears an open white lab coat over his uniform. Tight features, jaws blued by a heavy beard that probably looks the same way right after he shaves. Buzz-cut iron gray hair.

"You are?"

"Commander Glotser," he says. "Pleased to make your acquaintance, Volk."

He gestures for me to follow him into Building E, but I don't move. I motion toward the Mole.

"This man served in the 58th Army under General Nemstov. Why is he under arrest?"

Glotser appraises me, as though waiting for me to draw my own conclusion. His eyes are pale blue. One of them tilts off-center slightly. The effect is disconcerting, as if two men instead of one are studying me. I'm not sure which eye to look at.

"The first time I heard your name was during the fighting on the Dagestan border," he says.

I think he's referring to a 1999 uprising in Dagestan, one of the several reasons Yeltsin and Putin cited for reinvading Chechnya then. I saw action there.

"I was a lieutenant," Glotser says. "Sometimes I think that place was a breeding ground for the criminally insane."

"Are you trying to provoke me?"

"Awfully sensitive, aren't you? What makes you think I was talking about you?" He jerks his head toward the Mole. "I was referring to this deranged specimen."

The captain shifts his weight, and the Mole flinches and squeezes his eyes shut.

"What did he do?" I say.

"Why, he was the last man seen with a murdered journalist. He was *her* driver, too. She left with him and disappeared. A month later her body turned up buried in the mud on the banks of a river less than fifty kilometers from here."

Glotser regards me for a moment with his head cocked to one side so that I have no choice but to look into his crazed, off-kilter eye.

"Maybe you heard about it. The press played it up because she was one of their own. A rabble-rouser they called Kato."

Chapter Twenty-three

I watch without expression as the captain shoves the Mole ahead. They cross a barren field toward another low building a hundred meters away, the captain prodding the scrawny man with the barrel of his pistol. The Mole casts a frightened look over his shoulder before a push sends him stumbling forward.

"Shall we?" Glotser says.

I follow him into Building E.

Glaring lights. Tile floors, worn smooth in the middle where the traffic flows. Drop ceiling with rectangular panels hanging low enough to produce a feeling of claustrophobia. Plastered walls painted bilious green on the bottom and white above a rubber border, the paint smudged by countless hands. A reception area behind sliding glass windows to the right. Nobody manning the station.

Glotser says, "Follow me," and turns left and strides down a corridor, setting a brisk pace. Through the open doors on either side are offices, a kitchen, a break room, and a conference room with a table surrounded by mismatching chairs. Several rooms contain devices I don't recognize, and I'm unable to look closely as we pass each doorway.

The whole place smells stale and mildewy. Not much better than Oteri's morgue, and not at all as I imagined a modern nuclear facility would. Which is part of the problem, I think. Mayak is old. Modernized during the Cold War and maybe again in the 1990s, but out of date and run-down by current standards.

Glotser pushes through double doors into an empty room. He stops and offers me a false smile.

"I'm afraid you'll need to be searched here, Colonel. Regulations. You understand."

Two soldiers enter the room from a side door. Both armed with Kalashnikovs. A third person enters the room behind me. The captain.

"Is the Mole safely stowed away?" I ask him. "Or dead?"

He looks confused for a moment, then realizes I'm talking about the driver.

"Him? He's a problem for the police, not for us. They'll be here to collect him in a few hours."

The captain wands me with a handheld metal detector. It chirps when it passes over my belt buckle, then screams loudly when it comes to the titanium in my prosthesis.

"Strip," the captain says.

I remove my clothes. I have to sit and detach my prosthesis before I can pull off my pants. Glotser picks it up and turns it in his hands.

"They make better ones now, you know. Bioengineered with contacts and wires that allow sensory feedback between your nerves and muscle tendons and"—he breaks off and lifts my foot in the air—"and this thing."

My foot was state-of-the-art once, but not anymore. America's adventurism in Afghanistan and Iraq cost many of its soldiers their limbs, and prosthetic technology has improved exponentially in the years since then. The General hasn't offered to send me back there for a new foot. Besides, I'm used to mine, and I like that its relatively low-tech construction allows me to hide a slim-bladed knife in it. A knife that appears likely to survive another search undetected.

I stand, balancing with one hand on the plaster wall while the two soldiers paw through my clothes. One of them searches through my ID wallet. His partner finds a banded roll of rubles in the pocket of my pants and tosses it to Glotser, who catches it deftly with his free hand.

"Colonels make lots of money these days, I see."

He flips the cash back to the soldier, who reluctantly returns it to my pants pocket. Probably wondering why the spoils aren't being divided among the four of them—a natural assumption to make for a member of our deeply corrupted military.

"Put your clothes on," Glotser says.

I do. He hands me my prosthesis, and watches while I snug my stump into the socket.

"Still hurt?"

"Never." Not if you don't count the stabbing, aching, stinging pain in a foot that no longer exists.

"We've been ordered to show you what we showed the journalist, Kato. This is unusual for us, you see. Why allow guided tours of a closed nuclear facility? I would refuse the request out of hand, but…"

He shrugs.

I get the meaning. The General is not one who is easily denied, no matter how unusual his demands. Which raises an important question: Why was Kato allowed to tour this facility? But that's not a question I want to ask with more than one person in the room.

Glotser leads the way back to the hall, then pushes through double doors into a large laboratory. Lab tables, microscopes, beakers, washbasins, keyboards, computer monitors. The Captain trails us while the two soldiers hang behind him. In the brief moment we're alone after walking though the doors Glotser says, "Sorry for the theatrics, colonel," in a whisper.

Inside the lab several men and women wearing white coats are working around the tables and along a counter crowded with microscopes on the far wall. None of them appears to be moving very quickly. They seemed trapped in routine, bored.

Sliding glass doors on the other side of the lab open to admit us to a small lobby containing two elevator doors. We wait in silence for one of the doors to open, then ride the elevator down for a long time. No indicator lights to say how many floors we're passing.

"How deep?"

"Almost thirty meters," Glotser says.

We stop. The elevator doors open onto another lobby. The only way out takes us through a metal portal and into a changing room. We don heavy brown overcoats and face masks. Neither the captain nor Glotser bothers to button his coat, but I do.

From there we walk along another corridor while Glotser talks by rote, not looking at me.

"Nuclear reprocessing can potentially recover up to 95 percent of the remaining uranium and plutonium in spent nuclear fuel. It's then put into new mixed oxide fuel. This process is performed all over the world. Britain, France, China, Japan, and soon India. The point of it is to reduce long-term radioactivity within the remaining waste."

Glotser seems bored, uninterested in whether I'm following his monologue or not. I slow my pace to force him to reduce speed. My face mask smells ripe.

"Some reprocessing plants use techniques to divert plutonium to weapons building," I say.

"We don't need more nuclear weapons, colonel."

"What about our Third World partners?"

He doesn't respond.

We pass a control room. Half a dozen people inside in front of computers and consoles filled with switches, gauges, and monitors. Glotser makes no comment about it.

Thirty seconds later we arrive at a viewing platform with a large window overlooking a room filled with machinery and storage bins connected by metal tubes. Tables manned by figures dressed in what looks like pale blue plastic raincoats hanging from their neck to foot. Yellow masks over their face. Heads covered with something that resembles white shower caps. All of them move in slow motion, similar to the technicians in the lab. They look like pastel mannequins.

"The material undergoes various physical and chemical processes here," Glotser says. "You can see for yourself all the safety precautions."

Glotser motions for me to follow him. He leads us through a different set of sliding doors. Now we are looking down upon a room where people dressed the same way as those in the first room are mixing a yellowish substance in steel containers.

We proceed from the room and down a hallway. The rooms on either side contain banks of monitors and machinery lit with red, green, and yellow lights. White-smocked technicians fiddle with dials and stare at monitors and huddle in tight groups with clipboards in their hands.

We reach another viewing platform. This one overlooks an area that's about a quarter the size of a soccer field. The people inside are wearing gas masks, the breathing tubes hanging like long chins covering their neck. Between and around them are enormous steel pipes and canisters painted red and white. Large gauges are mounted on the side of each canister.

Glotser ushers me through more rooms. More of the same, none of which am I equipped to fully understand. Glotser rambles on about reprocessing techniques and methodology, but for the most part I tune him out.

I need to talk to him alone. Because he didn't whisper to me on a whim. Nor did he use the word *theatrics* lightly. He was sending a message.

When the tour is done, we return to the changing room and leave the heavy overcoats and face masks behind. We ride the same elevator back to the surface.

Three hours have passed. Glotser and the captain confer for a few minutes while I stand off to one side in the lobby. The captain salutes and marches away, leaving me alone with Glotser for the first time since he led me down the first corridor.

"He went to check on another driver for you," he says.

I step closer to him so that we're standing shoulder to shoulder. I don't see any cameras in the small lobby, but that doesn't mean they aren't there.

"Why Kato?" I say quietly, finally asking him what I've been wondering about. "Why would such a harsh critic of the Kremlin be allowed to see this place?"

Glotser frowns. Peers around with his offset eyes to see if anyone is near enough to hear us talking. Although we are alone, he too speaks in a hushed voice.

"How am I supposed to know something like that?"

I wait him out. I think he knows something. Maybe I'm reading too much into his hurried whisper, but I think he *wants* to tell me for his own reasons, although I don't know what those reasons might be.

He looks around again. Leans toward me. "I'm the man on the ground," he murmurs. "My orders come from the Chelyabinsk Military District. *They* do what the Kremlin tells them. They're no more autonomous than I am. You see?"

I nod.

"But people talk," he says. "By the time the stories get to me, who knows what's true and what's not? The second in command in Chelyabinsk told me that the top nuclear scientist in Russia gave the order to allow Kato access to this facility. Politicians bow and scrape before this man. Who are we to tell him no?"

The lines on Glotser's face deepen.

"I didn't like it, just as I don't like you being here now. We gave her the same tour we gave you. Bullshit. Nothing happens in this building. The others are the ones that matter. This facility turns out tons of radioactive sludge a day. Dumps it all over the Urals, some places secure, some not. Stand next to the stuff without protection for one hour and get a dose of radiation that will kill you in weeks.

"Me? My men? We're dead men walking. We've soaked up so much of the stuff we can't go near an ionization chamber without making alarms scream. That's why we've deactivated most of them. We bury our heads in the sand instead. When the alarms don't go off we can keep pretending we don't have a problem. It is the Russian way, is it not?"

"Who gave the order to let Kato tour this facility?"

"That's what's so strange. He didn't simply give the order. He came here personally. First time in years since he's been here.

After we finished with her, he toured her through other areas of the facility himself. They were alone together for nearly an hour."

"What's his name, this top scientist?"

"Lazar Solovie. He spends most of his time in Sarov. I hear they now have a facility as modern as any in the West. Everything new, cutting-edge."

Glotser keeps talking, but I'm not paying attention anymore. I'm hearing Kato's voice in my head. I feel as though I'm with her again, standing in the open-air market.

I went to Sarov and started asking questions. Instead of answers, the man I met with there fed me half-truths and lies.

Who?

The people at the facility I visited called him Solo. Just that, Solo. No sir, *no* doctor, *no* mister. *I don't know whether he is civilian or military. I don't even know whether that is his real name.*

Now I know for sure. Solo. Lazar Solovie.

Kato got to him. Pulled some magic out of her reporter's bag of tricks and got him to talk. Got him to bring her here.

Then what?

The only way to learn the answer to what happened between the two of them is to follow the trail. Now I've found the trailhead.

I have a target.

Lazar Solovie.

Chapter Twenty-four

Grayson Stone hates to fly coach. But first class was full by the time he booked the flight, so here he is. Trapped in a metal tube fighting for armrest space with scum who don't mind pressing their arms and legs against his. Lucky it's winter, and the chubby guy in the middle seat next to him has on a long-sleeve shirt. Stone's guts churn just thinking about flesh-to-flesh contact.

As the plane begins it long descent into Kennedy, Stone puts away his papers and closes his briefcase, considering what he knows about Lazar Solovie. The more he thinks about it, the more he likes Solovie for The One.

The One. Stone's name for the guy behind the scenes who's been fucking up his plans for years.

How long now?

Since the summer of '02. Maybe even before then, but that summer marked the first time Stone got kicked in the balls. The trouble in Bagdad, when he fired through the walls and took out the baby—that came later.

First came Kabul, Afghanistan.

North of Kabul, actually. The middle of nowhere, just miles of sunburned dirt and sand split by a ribbon of black asphalt that ended at the horizon in a shimmering mirage. Stone riding in the front seat of a Humvee mounted with an M2 machine gun, a Browning .50 caliber the boys called "Ma Deuce." Headed for a meeting in a village at the base of the mountains. A meeting with a village elder who harbored a grudge against a regional warlord named Zemar Waziri, one of the men at the top of the CIA's most-wanted list.

The village elder had his blood feud, and the CIA wanted Waziri dead. A "fortunate confluence of interests," according to a CIA analyst quoted in Stone's briefing memo. Fertile ground for a trade: the elder's information about Waziri's location in exchange for a bagful of U.S. dollars and the safe transport of a truckload of "crops," the euphemism du jour for opium. The spooks and the military brass would *always* look the other away for the right reason, and a chance to nail Waziri's hide to the wall was one of the best possible reasons.

No telling what started the feud between Waziri and his rival. A woman, a perceived slight, a fucking camel for all Stone knew or cared. All that mattered was that one towel-head wanted to narc on another.

Truth was, Stone really didn't give a fuck about *that*, either. Killing Waziri might be another notch in the gun for the CIA, but Stone had his own orders to worry about. Specifically: deliver the quivering fat boy riding in the seat behind him to a lieutenant colonel attached to the First Infantry Division, some of whose men had found a weapons cache out in a mountain cave in the middle of Bumfuck, Nowhere.

A cave loaded with AK-47s, RPGs, and enough high explosives to make hundreds of improvised explosive devices. And, way in the back, tucked in a corner where the sunlight never reached and covered with an oil-blotched tarp, three green barrels affixed with yellow-and-orange labels from the National Nuclear Security Administration, the United Nations, and RANSAC, the Russian-American Nuclear Security Council.

Fuck-ups all, in Stone's opinion. No room for debate about that.

Because no way, no how could a hundred and fifty kilos of HEU, Highly Enriched Uranium—weapons-grade stuff—end up buried in a cave controlled by a bunch of savages. Yet there it was. Three green barrels holding fifty kilos each. All of it supposedly inventoried and accounted for when it was moved under heavy guard to a protected site in the Urals more than a year ago.

Bullshit.

The cold truth: all 150 kilos stolen, diverted, disappeared during a top secret transport from a former East German research lab to the Mayak nuclear reprocessing facility.

American intelligence officials spent days burning up their secure videoconferencing equipment, pointing fingers at one another, at the Russians, at the duplicitous pricks in the U-fucking-N. Then they pulled together and decided to send in a team of specialists. Military, military intelligence, and nuclear scientists, all engaged in an exercise in ass-covering. You didn't need a busload of experts. Stone saw the pictures. The fucking *labels* told the story where the barrels came from.

Fatboy was one of the last experts to arrive, since he had to come all the way from Australia, where he was a well-known nuclear scientist. The kind of person the CIA didn't want anybody to know was in the desert.

So Stone had a mission buried within a mission. Kill Waziri. Deliver Fatboy.

Stone didn't need to be told which was more important.

An hour out of Kabul the convoy passed the hulking remains of a Soviet tank. Paint burned off by fire and wind-driven sand. Twisted metal bleached to a silvery white, like the bones of a prehistoric animal jutting from the sand.

The driver pointed. Said something about "the poor sons of bitches who fried inside that thing."

And then the world exploded.

The blast blew Stone out the side window. He landed five meters away on the other side of the road, the flaming Humvee between him and the remains of the tank. Pieces of which became shrapnel when the IED exploded, Stone realized. Shrapnel that pocked the Humvee with holes rimmed with the glowing white and orange of superheated metal.

Stone *heard* nothing. No crackling flames, no secondary explosions, no anguished cries. Turned out he was temporarily deaf in one ear, permanently deaf in the other.

But Stone *saw* everything.

Fire.

A mushroom cloud of black smoke against a dome of white-blue sky.

A boot with purple laces nearby—marking it as the property of Stone's Afghan interpreter—and the remains of a leg sticking out like the bone in a drumstick.

The perforations in the barrel support of Ma Deuce glowing like red eyes.

Gently falling debris that looked like fireflies.

But the thing Stone remembered most clearly was Fatboy. Stone wanted to look away, but couldn't. All he could think was, *Oh, you poor fucker.*

One second bouncing through the desert, wiping sweat, wondering what in God's name brought you to such a place. The next second all you know—all you will ever know—is agony. Fatboy. Nuclear scientist turned in an instant into a ball of flames, pinballing around the shattered interior of the Humvee like an incendiary dervish. Took him over a minute to still. Even then he seemed to collapse in on himself in slow motion, a melting wax figure.

Stone passed out. He awoke on a pallet in a hide tent. Camels bleated and groaned outside. Dark inside. Dim light from a candle. A face loomed over his. Cropped hair, a week's growth of beard, and hard, hard eyes.

"You'll live," the man said in English with a slight accent.

A Russian accent, Stone realized, still in the fog of concussion.

Stone listened to the man leave. Heard the sound of his voice but no words as he talked to the herder who would later take Stone to an American base outside Kabul.

Waziri lived, too. He killed more boys from Texas, Arkansas, Pennsylvania, and so many other places, wreaking private misery that metaphorically dotted a map of the United States like measles. Fatboy died, no help to the team analyzing the contents of the three green barrels.

Waziri lived, Fatboy died.

All of which gave Stone the reputation of being a fuck-up. Which still pisses him off. The international community lost track of 150 kilos of highly enriched uranium, Stone lost one fat scientist, and *he's* the fuck-up?

"Bullshit," he says under his breath as he steps off the plane into the jetway.

He hustles through the terminal. Hides behind a family as he approaches the baggage-claim area. Spots Jean-Louis leaning against a wall, hands buried in the pockets of his khaki pants, dark blue jacket tailored to fall in flattering lines.

The man dresses like a pansy, like Jimmy D but with flair. But it's not the clothes that Stone thinks about when he considers Jean-Louis. The clothes barely register.

Sometimes you brush up against evil so profound the memory of it stays with you like a stain on your psyche. Two years ago Stone watched the Frenchman work on a Filipino man who knew too much. They got their answers within minutes, but Jean-Louis kept at it for almost an hour. Made the things Stone did to Delvechio look like amateur hour. Stone still tastes the bile in his throat just to think about the euphoric look on the Frenchman's face with a bloody pair of pliers in his hand.

Jean-Louis sees Stone. A flash of distaste ripples across his features. Then the Frenchman smiles his oily smile and extends his hand in greeting.

"Grayson," he says. "Always a pleasure."

Stone grunts. The Frenchman's hand is soft, his grip limp, his palm moist.

"So," Jean-Louis says. "You have news for us? News about our Russian friend?"

Chapter Twenty-five

Glotser checks the halls and doors leading into the lobby, then turns to stare at me with his crazed eyes.

"Lazar Solovie," he says again. "That name means something to you?"

"Why shouldn't I know the name of your 'top nuclear scientist'?"

He laughs quietly, without mirth. "Because he doesn't want to be known. I met him in '95. He was nobody then. One more snooty scientist in a lab coat with his nose in the air."

Glotser cranes his neck to look through the window in the lobby door to see if the Captain is near. Whispers, "Then he killed Vladimir Nechai."

"I know that name."

Glotser nods. "He used to be the principal scientist here. You probably remember the headlines, like everyone else. Nechai was despondent, driven to suicide over lack of funds and the decline of Russian science. Lies. All lies."

"What's the truth of it?"

"Solo killed him."

"Can you prove it?"

Glotser scowls. The blued steel of his bearded jaw and the squint of his eyes give his face a Moorish cast. "Do you think I would be stuck here if I could do that? I would have a cushy job in Moscow. Or I'd be dead. Nothing in between."

"Why are you telling me these things?"

"For Nechai," he says simply.

He takes another peek through the window. Grabs my elbow and turns me to face the door. Through the window I see the captain approaching.

"You're going to walk out of here," Glotser says. "Those are our orders. If you talk about what I just told you, I'm a dead man."

"Cut the Mole loose."

"What?"

The captain stomps the snow from his boots on the concrete stoop outside the entrance to the lobby.

"I need him to take me to where Kato's body was found."

"I can't do that."

The captain enters. He looks from Glotser to me. Squints, starts to say something, then appears to think better of it.

"They don't want him," he says to Glotser.

"Who's 'they'?"

"The police. They've closed the file on the bitch reporter. The chief told me, 'We don't give a fuck who killed her anymore. Good riddance to garbage.'"

Glotser turns his crooked eye toward me. Deadpans, "I suppose I can cut your friend loose, Colonel."

I shrug. "One driver is the same as another."

The Mole looks the worse for wear. Limping. One eye bruised and a raised welt on his cheekbone.

He starts the Volga and drives out the way we came, wincing when he shifts gears. We have to stop at the red-and-white striped boom while the guards search the car. They make us stand outside. One of them rummages through the interior while another runs a mirror mounted on a pole under the carriage.

"Who did it?" I say quietly.

The Mole refuses to meet my gaze. "What do you care?"

Probably the captain, I figure.

"They're sadists," the Mole says.

I think of captured rebels tortured in bombed-out Grozny basements, of the gallows with the two soldiers accused of selling contraband to the Chechens, both of them dangling with their shoulders popped from their sockets, and of a cab ride in Manhattan when I snapped the fingers of Valya's beautiful brunette lover like they were twigs.

"Sadists everywhere," I agree.

The soldiers finish searching the car. One of them talks on his radio, looking at us. I think he's asking Glotser whether we need to be searched, too. The answer seems to disappoint him.

"Go," he says.

The Mole drives between the high berms. We stop again at the outside gate. The sentry in the guardhouse eyeballs us for a moment before he hits the button that rolls the gate back on its tracks.

The Mole looks at me. "Back to Chelyabinsk?"

"They told me you were the last person to see Kato alive."

"No. Her killer was the last."

"Where did you leave her?"

He jerks his thumb toward the east. "Over there. At a home outside a village called Metlino."

A woman stands with her daughter and grandson beneath a wooden alarm bell hanging like a man from a gallows on the banks of the Techa River.

"Is there a wooden alarm bell near there?"

His eyes widen. "Yes."

"Take me there."

He looks doubtful. Then a smile ghosts across his battered face. "Yes, sir."

Chapter Twenty-six

Ghosts.

The word takes me back to a trip I made to Afghanistan in the summer of '02. That was the first time I saw them, those nameless, faceless ghosts. Walking shadows.

The Mole drives away from Mayak in his slow, careful way. Both hands on the wheel as we wind through scrub brush and desiccated trees. No expression. But his eyes glitter, and I think his set features mask hard thoughts about the captain and whatever they did to him while they had him in custody.

I don't ask any questions. Instead, I let my thoughts drift away, remembering the first time I heard the word *ghosts* used to describe the women in burqas crowding the streets of Kabul.

The General had sent me to Afghanistan in the belly of an An-124 heavy transport plane, crammed in the cargo bay with a team of *Spetsnaz*, Army special forces, and a GAZ Zemlyak truck capable of carrying a payload of 4,000 kilograms.

"The Americans will fail in that hellhole," the General said when he briefed me in his subterranean quarters, the glow from his computer screen casting his blunt features into a ghoulish mask of darkness and light. "We'll help them along, just as they helped us thirty years ago."

I spent a month in Afghanistan. Arming, training, advising. Russian weapons and Russian techniques used by the Taliban in their war of attrition. A war fought on the margins, in mountains and caves, in valleys with sheer walls climbing into a washed-out sky. A war fought in cities and towns and villages among a civilian population that was ground to dust.

I kept to the periphery. Didn't fire a shot. Gave aid after firefights and IED explosions, mostly to civilians, but sometimes combatants. Among all those temporary alliances and shifting loyalties, the idea of *sides*, of one group being right and the other wrong, seemed hopelessly naïve and absurd.

But it was the ghosts that stamped an indelible impression on me.

Burqa-shrouded women.

Women who used to be doctors and lawyers and teachers imprisoned behind the mesh of their chador, faceless and anonymous, all but invisible in their flowing black robes.

Specters.

Ghosts.

One of them spoke to me once. Unaccented Russian. Low and controlled, but barely so, with a tremolo of suppressed rage. A disembodied voice that sounded like Valya's, probably because I was missing her desperately by then. Ferocious pain from my missing leg, an uncomfortable prosthesis that was a far cry from the titanium wonder I received later in the United States, and a month away from Valya were grinding me down.

"Please," the ghost said in her flawless Russian. "When will all this end?"

I didn't know what she meant by the word *this*. War? Humiliation and subjugation under Sharia law? But I knew this much. She wanted reassurance that her life could have meaning again. She wanted news of liberation, not just for her country but also for her gender, for the women entombed behind their burqas.

She wanted answers to questions I couldn't answer.

Her features were hazy behind her veil. All I could make out were her eyes, moist and pleading.

"Leave," I told her. "That is the only way."

I didn't intend for my words to sound harsh, although I'm sure they did. I was blunt because the way she talked and her erect carriage reminded me so much of Valya, and a woman like Valya deserved a straight answer. Or at least what I thought was a straight answer. A month in that place and I was ready to give up on the hope that centuries of culture could be changed in a generation.

An American intelligence agent named Brock Matthews once said something similar to me about Chechnya. We were riding in the back of a six-wheeled transport on our way to meet a Chechen rebel leader. We came across a boy on horseback, a Kalashnikov resting in the crook of his arm, crossed bandoliers over his chest, hate burning in his eyes.

"This is a generational problem, Volk," Matthews said, and all I could do was nod and agree. No other answer was possible.

"What are you thinking about?" the Mole says.

Ghosts. Hopeless ghosts. And I believe we are about to see more of them. Not the women who have disappeared in Afghanistan and all the other places in the world where women suffer Sharia law. A different kind of ghost. Those living in the shadow of a nuclear cloud covering thousands of square kilometers.

The Mole steers around a curve, waiting for an answer.

"Nothing."

He shrugs. We drive through a barren landscape. Patches of white snow and sickly brown dirt. Heath and scrub and gnarled trees. A light snowfall begins, quickly melting on the warmth of the Volga's windshield. One wiper works, the other flails uselessly in front of me.

"Ten more minutes," the Mole says.

"Why did they call you a terrorist?"

He concentrates on the road. Tightens his grip on the steering wheel.

"I joined a group of protesters in Moscow several years ago. Right after a series of revelations about what happened here—what's *been* happening here for decades—came to light. How many disfigured children must be born before the people in the Kremlin and the Duma acknowledge what they did to this place? How many generations must die young of some mysterious disease before somebody does something about it? Test, relocate? *Something.*"

The falling snow turns everything white. Clean.

It is an illusion. I know that. Kato knew it. She wrote:

> *We varnish the truth with lies and obfuscation. No light shines in our darkest corners. Governments change, administrations change, the world changes. But the truth about this place remains hidden. A secret known only to those who suffer and die young and the few people who peer beneath the blanket of lies and then choose to look away or even deny the existence of any problem whatsoever. Those who must live every day with the consequences of what we did cannot look away. They have nowhere to go.*

I reach beneath the seat, retrieve the Tokarev from its hiding place, and stuff it into the pocket of my jacket. Regard the Mole thoughtfully.

"You were arrested in Moscow?"

"Yes. Thrown into a holding cell with about twenty other protesters."

While he talks, I text an inquiry to the General. DESCRIBE JONAS KEPLER. Then I consider the Mole some more, several pieces falling into place.

"Kato was one of the protesters thrown in jail with you."

"That's right. That was the first time I met her, although I knew her by reputation."

Night falls early this time of year. The clouds press down on us. The snow falls harder, swirling in a vortex in the yellow light from the Volga's headlamps.

The Mole shifts his weight to angle his body more toward mine. "I didn't stop there. I continued to 'agitate' when I came back to Chelyabinsk. And I stayed in touch with Kato. Helped her identify the players here. Introduced her to some of the people hit the hardest, most of them ethnic Tatars and Bashkirs. I listened while they told her their stories."

"What sparked Kato's interest in this area?"

He glances at me. "You didn't read her articles?"

"Occasionally."

The truth is that I usually avoided reading Kato's columns and articles. The Kremlin called them "hate-filled diatribes" and "the delusional ramblings of a paranoid" who had "a deep-seated hatred" of her country. Not ideal reading material for a Russian army colonel and sometime Kremlin agent—especially not for a man who the Kremlin could trace and identify as her confidential source in Chechnya. One of her sources, at least.

All they needed to do was analyze what she wrote and when she wrote it, then compare that to where I was and what I was doing.

The Mole steers to the side of the road. Follows the shoulder around a copse of gnarled brush and birch and oak, then turns right onto a rutted dirt road. We follow the path for some time. The ground around us is the color of dead flesh. Gray snow with lines of black soil poking through.

When we are far enough off the road so that we can't be seen through the trees and brush, the Mole kills the engine.

"This is what fueled her interest in this area."

I look around, but there is nothing to see.

"What?"

"The burning lake."

PART IV

The death of one man is a tragedy.
The death of millions is a statistic.

—Joseph Stalin

Chapter Twenty-seven

The Mole leads the way through leafless oak trees bent by the wind or some other unseen force that has turned them into gnarled silhouettes.

Cripples.

Peasants hunched over a heavy job.

Clawed hands reaching for the sky.

Twisted limbs that look like the arms and legs of lovers entwined in an eternal embrace.

The snowfall stops. A dusting several centimeters thick covers the frozen ground. The soil feels like cinders beneath my boots. The earth and sky are gunmetal gray, as if we are in the bottom of a pewter ashtray that hasn't been cleaned in years.

We reach a curved stretch of sand. The Mole climbs a flat rock overlooking the dried bed of a lake. A checkerboard pattern is all that remains of ten thousand hollow concrete blocks planted there by the Soviets during the '70s and '80s to prevent sediments from shifting, now coated with silt. Gray streaked with black, puffs of ash lifted into the air by the wind in small eruptions that look like miniature mushroom clouds. They skitter along the bottom, rise in toy columns, whirl and dance, then dissipate.

A billion airborne particles swirling away.

That idea bothers me, but so does something else, a niggling thought I can't seem to grasp. Something is wrong.

"Lake Karachay," the Mole says. "We shouldn't stay here for very long. Even this much time, you might be sick tonight.

Nausea. You might vomit." He shakes his head. "Everybody reacts differently."

A flicker of orange appears near the center of the lake, burns in a wavering ribbon of flame that uncoils into the sky and vanishes like a snake disappearing into a hole.

"What was that?"

The Mole follows my gaze. "I didn't see anything."

"An orange flame. Like a Bunsen burner turned on and off quickly."

He shakes his head. Frowns. "Sometimes the night sky glows with a reddish color. I don't know the source."

Over his shoulder I can make out the dark shapes of the three smokestacks at the nuclear facility. Like the tines of a pitchfork drawn in a lighter shade of gray against the darker backdrop of the sky.

"Are they still dumping here?"

"I don't believe so. We've looked. We would have found the source."

"What if the source is underground?"

He raises his palms as if he is lifting the air. "How can we prove *that*?"

My phone buzzes with an incoming message. The General.

JONAS KEPLER: BORN 3 MARCH 1967. BROWN HAIR, BROWN EYES. 165 CM. 100 KG. NO OBVIOUS SCARS OR OTHER DEFINING FEATURES.

I return the phone to my pocket.

The Mole is younger, taller, and much thinner than the man described in the General's text. And his most distinctive feature—the mole on the side of his neck that caused me to give him his nickname—would almost certainly have made it into the General's file. The men who load descriptions into intelligence files don't miss marks like that one.

The Mole is not Jonas Kepler.

"We should go now," the Mole says.

"Where?"

"You need to meet the family Kato met while she was here."

I nod, but make no move to go.

The weight of the Tokarev pistol drags down the right side of my jacket. I can't decide whether to pistol whip the Mole for answers or let him play things out his way. My first instinct is to pile-drive him face-first into the lakebed. Make him breathe the irradiated earth.

Something stops me. Not the idea that the Mole appears to be no threat, or that he might be a good person trying to accomplish noble ends. Those considerations can't be part of the calculus, not if I plan to keep living this life I lead. No, the thing that stops me is that the Mole might give me answers if he's unaware that I know he's an imposter.

I contemplate the dried lakebed. I still can't put my finger on the thing that bothers me about it.

"What's going on here?"

His Adam's apple bobs. "What do you think?"

I study him. His gaze holds mine. Dark, vague eyes that still reflect something of the pain and indignity he experienced at the hands of the captain. Lips set firmly, almost defiantly. Rail-thin shoulders turned slightly away from me.

I decide to let him play out his hand. He may be an agent of the General's enemies. He may be a true-believing environmentalist, one of many men who admired and loved Kato from a distance impossible to bridge. Or he might be something else entirely. The quickest path to answers seems to lead through him, a man who somehow, some way, obtained false identification under a name that doesn't belong to him and knew enough about my travel arrangements to meet me outside the hotel on the streets of Chelyabinsk with a gun and take me to Mayak.

My phone buzzes. The General again. WHY THE QUESTION ABOUT KEPLER?

I wonder if the real Jonas Kepler is dead, perhaps one of the bodies laid out on a slab in Oteri's morgue, awaiting the saw blade.

"What do you think is going on here, Colonel?" the Mole says again.

A puff of wind riffles his hair. A scraping sound carries from the dried lakebed—the rattle of a wind-blown twig, maybe, or the scratching claws of a burrowing animal. No, not an animal, nothing lives here long enough to burrow. Nothing lives here at all.

That's when I realize what's been bothering me about the lakebed: its color, gray with black streaks. A dusting of snow coats the gnarled branches of the trees and covers the cindered ground around the lake. But the bottom of the lake is clear of snow.

Something warm resides underground.

The Mole shifts his weight. He scratches his cheek. "I told you, Colonel. One hour here is enough for a lethal dose. We have already stayed too long."

I text the General. JUST CONFIRMING. Close the phone and look at the Mole.

"Let's go."

From the corner of my eye I see another orange flame pop from the ash and sand in the middle of the lakebed, flicker there for a moment in some exotic dance, then disappear in the twilight sky.

Chapter Twenty-eight

"Are you happy, Alexei?" Kato asked me a long time ago.

We were in a hotel in Tbilisi. Light from the winter sun slanted through the window to paint a white rectangle that warmed the bed like an extra blanket. We'd been there for two days, scavenging food from the mini-fridge when we were hungry, sleeping only when we were exhausted between long sessions of lovemaking. Kato was built for speed, with the long limbs and the sharply defined muscles of a sprinter, but she had the sexual endurance of a marathoner.

Our long days and nights together started in Chechnya. Continued for another year or so all over the Caucasus whenever we could arrange to be in the same place at the same time.

I didn't respond to her question that day. She didn't expect an answer anyway. It was just part of her endless analysis of war and its consequences to its individual combatants and victims. "War is about people," she wrote. "Not politics or borders or economics. The frame must be small, the focus tight, lest truth be distorted by a failure of perspective."

I didn't need to respond to her question because she already knew the answer: No. Except for the interludes with her, I wasn't happy in those days.

Then I met Valya, and everything changed.

Valya became my obsession. She dominated my thoughts. My memories of her carried me through the worst time of my life, six months in a *zindan*—a mud pit—held captive by a rebel leader named Abreg, a man who still occupies the Stygian places in my mind.

Valya rescued me from that hell.

She cajoled, bribed, or tortured information out of every rebel she could find. When she discovered that I was alive and learned where I was being held, she assembled a group of men loyal to the General and me and led a night attack to save me.

Later, when I returned to Moscow, Valya stood by me while I learned how to walk again and struggled to rediscover some trace of my humanity.

Because Valya was the love of my life, I overlooked her occasional affairs with other women. How can one change that most fundamental aspect of one's nature? Even when one of her lovers turned out to have used Valya to hurt both of us, I forgave her, because she meant everything to me. No matter what I did with my life—soldier, spy, criminal, assassin—no matter all of those things, I had Valya, and my love for her laid claim to a small part of her mystical spirit.

But always, there was Kato.

Omnipresent.

Kato in the news, staring into the television camera and demanding that Putin meet her in Grozny to confront the horrors he had wrought. Challenging him to debates, denouncing his policies, skewering him with facts only she seemed able to uncover, damning him with her stories of lives ruined, families destroyed, villages reduced to rubble.

Wherever I turned, there was Kato.

Inescapable.

Kato's face on the cover of a magazine at the newsstand. Kato's image beamed over the airwaves on the nightly news, reporting from the front or from the site of the latest terrorist attack, often becoming part of the story. Kato's columns splashed all over the front pages of *Novaya Gazeta* and other newspapers brave enough to print what she wrote.

One night in St. Petersburg I saw her on television. My business there was done. A man with delusions of bidding for the timber rights near the Finnish border needed the facts explained to him. A bid? Fine, no problem. But this is the amount of your bid. This much, no more, you understand? Compensation? This is how much you will be paid. That much, no more, you understand? He couldn't seem to get the words out quickly enough. "Yes, yes, I understand, I understand," he stammered. During my years in the General's employ I had refined the science of persuasion to a fine art.

The caption at the bottom of the TV screen said Kato was in the studio, live at the station in Petersburg. I used the General's private codes to access the files of the Ministry of Internal Affairs. Their records revealed that she was staying at the Astoria Hotel, the guest of one of the American television news magazines. I waited for her outside the entrance, standing in the shadows. I saw her before she saw me. Erect carriage, fast-clipping high heels. The doorman held the door open as she swept past him.

The voice inside my head said, *Don't do this.*

I didn't listen.

I followed Kato into the bright lights of the Astoria's lobby. Stood next to her as she waited for the elevator, neither of us giving any sign that we knew the other. The doors opened, and we entered. She pushed the button for the fifth floor. We stood on opposite sides of the lift while it climbed with aching slowness. We walked together down the long hall to her room. She keyed the door, and I followed her inside. The only light came from the golden dome of St. Isaac's Cathedral framed in the window between the parted drapes. She stepped out of her heels. I pulled down the zipper on her back. She raised her arms above her head and let her dress slide from her body while I cupped her breasts and kissed her neck. She sighed and arched into me.

"Why has it taken you so long to come to me, Alexei?"

So that's the story of how I shredded my integrity. That's the story of how I betrayed Valya, the woman who saved me, the woman who is the love of my life.

Now I'm driving along a dark road with a man who is not who he says he is, crossing lethal ground on the edge of a burning lake, heading toward an uncertain destination to meet desperate people.

Why?

For Kato.

Kato animates everything, omnipresent and inescapable even in death.

Chapter Twenty-nine

Grayson Stone fumes while Jean-Louis lazily scans his menu, flicking away an imaginary fly, torturing the waiter with questions about how each dish is prepared, the freshness of the ingredients, the quality of the wines.

When Jean-Louis finally finishes, Stone orders the bone-in steak, rare, garlic-mashed potatoes, and oysters to start.

"No refinement," Jean-Louis says. "No refinement at all."

Stone kills the last of his scotch. Glenmorangie Signet. The cost of it will be on France's tab unless Stone decides otherwise, which depends on what the Frenchman wants and how much he's willing to pay. Stone rattles the ice in his glass on the tabletop. Looks around for the waiter, thinking he should have ordered another one before the guy took off. No telling when he'll be back after Jean-Louis' display.

"So." Jean-Louis drags out the word, his lips puckered as if he is about to deliver a kiss. "About our Russian friend."

"Fucking guy might be anywhere."

"Shakalov?"

"No, the fucking waiter." Stone grimaces. "Of course I mean Shakalov."

Jean-Louis picks lint from the lapel of his jacket. "You see, Grayson, that's not helpful. You are supposed to know things like that. That is why we pay a man like you, yes?"

Stone stares at a mosaic depicting a map of Europe, thinking that the boot of Italy would fit perfectly up the Frenchman's ass. "You pay me to take care of problems out here among the 'provincials.' Isn't that what you like to call us? It's your job to *find* the problem."

"Shakalov is not a problem, not yet at least. We are only concerned with what he knows about one little thing. That's all. One or two questions, one or two answers, his role is over." Jean-Louis flicks the air with his fingers. Curls his lips into his liquid smile. "Let Shakalov make his money on the drugs. We don't care about that."

The waiter brings Stone's oysters and the Frenchman's salad. Stone taps the side of his empty glass and says, "Double." He loads horseradish and red sauce onto his oysters and scarfs three in quick succession.

"What kind of questions?" he says.

Jean-Louis sips his wine. Sets the glass down carefully. Picks up his fork, puts it down, wipes nonexistent crumbs off the tabletop.

"We have a, ah…we have a small problem. It involves our Russian friends. Nothing for you to concern yourself with, you understand. Your role is to arrange a meeting. We will take care of the rest. Simple, eh? Easier than your last project."

Stone slurps another oyster to hide the excitement he feels. Damn right he *understands*. He understands that a great deal of money or international prestige is at stake. He stares at the mosaic.

"How much?" he says after a moment.

"For arranging a meeting? Not very much, but enough to make it worth your personal attention."

Despite his sadistic bent, Jean-Louis has talent. Stone will give him that much. He proved it that broiling day in Iraq, then again in Helsinki. Two Finns at a farmers' market holding hands, both killed with a headshot from seven hundred meters away on a rocking boat in the harbor. If Stone hadn't been kneeling next to the Frenchman on the deck below the gunwales—watching the Finns through powerful binoculars—he never would have believed it. Stone can't remember why the Finns needed to die.

Whatever reason he'd been given was probably bogus anyway. But he damn sure remembers those two shots.

"How much?" he repeats.

"One hundred thousand, but only if you're able to arrange a meeting."

"Why can't the Action Division get a meeting with Shakalov on its own?"

Jean-Louis pushes his salad away, untouched. "There was an *incident*. Two of Shakalov's men died. His policy is now one of aggression toward the Directorate-General for External Security."

So there it is. Action Division—and probably Jean-Louis personally—were the ones who tortured the two coyotes in the desert.

Why?

The answer to that question leads to the kind of money that buys jets and yachts and private islands where the movie stars like to hang out.

Stone thinks about the bloodbath in Iraq, and the Frenchman leaned negligently against the door jamb.

Associés? Partners?

Sometimes—when Jean-Louis and the men he works for in the Action Division are using Stone's services purely as a matter of convenience—he gets to say no. Not this time. No way. But that doesn't matter. Now that he's connected the dots from the torture-murder of the two coyotes in the desert to the *incident* involving Shakalov's two lieutenants, Stone *wants* this job.

Jean-Louis sips wine. Sets down his glass. Fastidiously wipes his lips with a napkin.

"Shakalov mustn't know you're acting on our behalf," he says. "That would be inconvenient for everybody. Make him believe it is a private arrangement." He wrinkles his nose. "Coming from you, he will believe it."

The waiter sets Stone's double Scotch in front of him. Stone drinks, closing his eyes as the smoky taste hits the back of his throat. Mami Kai will know how to find Shakalov. But Mami will want her cut. She's for sale, but she's not cheap.

"Quarter of a mil," he says. "Half up front. Thirty more for expenses, and I keep what I don't use."

"Out of the question. Our budget is nowhere near that much."

Stone considers what he already knows.

He starts with France's voracious appetite for nuclear power, contrasted with her politics of environmentalism. Schizophrenic, to say the least. He hopscotches across the globe to Mayak, a disaster area but still one of the world's largest nuclear reprocessing centers, part of the Russian culture in which anything can be bought and a devastating environmental problem can be denied with nobody to tell the story. He zooms in on the bodies buried in the radioactive mud on the banks of the Techa River, just before the last spadeful of earth covered the last face. He feels again the warm slide of Delveccio's blood, more cuts and more blood as the mobster couldn't explain why two Russians were tortured and killed in the desert.

He turns his mental lens to Solovie, one of Russia's most prominent nuclear scientists, ass-deep in a cover-up. A cover-up arranged by the men who pay Jean-Louis' *emolument*.

Conclusion: the French government, the Directorate-General for External Security, or a private consortium of French opportunists—one or more of them has waded into a river of shit. The Russians and the Americans may be in the same shitstream, and they may have an open checkbook, too—he'll have to look into that—but the French are right here in front of him.

"Oh, I think you *do* have the budget."

The waiter delivers their meals with a flourish. Jean-Louis ignores him, just watches with his lip curled while Stone tears into his steak. The Frenchman no longer bothers to hide his distaste.

Stone signals the waiter and asks for A-1 Steak Sauce, enjoying the frozen look on the waiter's face almost as much as he relishes watching Jean-Louis squirm. The Frenchman scares him like nobody else. The man is vile to the depths of his soul. This moment may cost him in the future, but Stone likes that he has won a small victory. Small wins lead to bigger wins.

"Look at the bright side, man," he says, shoveling a load of potato and sour cream into his mouth, talking around it as he chews. "Dinner's on me."

Chapter Thirty

The image of orange flames spiraling into the sky above Lake Karachay won't leave my mind, even as the Mole pulls back onto the main road and continues northeast. There's nothing to see outside anyway, only a fresh fall of swirling snow captured in the headlights. The tunnel of light cocoons us within the darkness.

I lean against the passenger-side door and close my eyes, the flames from the lake bottom burning on my retinas—alien and unreal, like a breach in the fabric of reality, something that's not supposed to be there. Not now. Fifty years ago, maybe, when the polluted lake overflowed into the Techa River, or when the dust from the lake bottom blew across populated areas.

Another page from Kato's notepad appears in my mind's eye, each word committed to memory.

> *Hundreds of thousands were exposed to radiation poisoning. In their air, their water, their food. The bureaucrats call the area of devastation a "nuclear footprint." Such masters of the language, these people who use words to obfuscate rather than elucidate.*
>
> *Here is the cold reality of it. If you were born here or if you live here for longer than a year you will die young of cancer or some unexplained illness. Your children will emerge from the womb looking sickly, already suffering from some physical or mental defect.*

*Take young Abram, one member of the third generation
since the disaster. Partially paralyzed. Skin that droops over
the bones of his face like the peeled hide of a dead animal.
Joints that ache with bone-deep agony medicine can't cure
or alleviate. A life ruined before it had a chance to begin.*

*We expect the final chapter of our collective disasters to end
in a quiet coda, a heart-rending dénouement, or an elegiac
epitaph that wraps the unexplainable in something comfortable and familiar. But then you realize the truth of it. We
don't have the courage to confront our failures, to right our
wrongs. So this tragedy, this suffering, has no end.*

"Normally we would arrive in an hour," the Mole says. "But
in this weather…hard to say." He shrugs an apology.

"Tell me about the time you drove for Kato."

"The first time? Three years ago."

"The *last* time. I want to know what happened the last time
you saw her."

"She visited someone at the Child Regional Hospital. A pretty
place on the outskirts of the city. Pine forests all around. I think
the children must like it there."

"Who did she visit?"

He shrugs. "How should I know? I waited outside in the car.
She was gone for a long time. More than two hours."

"A patient? A doctor?"

"A patient, I think. One not doing well."

"What makes you say that?"

The Mole glances at me, then turns his attention to the road
again. "When she got back into the car, I could see that she had
been crying."

In all the years I knew Kato I saw her cry just once. We'd spent
two days uncovering a mass grave on the trail of blood leading
from Grozny to the sanctuary of the mountains. Bodies piled
together, topsoil bulldozed over them like frosting on a cake
made of human remains. Women, children, and men too old
to fight. Kato never shed a tear. She barely changed expression,

even when we pulled what appeared to be a porcelain doll from the lifeless arms of a woman in a red scarf, and the doll's head lolled back to reveal sand and dirt packed into her mouth by her frantic attempts to draw a breath. That night in a camp under the stars I felt the wetness on Kato's blanket.

"The little girl saw her mother shot, and then she suffocated," she whispered.

I didn't answer.

"Now I must write her story," she said.

She was quiet for a time. We listened to the sounds of the night: the drone of a military plane overhead; the snores of her companions from Memorial; a barking dog. The whites of her eyes glowed in the starlight when she looked at me.

"I am afraid, Alexei."

I didn't ask what frightened her. There in the ruins of a nation, surrounded by the dead, by contract soldiers and bandits and rebel fighters and unexploded ordinance and landmines spread everywhere like lethal seeds, what was there not to be afraid of?

Lightning flashed over the distant mountains. Kato shifted her weight to stare at the jagged flashes of light. I had to strain to hear the sound of her voice when she finally spoke.

"I am afraid to my bones that my empty words can't do her justice."

I realize I have been quiet for a long time. The Mole is studying me with sidelong glances. He shifts his gaze back to the road when he sees me notice him.

"I know when a woman has been crying," he says.

"Okay. Kato visited the hospital. She cried there. Then what?"

"We made three more stops in Chelyabinsk that day. Two apartment buildings and a commercial center, all of them many stories high. I could take you to each place, but I don't know which flats or offices she visited."

Kato could have been seeing anybody. A source. An old friend. A lover. She undoubtedly knew people in every major city in the world. What surprises me is that she needed help getting around.

"Why would she hire you to take her around Chelyabinsk? Why not public transport or a cab?"

"She trusted me, I think. She hired me for three days on that trip. We spent the first day in the city. The second two we came here. First to the Mayak nuclear facility, then to the village and the house I'm taking you to now."

"Who did she meet with at Mayak?"

The Mole flushes. His fingers tighten on the wheel. "Those same assholes you just met. The captain and his commander."

"Anybody else?"

"Not that I know of."

If the Mole is telling the truth, he doesn't know the scientist Solovie. If he's lying…well, he's been lying about a lot of things. Why should this be any different?

He slows the car to a crawl, peering through the windshield for nearly a kilometer before turning left on to a dirt road. We bounce along for several minutes, still encased in the white cocoon of our headlights, then he steers right at a fork and stops at a fence and a gate made of stretched wire and rough-hewn wooden poles.

"Wait here."

He pulls on his jacket, flips up the hood, and climbs out of the car. He trudges through the snow with his head bowed. He reaches the gate, fiddles with a piece of wire someone has wound through the latch to prevent it from coming loose, then opens the gate, the lights from the car blaring against the reflective stripes on his jacket as he passes through the beams.

When he returns to the car he brings a salvo of cold air and snow with him.

"Not much security," I say.

"That's not to keep people out."

He drives through the gate and executes a three-point turn to shine the headlights back onto the gate, then he gets out of the car and closes the gate behind us, carefully twisting the wire back into place. That done, he settles back behind the wheel, turns, and drives ahead several hundred meters, the soft suspension tossing us around as the car jounces over lumpy ground.

A smudge of yellow light appears in the windshield. As we approach, the light resolves into a kerosene lantern hung on a hook outside a tumbledown dwelling.

"Who is the fence meant to keep *in?*" I say.

"Abram." The Mole scratches the side of his nose, cutting his eyes at me. "I think you'll like Abram. Kato did."

Chapter Thirty-one

Stone follows Jean-Louis after they part at the restaurant. The Frenchman hurries down Fifty-ninth for several blocks, makes several abrupt turns and crosses the street against the light, then jumps into a waiting cab in front of a hotel. There are no other cabs in sight. If Stone hadn't been prepared, Jean-Louis would have lost him right there.

But Stone is prepared. One of his Manhattan-based operatives, Jessica Campbell, slides a dented beige sedan to the curb next to him, and he climbs into the passenger side.

"You got him?" he says, and she nods.

The cab makes sudden lane changes and turns. Cruises near the park for a few minutes, then heads east. Campbell takes her eyes off the road for a moment to look at him.

"These are the guys paying us, right?"

"Uh-huh." He studies her profile. Big nose, tight lips, narrowed eyes. Mid-forties, fifteen-year career as an analyst in the CIA, three years with Graystone Security. Good for logistics and, in a pinch, light surveillance, but not much else.

She turns right to follow the cab.

"So tell me again why we're wasting time chasing the people who sign our paychecks instead of the bad guys?"

"There are no good guys and bad guys. It's all a matter of perspective." He shifts his weight to get a better view of the cab, thinking that one's *perspective* changes in a fucking hurry once you realize you're the guy who's been manipulated, worked, steered—pick a word—to take the fall for everybody else. "Don't they teach that at the CIA anymore?"

The cab makes more evasive turns and double-backs. Campbell follows, staying a discreet and varying distance behind it.

"Where are the boys?" Stone says.

"Gibson's still in Vegas."

That makes sense. The feds will keep him there until they're finished with Delveccio and Jimmy D, a job that will take a while, because now that Stone is out of the picture the FBI will start playing by the rules. Just as well, though, because every hour Gibson stays on the job means money in the bank for Graystone Security. Big money. None of Graystone's services come cheap.

"Baker's on his way to Moscow," Campbell adds. "Jackson went to L.A. to work with the FBI field office on the problem in the Port of Long Beach. Graham is MIA."

"Daphne Graham quit."

Campbell takes her eyes off the cab to stare at him. "You're kidding. Why?"

"She didn't say."

Jean-Louis must have instructed his cabbie to head directly to the destination now, because the evasive maneuvers end and the cab heads straight down Fifth Avenue. It stops outside the Consulate General of France, and Jean-Louis gets out.

Stone signals for Campbell to speed ahead and double-park at a place where he can watch the entrance to the building.

"Now what?" Campbell says.

"We wait."

Stone considers. Just because Jean-Louis came here doesn't prove he's not free-lancing this one. But it does make Stone feel better about the idea that the French government is behind this...what? Whatever it is that everybody is trying to hide.

Two hours pass.

A man Stone knows from his days working the Russia desk hurries along the street, overcoat flapping in the wind like the wings of a giant bat, his head pitched down, but casting his gaze right and left. Stone can't remember his name, only that he is a flunky for one of America's top diplomats in Moscow. He pauses, looks around one last time, then turns and enters the Consulate.

Campbell leans back her seat. "So Daphne quit. It didn't have anything to do with your charming personality, did it?"

"Of course not."

She blows air through her lips. "Tell me again why I left government service for this?"

He gets out of the car. A cold wind funnels through the high-rise canyon and snaps his coat behind him. Campbell opens her window, and he leans in.

"You're in this because of my *charming personality*," he says.

"Yeah, right."

"Okay, here's the real reason. You're in this because you want the big bucks." He grins, thinking that the bucks just got bigger, because now he knows for sure that this is not just a French problem. It's an American problem, too. "And because you're already wondering who's going to take Graham's place."

She colors, but doesn't protest.

He straightens. "We'll give him a few hours. See where he goes from here. After that, I've got a plane to catch."

"Where to?"

South, baby, south of the border and into a different world to look for a Russian gangster named Shakalov. Just for a night, but he can have a lot of fun in one night, especially with the right person there to arrange the details. A person like Mami Kai.

"Back to Vegas," he lies. He thumps the top of the car with his hand. "Stay close."

Chapter Thirty-two

Kato wrote few details about the family at the heart of her Mayak story, at least only a few that found their way onto the surviving pages of the red notepad she gave me.

Except for Abram. She devoted several paragraphs to him alone.

Abram fishes the polluted Techa River almost every day. He sits on the branch of a giant oak with his back propped against the trunk, one end of his fishing pole wedged in a crack in a split in the bark, the other end dangling carelessly over the muddy water. He catches three bottom-feeders. Strings them and carries his prize home.

Home. Thatched roof mounted on crooked poles, wood siding weathered to a silvery sheen, a stoop made of planks laid on top of fieldstones. One large room divided by blankets hung from the ceiling into a kitchen, bathroom, and living/sleeping area. Plank floor that shows the raw dirt beneath in the places where the knots have fallen out.

Abram cleans the fish and sets the table. His mother cooks. His grandmother peels five potatoes, two more than usual because they have two guests tonight, and they want to make us comfortable. They've already offered to give us their beds for the night. This family has done so much with so little to make their guests feel at home. Now we have no choice but to insult them.

*My traveling companion and I back away from the table.
There is no way to say it gracefully.*

*"We can't eat this food. Thank you for the offer and for
your hospitality. We're sorry. We can't eat the food here."*

The dwelling lit by the lights of the Mole's Volga looks much
as Kato described it in her notepad. One step up to a stoop and a
battered door, warped gray planks all around, thatched roof with
a homemade weathervane mounted on top, the whole structure
maybe twenty square meters. Chinks in the wall filled with dried
mud. A small garden on one side, the stakes spiking the night
air like a row of filed teeth. Scrub brush on the other, the nose
of a rusted wheelbarrow poking from the snow-covered brier.

The Mole kills the engine and the lights. The world shrinks
to the pale circle illumed by the kerosene lantern. We climb
out of the car into the cold. As we approach the door opens a
crack. A woman peeks out. Her features waver in the poor light,
indistinct, but she appears to be very old.

The Mole steps to the foot of the tiny porch and stands where
the glow from the lantern reaches his face.

"Helen? It's me, Misha."

"Go away."

She closes the door with a bang. A bolt scrapes into place,
and a chain rattles.

A twig snaps in the darkness behind us.

The Mole turns to me with his palms up, his eyebrows arched.
"She's never done that before." Apparently he didn't hear the
twig break.

I reach into my pocket for the Tokarev. Slowly ease it out
and hold it against the side of my leg. A crunch sounds behind
me, a careful footfall in loose rock and thistle.

The Mole still doesn't react. He turns and pounds on the door.

"Helen! Open up. What's wrong?"

I take one step to the side. Drop and roll, moving *toward*
the sound in the darkness. I spot the black silhouette of a man
against the moonlight filtering through the overcast. Keep driving forward, bent low.

My shoulder rams into the midsection of a wiry body, a small man by the feel. The air whooshes out of him and we both slam to the ground, me on top. Without giving him any time to recover, I grab his wrist and crank his hand so that he has to go with the motion and I have him facedown in an arm lock. I drag him a few meters into a bramble thicket and clamp my hand over his mouth in case he's not alone. Grind the barrel of the Tokarev into his ear.

"Move and you're dead," I hiss to keep the sound low.

"Volk?" the Mole calls out.

He's still standing on the tiny porch, a thin shape bisecting the lantern light. He shields his eyes, peering into the darkness.

The man beneath me moves, whimpers. Normally that would result in a smack with the flat of the barrel, but I hesitate. His face feels like pebbled leather beneath my finger. I have a bad feeling I know who this is.

I put my lips next to his ear. "Abram?"

He doesn't move or respond. His body stays rigid. I release my hand little by little. Draw back so that I can see his face.

"Please don't hurt me anymore," he says.

He has the body of a man and the voice of a child. He muddles his words. He is, I realize, either completely or partially deaf.

I ease my body off his. Squat next to him in the dirt, both of us breathing hard. The whites of his eyes look like large white marbles staring up at me.

"Please don't hurt me anymore," he says again.

I stand. Help him to his feet. Brush him off and walk with him toward the Mole.

The door to the shack bursts open. Helen crashes out onto the stoop, carrying a shotgun that seems taller than she is. She lifts the barrel and cuts loose just as I dive back on top of Abram, figuring she'll aim away from him.

Her shot goes wide.

The Mole grabs the barrel of the shotgun and tries to wrestle it away from her. She fights him with the raging fury of a mother bear protecting her cub.

I blast a round from the Tokarev that splinters the wood at their feet.

"Stop! Now!"

The shot doesn't slow Helen down. She doesn't seem to have heard a thing. She keeps fighting over the shotgun with the Mole and kicking his shins. Then she sees Abram at my feet, struggling to rise. Her eyes widen, and she lets go of the shotgun and runs to him with a keening moan, drops to her knees in the dirt and snow beside him.

I walk over to the Mole. His breath comes out in ragged gasps. He holds the shotgun at arm's length, studying the chased silver on the stock and the elaborate etchings on the double barrels.

"I'll bet a Bolshevik took a few potshots with this thing during the Revolution."

It's a bird gun. Probably wouldn't have killed me unless she'd scored a head shot. I take it from him, open the breech, remove both shells, and lean it against the shack.

"Check to see if there's anybody else in there. Next thing you know, somebody will come out with a cannon."

He nods, but he doesn't move right away. Instead, he watches Helen rock Abram in the dirt in front of the house, her tears of—what, relief, joy, fear, rage?—shining in the light from the lantern.

"Poor kid," he says.

"Did you have a mother like that?"

"What's that supposed to mean?"

I don't answer, letting him work out for himself who is poor and who is not. I walk over to where Abram is now slowly getting to his feet. I stand where he can see my face and read my lips.

"My name is Volk. I am a friend of the journalist named Kato. We don't mean to harm anyone."

Helen has a long torso and short arms and legs that remind me of the General's dwarfish limbs. She looks seventy, but according to Kato's journal she's only forty-two. She steps closer and looks up at me as if she is preparing for a kiss. She hacks phlegm and spits it into my face.

"Why won't you animals just leave us alone?"

She helps Abram to the stoop, a protective arm around his waist. Shoots a last malignant look over her shoulder. Slams the door behind her, leaving us out in the cold.

Chapter Thirty-three

The Mole stares open-mouthed while I wipe the spit from my face. "You're just going to let them go?"

My phone buzzes an incoming message. Valya.

I NEED TO KNOW WHAT REALLY HAPPENED BETWEEN YOU AND KATO.

I slip the phone back into the pocket of my jacket. Stare into the eddying snow and the darkness. The moon and the stars have lost the battle against the low-hanging clouds. The night has suddenly turned blacker.

"Who was that?" the Mole says.

Now that the adrenaline rush is gone, I feel cold again. I climb into the car. The Mole follows. His gaze drops to the Tokarev in my lap, at the muzzle that's aimed at his thigh. He raises his eyes to meet mine.

"The truth," I tell him. "No more lies, no more misdirection, no more pretending to be someone you're not."

He stares at the gun again, then looks through the windshield at the lonely shack in the gathering snowstorm.

"Well, first of all, I'm not Jonas Kepler."

"What happened to Kepler?"

"Died of natural causes four years ago while living in a communal flat in Chelyabinsk. The landlord buried his body in the woods and started cashing his pension checks. I found out about it and made a trade. You keep the pension money, I get everything else, including his identity. Mail, credit cards, driver's license, even a passport."

I know the identity-theft business. I used to run a porn operation that made some of its money stealing the identities of those foolish enough to purchase our products with a credit card.

"That's what you do? Identity theft?"

He shakes his head. Ponders the question for a long time, as if trying to make up his mind about something.

"I work for Memorial," he says finally. "The human rights group."

The lantern hanging over the stoop flickers and dies. We're silent for a time, listening to the wet brush of wind-driven snow against the windows, the fog of our breath filling the car, illuminated by the blinking red alarm indicator in the center of the dash.

I know Memorial, of course, and not only from the two days I spent with Kato helping them dig bodies out of the ground. One of its more famous and vocal members, Natalya Estemirova, was abducted and killed in a Grozny suburb a year ago. Taken at gunpoint as she got into her car. The police found her body four hours later, gunshot wounds in the head, her purse with all her money lying next to her. An execution, pure and simple, with no pretence of robbery or kidnapping for ransom, committed by men who believed themselves immune from the law. A message delivered and, if the paucity of stories coming out of Chechnya and the surrounding republics is any indication, a message received by human rights activists and journalists in Russia and the southern cauldron.

"We knew Kepler was a Kremlin man," the Mole says. "We kept an eye on him, followed him to learn what we could. When he died, but didn't die officially, we took advantage of the opportunity."

He watches my reaction to his words, looking wary and uncertain. When I don't show any emotion, he shifts his weight so that the Tokarev isn't pointed directly at his thigh.

"Kepler *still* receives occasional assignments via courier," the Mole says. "Two or three a year, never more than that. I handle them in whatever manner best suits our purposes. Three years ago I received a communiqué to pose as a driver and pick up an unidentified woman at the same hotel in Chelyabinsk where you stayed. I—or Jonas Kepler—was to prepare a written report of her movements, who she met, and anything I heard. The woman turned out to be Kato, of course."

The temperature inside the car has dropped to near freezing. My breath mingles with the Mole's to smoke the inside of the windows. I feel colder on the inside than I do on the outside.

I remember thinking when I met him that men change. Figuratively, or so I was imagining then; this man had changed literally. How many of the General's operations have been breached this way? Even assuming the Mole is being entirely truthful now, which I doubt, at least four and as many as six have been compromised in Chelyabinsk alone. I shudder at the thought of the wider implications for the General's far-flung apparatus and the danger it poses for his most at-risk operatives, including me.

Kato would have believed her driver was clean. With her security always in peril, she'd probably gone to great lengths to ensure as much. Meanwhile, the General believed her driver to be one of his men, planted there to keep tabs on the opposition, Kato being perhaps the most vocal critic of the General's precious 58th Army.

They were *both* wrong.

"Did Kato know?"

"Eventually. Then she became a regular visitor and we talked all the time."

"About what?"

He gestures toward the shack with a motion that takes in the whole area. "How we could help these people."

My phone buzzes again. The light from the display burns my eyes. The Mole watches me read the message.

GODDAMN YOU, ALEXEI.

I wonder how she found out. Valya isn't one to overreact to sketchy information. She knows. Somehow she knows about Kato and me.

I text back: WE NEED TO TALK ABOUT THIS WHEN I COME HOME.

The Mole waits until I'm finished.

"So," he says. "Now that she's dead, maybe you can fill the void? Or maybe you know somebody else who can?"

I stare at the tiny screen on my phone for several minutes. Waiting.

No response.

"What do you think?" the Mole says nervously.

I hate the weakness in his voice. I despise the fear in it. These people with their noble ideas and their intrigues that lead nowhere remind me too much of my own failures, remind me too much of the distorted image that peers back at me from the mirror.

I laser him with my eyes.

"Tell me," I rasp. "Why the fuck would I want to help these peasants?"

Chapter Thirty-four

Stone prowls the streets outside the French Consulate General, but Jean-Louis fails to emerge. After two hours, Stone orders Campbell to drive him to Kennedy. He fidgets during the drive. Checks email on his Blackberry. Starts to call Matthews, glances at Campbell, decides against it.

France, Russia, America. If anybody knows what they're up to, it'll be Matthews. But Matthews isn't going to tell Stone shit. Stone is going to have to figure things out for himself. *Then* he'll call Matthews and turn the tables on the smug bastard.

Break it down. First he has to get to Mami Kai in Tijuana. Not an easy task. Then he'll have to convince her to cooperate. That shouldn't be a problem. Mami worships at the altar of money. For enough money, she would arrange a meeting with the devil himself—or with Shakalov, the devil's doppelganger.

Second, he has to *survive* the meeting with Shakalov. Easier said than done. The Russian gangster lives with bounties on his head from the DEA, the FSB, Interpol, and God knows who else. He's notoriously reclusive and deadly paranoid. Stone's best bet: arrange to meet him without seeing his face. Still no guarantee of survival, but better. Safer.

Finally, take away something valuable from the meeting, preferably that tidbit of information that unlocks the mystery of whatever the fuck is going on. Then use the information to work the angles between the players.

That could be the biggest score of all.

Chapter Thirty-five

We spend the remainder of the cold night in the Mole's Volga. Before daybreak I get out of the car and relieve myself in the woods, then sit on my haunches and watch the stars disappear and the clearing turn into murky shapes that might have existed during any time in the past thousand years.

The shack lists, its crudely built walls and sloping roof interrupted by a bent flue pipe, a curl of smoke trailing away. The whole thing looks as if a hard wind would blow it down easily. Leaned against one wall, a rusted plow with dangling leather traces. In the clearing behind the shack, an outhouse, little more that four posts and a thatched roof with walls made of cured leather hides. In the distance, a cleared plot of land blanketed with snow beneath tendrils of mist.

A place of basic shelter, a hardscrabble existence, and life lived on the far margin where hunger, severe weather, and accidents are serious threats. The difference being that here the modern world has intruded in the form of radioactive soil, plants, animals, and people.

The Mole starts the engine. It winds up for a few seconds, coughs a cloud of black smoke, and churns to life. It sputters for a minute or so, then clunks, I think because he has turned on the heater.

I walk the perimeter of the property inside the wire fence. Arrive at the cleared plot. Look at the animal tracks. Deer, rabbit, rodents, life everywhere, abundant. I recall the feel of Abram's face beneath my hand. Grainy, soft but firm, like the leathery shell of a baby turtle. I hear his childlike voice. *Please don't hurt me anymore.* Life goes on, yes, but it has been shortened, altered, *perverted*, by the things that were done here.

The Mole gets out of the car. Slams the door and trudges toward me. He stops nearby and exhales a white cloud into the air overhead.

"I made a mistake," he says quietly. "Kato told me a little about you. I thought, maybe. You know?" He scowls and takes another deep breath, holding the air in his lungs for a long time. "I want this to go away. I'll stop being Jonas Kepler. I never did anything that made a difference anyway. Tell your friends in the Kremlin that, okay? I'll take you back now, and we can both forget these people and this place."

"Where was she killed?"

He looks at me. The cuts on his face are beginning to scab. The bruises look more colorful, purple in places.

"I can show you where her body was found. I can't tell you whether she was killed there or dumped there."

"Let's go."

The same private smile ghosts across his face. "Whatever you say."

Just as we start back toward the car, a voice startles us.

"Did you come here to hurt me?"

Abram. Standing in the mist, nearly invisible. I don't know how he managed to approach us so quietly. I glance at the Mole. I can tell from his expression that he's thinking the same thing I am: the boy could have done almost anything and we wouldn't have had time to react.

Abram looks worse than Kato described him in her notepad. Hunchbacked, skin sloughing off his lumpy face, pain lurking deep behind his eyes. I don't think I caused the pain when I wrestled him to the ground last night. I think it's always there.

"No," I say. "We're not here to hurt you."

The Mole steps closer to him, moving slowly, as though he is afraid the boy will startle like a deer. "This man is a friend of Kato," he says.

Abram's granular features brighten, then cloud over as if a bad memory has intruded on his thoughts. "She was always nice to me."

The Mole darts a sidelong glance at me, raising an eyebrow at Abram's use of the past tense. *How does he know she's dead?* the look says.

Abram raises his head. His nostril's flare. "Breakfast!" he announces, and then scampers off toward the shack. The Mole and I follow at a slower pace, wary of another gun. By the time we arrive at the stoop, Abram has disappeared inside.

"Now what?" the Mole says.

I step up to the door and knock.

A rustling sound of movement from inside.

"Go away." A woman's voice, probably Helen's.

"We need to talk to you for a minute," the Mole says. "It's about Abram."

"Abram is right here."

"Yes, we know." He gives me a worried look, as though he's not sure how I will react to what he's going to say. Then he sets his jaw. "I need another test, Helen. It's important."

"No more tests."

"What kind of test?" I say quietly, so that the sound of my voice won't carry through the door.

"Blood," he answers in the same way. "We need multiple samples over a period of months to measure drops in the white blood cell count and abnormal changes in the DNA of the blood cells. That tells the doctors the degree of bone marrow damage, gives them a window into the level of the absorbed dose."

He gives me a pained look. "Abram has been a project of ours for almost a year. I don't know why Helen is acting this way now."

"No more tests," Helen says again through the door.

"Abram is sick," the Mole says. "These tests will help him." He cuts his eyes at me. "Not him, maybe," he says under his breath, sounding defensive. "But someone else, certainly."

I don't respond. Who am I to question the lies told by another?

"Cancer markers, tumor growth, long-term genetic

damage—we need to measure those things," the Mole says in the same quiet voice. "These people keep dropping babies. Maybe we can help *them.*"

Radiation sickness, creeping dose exposure, acute and chronic radiation poisoning—all are terms I've heard before, but I don't know the science or the medicine.

Years ago I met Alexander Litvinenko in London, back in the time when his former masters in the KGB and the FSB thought they could control him with threats and money. They chose the General to act as an intermediary, and he selected me to accompany him on the trip, probably because my English is passable. Litvinenko refused to compromise. Later he intensified his attacks against the Kremlin in the media, his opposition growing more strident until it reached a crescendo with the accusation that Putin ordered the murder of Anna Politkovskaya.

A year later he paid the price of dissent. A cup of tea in a London hotel that coiled like a hot snake down his throat and caught fire in his belly. I recall the photos of Alexander Litvinenko on his deathbed, burning alive on the inside from a dose of Polonium 210 that left a radioactive trail—from hotels, restaurants, and planes—back to Moscow.

"Helen?" the Mole says to the door. "Let me help Abram, Helen."

A strange sound seeps through the split wood siding of the shack. Like the mewl of a wounded animal. The Mole doesn't seem to hear it. He places one hand on the doorframe, bows his head, and sighs. I nudge him aside and put my ear to the door.

Crying. Helen is crying on the other side of the door.

"Let us in, Helen," I say with my mouth close to the handle, where the wood has been worn to a satiny gloss. "I will protect you."

"Protect her from what?" the Mole says. "Why does she need protection?"

I can't hear her sobs anymore. She's listening, I think. Trying to make up her mind.

"Let this man do his tests," I say. "Abram's blood might save him, or it might save the lives of other children."

Nothing. More than a minute passes. Sunbeams pierce the clouds and touch the ground, offering the false promise of warmth.

Then come the sounds of a sliding bolt and rattling chain. The door opens a crack, and Helen peers at us. She's wiped away the tears. Deep lines crease her forehead and the skin on both sides of her mouth. Her eyes droop with weariness and worry.

"They told us never again. No more tests. No more talking to writers."

"Who told you that?" the Mole says.

She turns her tired eyes to him. "KGB," she says.

The Mole lifts his brows. I shake my head at him. *Think about it.* He nods to say he understands. Like many older Russians, Helen refers to the secret police by their former name, disdaining the new acronyms *FSB* and *SVR.*

"Let me get my things," the Mole says. He returns to the car, opens the trunk, and rummages among whatever it holds.

Helen watches him, shakes her head, then sets her jaw and nods. She is the picture of a woman at odds with herself.

"They told me they couldn't protect me if I allowed the tests and talked to reporters. Now you say you can. Who am I supposed to believe?"

"*Protect* you? The KGB said it couldn't *protect* you?"

Frozen ground crunches behind me as the Mole returns with a white Styrofoam cooler in his arms. I'm not paying any attention to him. I'm coming to the slow realization that I misunderstood Helen. I thought she believed the *KGB* was threatening her. But she hadn't meant that at all.

"Who are you afraid of, Helen?"

She looks me straight on. Her face is worn out. Too much stress for too long. And only the devil knows what chemical cocktail is surfing her bloodstream, killing her like Litvinenko, except even more slowly, death on the installment plan. Her gaze holds mine without subterfuge, like the stare of an old cow. She coughs once, then twice more in quick succession.

"The CIA," she says at last.

Chapter Thirty-six

"What did she say?" the Mole asks.

Helen coughs some more—wet, rattling sounds. She pulls a handkerchief from a pocket in the front of her dress and holds it over her mouth.

"She said the KGB warned her not to allow any more tests and not to talk to journalists because if she did they couldn't protect her from the CIA."

"She's crazy," he whispers.

I don't say anything.

"You don't believe her, do you?"

Helen stops coughing. Stares at the sputum in the handkerchief.

"I saw one of the CIA," she says. "With the beautiful woman, the reporter. Then she disappeared, and when they found her, she was dead."

"Volk, let's do the test and get out of here. I'll show you where—"

I hold up my hand to shut him up. Focus on Helen. "What did he look like?"

"A demon."

The Mole groans. "Helen, can I go inside now?"

She hesitates, then opens the door and stands aside.

I follow him.

Into a square room divided by animal hide blankets hung from the rafters. Light leaking between the gaps in the slatted sides, a table surrounded by unmatched chairs, a glowing iron stove in the corner with a cooking pot on top, from which comes the burble of boiling water and the smell of potatoes, celery, and carrots.

Abram's grandmother sits in an armchair, white stuffing popping out of the brown Naugahyde like mushrooms from the soil. Small and frail, shrunken so much that her clothes are too big for her body, little more than a burlap sack of bones. She wears a green scarf with wisps of white hair sticking out.

Abram stands in front of the stove, stirring the pot. He notices the Styrofoam cooler in the Mole's arms and wordlessly begins to roll up his sleeve.

Helen closes the door against the morning chill and follows me into the room. She offers me a seat on one of the mismatched chairs at the head of the table, ladles a steaming serving of soup into a chipped china bowl, and slides it in front of me along with a metal spoon. Chicken stock, shaved carrots, chunks of potatoes and celery.

I don't eat, just watch the Mole prep a syringe and tie a rubber tourniquet around Abram's thin bicep. Helen stands next to me, observing in silence. Abram's grandmother drifts off, her eyes half closed.

"What did the demon look like?" I say to Helen.

"Cruel."

The Mole swabs Abram's forearm below the elbow joint.

"Big or small, black hair or blond?" I prompt her.

Helen purses her lips. Winces slightly when the needle slides into the flesh of her son. "Average."

"What made him look like a demon?"

"Fierce eyes. Like you. And a terrible, evil smile."

"What else?"

She waves away the question. *I don't know.* She tracks the well of blood into the vacuum tube. The Mole removes the first tube as soon as it's full, and attaches another one to the hub.

"Old or young?" I say to Helen.

"Neither."

The Mole fills three tubes, placing each one into a hole in a foam brick that fits into the bottom of his cooler. He loosens the tourniquet and withdraws the needle while pressing a cotton ball to the puncture. All the while Abram stares vacantly at an empty spot on the far wall.

His mother goes to him and lifts the cotton ball to check for bleeding. Just one small dot of blood on it. Satisfied, she presses it back into place.

"Abram!" I shout.

He startles at the unexpected sound, then turns to face me, his eyes wide.

"What did the man—this demon—what did he look like?"

Helen steps between us. She smells like potatoes. "No! No questions for him."

The boy starts to say something, but she cuts him off with a raised finger.

"I will answer, not him. Leave now if that's not good enough."

Abram goes back to staring at the wall above the Mole's head. Whatever spark I thought I saw in him is gone.

"You're not giving me clear answers, Helen."

"The demon cut Abram," she says, as though that explains everything.

"I don't understand."

"Right here." She lifts his shirt and shows me an inflamed red scab running from just above his hip to a spot a few centimeters below his nipple.

"It looks infected."

Helen nods. "He dirtied the blade with dung before he cut him."

"Why?"

"'Let this be a lesson,' he said. 'I'll peel his hide and hang it on the wall if you don't do as I say.' This was not a man. This was a demon. Now you have your blood, and I am finished answering the questions."

"Was he KGB?"

"I *told* you. CIA."

"He spoke Russian?"

Helen rolls her eyes, looking exasperated by such a silly question. "The KGB man talked for him."

The Mole purses his lips and shakes his head. *She's crazy.*

"I need more," I say to Helen. "I need to be able to find this man if I'm going to protect Abram."

Her eyes shift while she weighs the risk of saying nothing against the risk of saying only a little. I see the decision in her before she answers. She wants to hedge her bets. She fears the man she calls "the demon," but she wants the protection that talking to me might buy.

"There was another man with the demon," she says. "They named him after a rock. Maybe because he has no feelings and no heart, like a rock."

"You heard his name?"

"Abram"—she breaks off and looks quickly at her son.

"*I* heard what the demon called him," Abram says. "He called him *kamen.*"

Stone.

I exchange glances with the Mole. We both shake our head. Neither of us knows the name. It could be a nickname. More likely, Abram simply misunderstood. But the gist of his story fits with what I already suspect. Two men. One mechanic, one cleaner. And they must have had a Russian guide and interpreter.

But I can't prove any of it. Abram and Helen have too many problems to be credible witnesses.

Kato knew it, too, according to her notes.

Nobody will listen to these people. They are bullied and harassed into silence by a fearful government that fails to acknowledge their essential helplessness and turns its back on their fundamental hopelessness.

My cell vibrates. Valya.

Fuck you, Alexei.

Chapter Thirty-seven

Stone flies from Kennedy to San Diego's Lindbergh Field. Waits for nightfall. Cabs to the U.S. side of the border, then walks into Tijuana, flowing along with a crowd of day workers, Mexican shoppers heading home, and clumps of American partiers. The crowd passes single-file through turnstiles made of tubular metal that feed everyone onto a wide ramp filled with street vendors, beggars, pimps, and cabbies. He signals for a cab, follows the driver to a dented Ford, climbs into the back, and says, "Adelitas."

The driver glances at him in the rearview. "They have the prettiest girls there, *señor*."

Stone doesn't answer, just stares out the window at the crush of vehicles snarled where the road narrows to funnel the border-crossers toward the center of town.

Five minutes later they arrive at a boulevard lit by streetlights and neon signs. Two lanes clogged with traffic on both sides of a concrete median, music pumping from the nightclubs lining the road and a low-rider Chevy next to the cab. Rock, rap, salsa, and reggae: competing beats, competing generations, competing cultures.

Stone pays the fare in dollars, standing in the neon-green glow of a mermaid sign advertising a strip club. Two teenage boys wearing wife-beaters stroll past, rolling their hips and shoulders, eyeballing the large denomination bills in his money clip. He pulls the flap of his jacket aside to show the butt of his Glock, and they cut away, looking for easier prey.

Stone winds between the jammed cars to the other side of the street. He passes a small pickup riding low in the back with the weight of six *federales* armed with machine guns. Dead-eyed, holding their weapons like lovers. Hats low, uniforms buttoned tight to the throat, dried sweat rings under their arms. Scanning the crowd for marks. Not tourists, the tourists bring the money for the women and the drugs. They're looking for weaker members of their own tribe to cull from the herd and carve up.

They remind Stone of the urban soldiers he has seen all over the world, from Afghanistan to Somalia. Predators all. The feral look crosses cultural lines.

Hawkers greet Stone at the entrance to Adelitas: a fat man in a dirty T-shirt and black vest and two rail-thin boys who work as his runners. To the right is a passageway with stairs heading up. The stairs, Stone knows from past experience, lead to the lobby of the attached hotel, where the Adelitas girls are expected to turn more than ten tricks a night. Seventy-two American dollars buy a girl for a half hour and a towel to use when you're finished. Twenty for the room, twenty-five each for the house and the girl, two for the boys who clean the room, tips optional but strongly encouraged.

A bouncer holds open the red velvet drapes at the entrance to Adelitas. Stone enters the bar, then stops there for a moment while his eyes adjust.

The club is crowded, smoky, and loud, the speakers blasting the wailing guitars and thundering drums of an old Scorpions song. A pole dancer works the stage. Next to a long bar, two rows of girls dressed in G-strings, bikinis, cut-off jeans shorts, skirts slit to the waist. Fourteen to forty years old. All that flesh mixed with drugs, alcohol, and high-octane lust in the form of American and Mexican boys and men of all ages and various states of intoxication.

Stone snags a beer from a metal bin filled with cracked ice. Pays the girl standing on a wooden box next to the bin. Tips her enough to earn a press of bare thigh against his cheek. Slams the beer and pays for another, all the while watching, waiting. In five minutes at least twenty girls head out the door for the hotel next door, their john in tow, and the same number return, usually alone, scanning the room for their next customer.

A girl cuddles up to him. Bottle-blond, light-skinned, pancake makeup over old acne scars. Soft skin, fake tits hard as softballs, busy hands.

"Buy me a drink?"

Stone pushes her away. Walks toward the back of the bar, running the gauntlet between the two rows of girls, their fingers plucking at his shirt as he passes. They tug at the shirts of *every* man who passes, of course. Guy could be a Calvin Klein model or three hundred pounds of unwashed flesh, none of that means shit to these girls. Who can afford to be picky these days?

The worst customers for them, Stone knows, are the men who can't perform, then take out their fear and frustration on the girl. Beatings have a price tag, too. If the guy has money he pays off one of the bouncers and walks away. Costs him more than sex, but unless he does real damage it's affordable enough. If he can't pay, the bouncers knock him around a little. Either way the men go home, back through the customs lines on the American side, back to wives and girlfriends, back to the lives they pretend are unaffected by the things that happen down south.

The rear of the bar is jammed with orange vinyl booths and a standing-room only crowd. Stone elbows through the crowd to an unmarked door in the back. He stands with his back to the door to see if anybody is paying attention to him. Sees nothing unusual.

He presses the panic bar and slips through the door into a hallway cluttered with cleaning supplies, wet cardboard boxes, a used condom still draining its contents onto the painted concrete floor, and a passed-out prostitute, her back against the wall, legs splayed across the floor. He steps over them as the door closes behind him, muting the music to a throbbing growl.

The hall leads to another door, this one locked. Stone uses a pencil-sized jimmy to crack the wood beside the deadbolt. The girl in the hallway behind him mutters something. Stone knows enough Spanish to catch the drift. She wants her mother. She wants to go home.

He pushes through the ruptured door. Concrete steps lead down to a tunnel that takes him under the street behind Adelitas, a street famous for its long line of prostitutes who work for much less than $72 a pop. Those girls and boys turn tricks for as little as $5, sometimes kneeling to give a blowjob in an open doorway.

The tunnel slants upward, then levels off at a wooden door with a peephole covered with a metal slide on the other side of the door. Stone knocks—three quick taps, wait a beat, then two more. The metal panel slides away. A bloodshot eye under a bushy black brow peers at him.

"What?"

"Grayson Stone for Mami Kai," he says.

The panel slides back into place.

Stone waits.

Five minutes later a chain rattles on the other side of the door, then a key turns in the lock and the door opens. The man inside is Mexican, short and slight. He wears square unframed glasses, jeans, and a white shirt with the sleeves pushed high on his forearms.

"Long time, Stone."

Stone grunts. Looks over the man's shoulder at a small foyer and, in the back, another set of stairs going down. This stairway leads to combo strip club and whorehouse called the House of Hong Kong. Mami hails from Bangkok, but what the hell.

"She here?"

"The question is why are *you* here?"

Stone turns his attention to the man.

Ernesto Garcia. Ex-PRI. One of the big boys during the days when Zedillo's government was in power. Not a thug. Garcia made himself useful in another way. He kept the books. Laundered the money and kept track of where it was hidden—including a 10 percent spoilage fee for what was lost, stolen, or eaten by insects and rats. Bundles of cash stacked high enough to cover the beds of a thousand pickups, all of it needing a home. Stashed between the studs in a plaster wall, lowered to the bottom of a dry well, packed in a mattress. But hiding places like those were risky.

They also required detailed recordkeeping.

In '01, the DEA caught Garcia in a Chevy Camaro with the door panels loaded with black tar heroin. Garcia flipped. He stayed in place, snitched to the DEA for five years, the last on Stone's watch after the Russia connection became clear. Back then Stone was one of the few guys with that kind of experience who could be trusted to work on the outside, where the rules didn't apply.

Then one night in Guadalajara somebody fucked up. Garcia got fingered. Two guys armed with PP-19 Bizon submachine guns unloaded on his Porsche. Garcia caught a bullet with his crotch. Stone still winces just to think about it. The Bizon being a Russian product—and not commonly found in the middle of Mexico—Garcia believed that the *somebody* who had fucked him was Grayson Stone.

Stone looks past him. "Get out of the way, Garcia. I've got business with Mami, not you."

Mami Kai. Pronounced *Maim Me* by the boys in TJ, but never to her face. As far as Stone has been able to determine, the nickname refers to her prowess in bed, not the wet work she's done to extract information or remove a problem. But nobody doubts that Mami is capable of such violence. Stone certainly doesn't doubt it. One doesn't build a trans-Pacific drug network with clean hands, even with help from Shakalov.

Garcia steps to one side and gestures toward a wooden table at the top of the stairs. "No weapons."

Stone unloads his Glock and a switchblade onto the table, then lets Garcia pat and prod to satisfy himself that he's now unarmed. As soon as Garcia finishes the task he shoves Stone away from the table. He reaches behind his back and pulls a revolver that looks like a cannon. He jams the barrel under Stone's nose, forcing his head back.

"Do you have any idea how long I've been waiting for this moment?" Garcia says.

Chapter Thirty-eight

Betrayal.

At least one of the clichés about infidelity turned out to be true in my case. The first time was the hardest. After that, I lived with guilt the same way Abram and his family live with low-level radiation. It simmered and curdled in my bloodstream like a venomous broth. Not enough to kill me, just enough to reduce me to something less than the man I was before that night in the Astoria Hotel. And each assignation with Kato diminished me a little bit more.

Valya sends five more text messages during the time we spend in the shack with Abram and his mother and grandmother. Each one is a variation on the same theme.

How could you do such a thing?

"Don't be naïve," Valya once told me during a long ride on the night train to St. Petersburg when I questioned her about how her affair began with a woman named Yelena Posnova. I suppose I could make the same argument now, but what's the point in being right if it means losing her? Especially now that I've lost Kato as well.

I don't know what to say to her, so I don't respond to her messages.

"What next?" I ask the Mole as soon as he finishes loading his Styrofoam cooler into the back seat.

"You want to see where they found her, right?"

No. "Yes."

Five minutes pounding over rutted roads. The Mole loses his way once, and we have to go back between the colonnade of trees along the narrow lane. He turns onto a road that's little more than a trail, and we drive another few kilometers, bare branches scraping the side of the car. He parks and points into the woods.

"That way."

We push through the tangled branches and brush. The forest thins. The snow lies heavily on the ground between the tress. We emerge on the bank of a river, less than fifty meters across, the muddy water flowing sluggishly. Upstream, in shallower water, small rapids gurgle as the water flows between the rocks. But at this spot on the waterlogged banks the river looks lifeless and sludgy.

The Mole points to a fallen tree half buried in the loamy ground near the bank.

"There."

Ankle deep snow covers the open ground around the fallen tree, concealing whatever lies beneath it. The snow weighs thick on the branches of a nearby sapling, drooping its limbs. Fluttering from one of its branches, a strip of crime scene tape. Peeking from the snow are bits of paper and wrappers and empty plastic evidence bags, all left by the investigators.

I walk close enough to see the ground on the other side of the dead tree. When I stop, my boots sink into the muck beneath the snow.

Here is a hole, two meters in diameter, one meter deep. Snow coats the bottom like a residue of milk left in a bowl. The snow all around the hole is uneven, the lumps and hollows marking the places where police and crime scene technicians trampled the mud, probably erasing any sign of the person or persons who dumped Kato's body here. Most likely making it impossible to determine whether the three students were dumped at the same time or, as I suspect, killed later and left here to confuse the scene.

A shallow depression and churned up ground are all that remain of Kato's temporary grave.

"So close to their home," the Mole says, looking back in the direction of the shack. "Maybe Helen really did see the killer."

"I don't think so."

He arches an eyebrow.

"Abram," I say, thinking of how easily the boy crept up on us in the field outside the shack. "Abram saw the killer. Maybe even saw him pull the trigger. I think that's why Helen won't let us talk to him. I think that's why she's so afraid."

We stay that way for a few minutes, him resting his hip against the tree trunk, me standing near the riverbank, closer to Kato's grave. A clump of snow falls from a pine bough. The wind riffles my hair.

I step into the hollow and drop to my haunches, subconsciously mimicking the way Kato squatted in the mountains of Chechnya on that long-ago day.

"Go away," I tell the Mole.

When he's gone I feel through the snow in the grave. I don't know what I'm looking for. Maybe I just need to get as close as I can to the soil that cradled her flesh.

Men go and come, but earth abides.

I don't know the Bible by chapter or verse; Soviet schools didn't teach such things. Ecclesiastes, I think. The line appeared in one of Kato's early columns, one of many I read before deciding to deliver her notepad to her editor a decade ago. The words resonated then, and they do so again now as I squat in her grave, feeling the earth where she bled out her life.

Except for the detritus of the investigation, there's nothing to find here, of course. First the insects and the animals and then the police and forensics teams removed all traces of evidence from this place.

That's not what I'm searching for.

I'm searching for absolution.

I close my eyes. I recall the way she cocked her head when she was skeptical or curious. How she walked with a dancer's step. How she squared her shoulders when faced with a difficult question. I allow myself to fall into the memories: the softness of her skin under my hands, the smell of her after a jog, the taste of her when we made love.

That's the thing.

I never told her how much she meant to me while she was alive. During that first year we came together like cymbals, no time during our brief interludes to think about the deeper meaning of things. Then, after Valya and after the Astoria, my guilt consumed me. I loved Valya completely. How could I possibly love another?

I didn't know the truth of it myself, not while Kato was still alive.

I scoop a handful of black earth and let it sift through my fingers.

Chapter Thirty-nine

Garcia rams the chromed barrel into Stone's nostril. The odor of gun oil fills Stone's nose. He stares at the ceiling. Cracked plaster and flaking yellow paint. Garcia pushes harder.

"You think you can—"

But Stone doesn't give him time to finish. He jerks his head aside, grabs Garcia's wrist, and wrenches the gun away from his face.

Garcia yelps and pulls the trigger. The revolver spits flame in a deafening roar that drops a plaster rainfall onto them. Stone clamps Garcia's gun hand under his arm and spins, using his weight to bend Garcia's hand back until bone cracks like a small branch. Stone doesn't hear the sound. The blast from the revolver has put his one good ear out of commission. But the break telegraphs itself from Garcia's wrist to Stone's hands.

Garcia's mouth opens in a scream Stone can't hear. His legs give way and he drops the gun. Stone follows him down until they're both on their knees. Stone ratchets up the pressure, bending Garcia's wrist farther back, playing him like a musical instrument.

"I told you, shithead," Stone says, punctuating each word with a crank on the hand that convulses Garcia's body with agony. "Guadalajara wasn't on me. Somebody else ratted you."

Now Stone can hear again, although everything is muffled. Garcia moans like a wounded animal, gasps for air, and shrieks again. Feet pound up the stairs toward them. Three or four by the sound of it.

Without releasing Garcia's hand, Stone feels around for the revolver. Finds it under the table. A .357 Magnum with a rubber grip that fits his hand nicely. He aims it toward the stairs.

Garcia is still screaming. Music thumps from so many places that Stone can't locate the source of any one sound.

The sounds in the stairwell stop. They're either on the landing below the last flight or creeping up the stairs.

Betting on the latter, Stone releases Garcia, stands, and drags the whimpering man to the corner closest to the top of the stairs. He pins Garcia's broken wrist with his boot so he can increase the pressure by shifting his weight, and he does that now, ignoring Garcia's cries of pain, poised with the .357 aimed down the stairway.

"Ernesto?" a voice calls out.

Stone rocks his weight, and Garcia wails. Like working the pedals of an organ.

"Come and get him," he yells.

"Mr. Stone?"

A different voice this time. Stone grinds Garcia's wrist. He has to shout to be heard over Garcia's shrieks.

"This is how you treat a friendly visitor?"

Nearly a minute passes. Through Garcia's whimpers he can hear them moving around at the bottom of the stairs, maybe preparing for a charge. The .357 holds six rounds. He'll have to make every shot count.

"Mami wants to talk," the second man hollers up the stairs. "We'll take you to her."

"No deal," Stone shouts, knowing that if Mami wants him dead she'll let him kill a hostage to get the job done. "Tell her to come here herself."

Stone glances at Garcia. He's squinting. Stone remembers that he can't see shit without his glasses, which are shattered on the floor nearby. But the thing that makes Stone's heart leap is that Garcia is looking behind him, at the door that leads back to Adelitas.

Stone whirls, leveling the .357, his finger tightening on the trigger.

"Okay, you got me," Mami Kai says.

She's standing in the doorway with her hands in the air. Wearing a bright red, ankle-length dress with a gold dragon wrapping her slender torso. Her raised arms tighten the dress around her curves, accentuating her hips and breasts. She knows the effect she has on men. Stone's seen it work many times, but that was a long time ago in Shanghai.

"You've still got it, Mami," he says, making no attempt to conceal his admiration.

Her smile widens.

Cold steel presses against the back of his neck.

"And we've got you, Stone."

Chapter Forty

I don't know how long I sit in Kato's grave. More than an hour, I think, before I'm struck by a revelation.

I have been thinking about Kato in terms of the past. So many memories, so many experiences of war and strife and hardship, many of them captured in Kato's stories with diamond-like clarity and full-bodied resonance. So many yesterdays, but no tomorrows. Now I realize that it might be possible for her to have a future. The story that led to her death can project her forward in time.

Kato can keep living through her stories.

My job is to see that she does.

The winter sun is already on its downward trajectory by the time I climb out and stand next to the log, surveying the area. On the left a set of tracks disappears into the forest, pointing the way to the Mole and his Volga. To the right a game trail leads in the other direction.

Abram is the type of boy who would go by the road less traveled, I think.

I follow the game trail into the woods.

All footprints and other signs would have been wiped out weeks ago. Instead of looking for them, I skirt along the tree line in a half circle, catching glimpses of the fallen tree trunk between the boles and branches, scanning the ground, looking for anything unusual.

Nothing.

I make a wider arc. The forest grows denser. Kato's gravesite disappears except for occasional snapshots framed by the foliage.

Still nothing.

I swing wider still. Pine, birch, and oak are thick and tangled here, forcing me to push my way through their branches in spots. I can't see the river's edge at all. A hundred meters.

Two hundred meters. The forest eerily silent, wet flakes of new snow sifting down. Three hundred. I stop on the edge of an impenetrable thicket. Scan all around.

Decide I'm wasting my time.

I backtrack. My footprints in the snow provide a clear path. I scrape under the branch of a scrub pine. A dislodged clump of snow hits the back of my neck and slides under my parka.

"Shit."

I shake off the snow and tramp onward.

Stop dead.

It takes me a moment to register what I'm seeing. Tracks in the snow crossing the ones I left not ten minutes earlier.

Moving without haste, I crouch and crab away to put a pine tree between the tracks and me. Big tracks, almost certainly left by a man, crossing mine at a ninety-degree angle. I can see where he paused to look at the trail I left, shifting his weight from side to side, leaving a cluster of footprints. Then his tracks head away, with more space between each step—a man in a hurry.

I draw the Tokarev. Slip as soundlessly as I can through the vegetation parallel to his course, wary of a trap.

In the distance comes the sound of the Mole's voice.

"Volk! Volk!"

The cry echoes across the snow and breaks apart in the trees, so it's difficult to pinpoint his location. Probably on the riverbank where Kato's body was found, but it's definitely not coming from the place where the tracks lead.

Nothing moves. No squirrels, no birds, no deer. The footprints zigzag around obstacles, still leading steadily in the same direction.

Whoever it is has a five-minute lead, no more. I backtracked after going less than two minutes past the point where his tracks crossed mine. Figure two minutes out, two back, then assume he's widened his lead because he's moving faster than I am. Five minutes won't be a problem. Snowflakes drift through the air, but not enough is falling to cover his tracks. As long as I stay on the trail, he has nowhere to hide.

"Volk!"

The sound of the Mole's voice has faded. I'm moving away from him at a forty-five-degree angle. Three hundred meters later I pause and squat behind a tree on the edge of a clearing. Fifty meters of open ground bisected by fresh tracks. Uneven terrain covered with snow, the only way to make it across quickly is to fly.

I'll be exposed for twenty to thirty seconds. An easy target. But I'll lose too much time if I go around. Chances are he's still moving away from me, not waiting.

I charge ahead. Each jolting step sends a lightning bolt of pain through my stump into my thigh. I stumble. Right myself, then catch my toe on a root buried in snow. My momentum throws me forward onto my chest. The snow cushions my fall, but the impact blows the wind out of me.

While I'm still trying to catch my breath a puff of snow mushrooms in front of my face. I jackknife to the side, roll to my feet, and charge toward the nearest stand of trees. Just when I think I'm going to make it, a sledgehammer blow buckles my leg and spins me around.

Chapter Forty-one

Moving slowly, his gaze never leaving Mami's, Stone lowers the .357. The man behind him takes it.

"I came to talk, not fight," Stone says. "Garcia wanted a piece of me. I had no choice."

Her smile remains in place as she approaches him. She stands so close he can smell jasmine. She must be in her late thirties by now. She looks like a toned twenty-five.

She stares up at him. Lightly plays her fingertips across his chest.

"Grayson Stone," she says. She glances down at Garcia, huddled and whimpering. "Still an animal, I see."

"Been a long time. Since Shanghai."

"Shanghai? In 1999, right?"

"Right."

She flattens her palm against his chest. Slides it lower. Her eyes glow. Her pupils are black pinpoints, so small they seem to vanish in the lustrous light of her irises, which in the glare from the desk lamp appear to be the brassy color of the sun melting into the sea. But they leave Stone with the same cold feeling he gets when the sun disappears behind the horizon.

"I remember," she says.

Her hand glides over his belly, pauses, then continues its journey south. She squeezes him. Despite the gun against the back of his head, despite the fact that he should just plain know better, Stone is aroused. Just as stupid as that fucking halfwit Delveccio letting an attractive redhead get to him in the Vegas casino.

"So." She strokes him. Her lips curl into a smile as she feels his reaction. "What did you want to talk to me about?"

"Shakalov."

Her hand stops moving. The man behind Stone digs the barrel under the base of his skull. Mami stops him with a look.

"You DEA again, Stone?"

"I don't care how many tons you move for him." Stone grins at her. "Addicts, prostitutes, tortured gang members, murdered cops, billions of dollars—no small percentage of which gets siphoned off to fund terrorists—what's not to like about the drug trade?"

"Then what you want with that man?"

Mami's English goes to hell when she's stressed, Stone remembers. The tone of her voice changes, too. It becomes more guttural, more like her native Cantonese.

"He won't come here no more," she says. "Big shot now, stay on his yacht or at one of his houses. Dubrovnik, Malibu. What you want with him, anyway?"

"Turns out we have friends in common."

"Who?"

Stone nods toward the men standing behind him. "Let's talk in private."

She holds his gaze for another moment, then steps away, her brief seduction routine forgotten. She claps her hands together once.

"*Vamos!* Go, go, go!"

The man holding the gun on Stone waits while the others carry Garcia down the stairs. Once they're gone he offers his pistol to Mami, who takes it from him and aims it at Stone's forehead.

"Bang," she says, and laughs. "That is what Shakalov will do to you. Don't think he won't. And don't think you can stop him. You can't. Not anymore. Nobody can."

"I told you, I don't want to stop him. I just want to talk."

She tosses the gun back to her man.

"Come," she says, and she leads the way back through the door and down the hall to the rear of Adelitas. The passed-out prostitute is gone, probably hauled away by one of Mami's men.

They enter the bar, into a sweaty press of bodies and a wall of sound. Mami leads the way to an orange vinyl booth against the far wall. One of the bouncers has already shooed away whoever was sitting there before and now stands next to the booth with his hands clasped in front of his body. They slide in across from each other.

A waiter appears. Mami orders drinks. Stares impassively at the waiter's back as he walks to the bar.

"I need a face-to-face with Shakalov," Stone says.

"Why you want trouble, Stone?"

"How many times do I have to say it? No trouble, just talk."

Mami cocks a plucked brow. "Money?"

"Maybe."

"How much?"

"For you or for Shakalov?"

"Me."

"Ten thousand. All you have to do is arrange the meeting."

"You have it on you?"

"No. I left it in San Diego. Figured this would take a few days."

The drinks come. Scotch for Stone, something brown and steaming for Mami. She stirs it. Sucks the end of her swizzle stick, then taps her teeth with it, looking thoughtful.

"How much for Shakalov?"

"That's between him and me. You know that."

She appraises him. "I wonder."

"Don't. That's nonnegotiable."

"If you split profits with him, why not with me?"

"You're the middleman. He adds value."

"Twenty."

"Done."

She sets the swizzle stick aside and sips her brew. "Drink, drink. Maybe the alcohol clears your brain."

Stone knocks back the shot. He likes the burn in the back of his throat and the warm glow in his belly. Mami signals the waiter to bring another round. With her arm still raised she circles her hand to take in the whole roomful of half-naked girls, more of them than customers, a swirling bounty of flesh.

"Which one you want?" she says.

Another drink arrives. Stone kills it, swipes the back of his hand across his mouth, and holds up the glass to get another one.

"You're still off limits?"

"What do you think?"

He nods. Points to a girl in cut-off jeans and a white tank top. "Her."

"Okay."

The waiter sets another shot in front of him. He downs it. Aims the bottom of the glass at another girl in a Budweiser bikini.

"And her."

Mami smirks. "Like I said. Still an animal."

The first girl glides over to the booth and sits in Stone's lap. She's warm. The bare skin of her belly feels silky and soft. He fingers a tiny gold chain dangling from her belly button. The Bud girl approaches and kneels on the seat of the booth behind Stone. She leans over him and slips her hand under his shirt.

Mami slides out of the booth.

"Come see me tomorrow," she says. "I'll have answer for you then." She glances at the girls. "This is my gift to you tonight. Don't forget the money tomorrow."

She slinks away. The girls hold Stone's hands as they lead him through the crowd and up the stairs of the hotel next door, bypassing a long line of hookers and their johns to go straight to a room on the top floor.

King-size bed, a dresser and mirror combo. A sink off to the side, then a door opening into a bathroom with a commode and a shower stall.

Stone flops onto the bed. The girls undress him. They undress each other and kiss.

Stone watches. He directs them, using hand signals to tell them what to do. He arranges them into different positions. He moves in and out of the action. He pulls one of them on top of him. He thinks it's the Budweiser girl, but now that their clothes are off he can't be sure. They're both long-limbed and dusky, black hair swinging free.

Then the spreading warmth in his groin fades, replaced by a strange vertigo.

"What the fuck?" Stone says.

"You want to fuck?"

He opens his eyes. One of the girls is hovering over him, stroking him to smooth on a condom, her hair brushing his belly. The ceiling spins one way, the bed spins another.

"That fucking bitch," Stone says.

The girl misunderstands. She straddles him, reaching between her legs to put him inside her. He bucks her off. Bellows Mami's name, but all that comes out is a croak.

He tries to get up.

Can't.

He's at the bottom of a giant whirlpool and all he can do is wonder where he'll be when he wakes up.

If he wakes up.

Mami, you fucking bitch!

Chapter Forty-two

I land with a thud, exposed in the clearing, screened only by mounds of snow.

Another round scorches the air just above my head.

I scramble behind a mound no taller than a tripwire.

Use the mound for cover and drag myself to the bole of an oak. Press back so hard I'm surprised the bark doesn't crack open to let me inside.

My left leg is numb, my boot torn open to show the titanium frame of my prosthesis beneath the foam piece shaped like a calf. No blood. The bullet hit the mechanism and cosmetic paraphernalia.

I get to my knees, draw the Tokarev and hold it with both hands. My heart is beating so loudly I can't hear through the rush of blood in my head.

Calm. Be calm. Use your head and you might live. Panic and you die.

Nothing hard about that.

I bring up my leg and test the prosthesis. It seems to work. But now I'll have to find out whether it can support all my weight.

The shots came from a suppressed rifle, in front of me and slightly to my right, I think, remembering the way the snow jumped from the first round. No sound when he fired, no way to judge the distance. The shooter knows I'm alive. He probably thinks I'm hurt worse than I am, but he'll be cautious. In his position I would work around to try for a clean shot. Take advantage of the accuracy of his rifle from a distance. No need to risk coming in close to kill a wounded man.

First thing, change positions.

I shift around the oak tree to give myself more cover, still guessing at the shooter's location. The oak stands five steps away from a copse of trees rising from thick underbrush. Keeping the trunk between the likeliest spot for the shooter and myself, I dive into the thicket and burrow into the densest part of it.

The ground falls away on the other side. I sled on my back and land in a trickle of water at the bottom of a V-shaped gully. My foot works. I scramble along the stream bed for forty meters, climb over a tumble of boulders, and find a sheltered place to rest.

I started with three rounds in the Tokarev. Fired one into the planks at Helen's feet. Two rounds left. That's all I have to work with.

So what's the plan?

The shooter thinks I'm injured, less mobile than I am. So I need to move. I need to attack.

"Volk!" the Mole shouts, still some distance away.

I claw my way out of the stream bed and into the woods again. My leg aches. I tear off a length of cloth from my undershirt and stuff it into my mouth to muffle the chatter of my teeth. Slip as silently as I can through the woods to the spot where I believe the shots were fired, searching the ground for marks.

I find an area of churned snow where the shooter had waited for me to appear in the clearing. He laid flat, steadied his gun on a rock. Picked up his brass. Quartered to the left after his shots, trying to get a better angle, just as I suspected, leaving a clear trail behind him.

"Volk!"

The Mole again, still calling, closer now, almost to the edge of the clearing opposite me where I first came out of the tree line. I want to warn him, but I can't do that without giving away my position. Me with a pistol, the shooter with a rifle…He'll make short work of both of us. But maybe the shooter won't take a shot, either, because that would give away *his* position.

I back away. Follow the fresh prints in a wider arc as they head north, then east.

"Where are you, Volk?"

I spot the Mole through the trees just as he steps into the clearing. He hesitates for a moment, then takes a few tentative steps forward, staring at the marks in the snow where I hit the ground and then scrambled away.

I get going again, moving faster. Faster than I should, because now I think the shooter may not care about giving away his position if he thinks I'm hurt and holing up on the far side of the clearing.

The Mole screams. Clutches his leg and goes down. I don't hear the shot, but I see a puff of smoke drifting into the air less than fifty meters to the east. The Mole screams again. I take off running toward the smoke. I can't see the Mole through the blurred branches. All I can hope is that his cries mask the sound of my approach.

I slow when I'm within fifteen meters of the spot where I think my quarry is hiding.

Control my breathing. Hunker down, looking for movement, see none.

I creep forward. Everything is still and deathly quiet except for an occasional cry from the Mole. I can't spot the shooter. I move in slow motion.

Then I freeze. I can *smell* him. Or rather I smell his chewing gum or breath mint. Peppermint. He's close. I'm almost on top of him. I must be. But *where* is he?

A whisper of snow drifts to the ground from a tree branch, followed by the slightest movement.

White on white.

He's wearing a white camouflage suit. He's burrowed into the snow behind a low mound, screened by a stand of poplars.

I raise the Tokarev. Squeeze. Feel it jump in my hands like a living thing.

Chapter Forty-three

The round from my Tokarev strikes the shooter in the middle of his back. A downy white puff, a smoking hole that instantly turns red. He rolls, his body stiff, his feet jerking spastically. An AK painted white lies where he dropped it in the snow.

I rush toward him, prepared to fire my last round.

No need.

His eyes are open wide in shock. He coughs up a gob of blood that spills down his cheeks. I put the muzzle of the Tokarev against the side of his head. Turn him onto his side and tear a wider hole in his camouflage suit to see the entry wound. Pale skin, a hole the size of my thumb colored purple and red with white bits of bone from his shattered spine poking through the gore.

I let go of his shoulder, and he flops onto his back. His sightless eyes roll back in their sockets. He makes a ragged gasp for air. More blood froths from his mouth.

I pick up the AK and carry it into the clearing where the Mole fell.

He's dead.

The first shot cut him down, the second ripped away his jaw. The sounds he was making weren't cries for help. They were the sounds of an animal dying in agony.

I trudge back to the shooter. He's dead now, too.

I check his pockets. Find a wallet loaded with a thick sheaf of rubles, no ID. I unzip the top half of his camouflage suit. Rip open his long underwear, popping buttons, and expose his chest.

Tattoos cover his upper body. So many that he appears to be wearing a body suit the color of blue prison ink. The story of his life is there. Prison, army service, foot soldier for the *Solntsevskaya bratva*, prison again.

A résumé not altogether different from my own, although my days as a gangster were undercover for the General, and I never worked for any of the animals in the *Solntsevskaya bratva*.

Dog tags cradled in the hollow of his neck, nestled in a patch of black hair. The tags are homemade, made of melted steel scored with his personal information. A souvenir from Chechnya, I know, because army-issued tags are made of aluminum, which melts too easily in fire, meaning no one can ID your body. Nobody wants to be an unidentified lump of meat in a refrigerator. So soldiers go to Mozdok and other towns and buy their own tags made of galvanized steel. Engravers mark them with their name, DOB, address, blood type. If they don't have the money for a tag like this, then some soldiers break up ladles and spoons, melt the metal into the desired shape and thickness, and use a nail to inscribe their name and blood group.

That's what this man did. His tags identify him as Vtoroi Solmanov. Born 5-5-84. Blood type AB.

He had hooked a silver locket on to one of the links of the chain. The locket opens to reveal a miniature portrait of a woman with bobbed hair. Mother, wife, girlfriend, who knows? All the ties made over a lifetime have been severed here on the edge of a frozen clearing.

I jerk the chain from his neck. Search him without finding anything else useful except a protein bar still warm from his body, with only a smear of blood on the wrapper. I settle into the snow, rip open the wrapper, and take a bite. Check my cell for a signal. Weak, but it's there.

I speed-dial the General's number. He answers with a grunt while I'm in mid-chew.

"I need you to run a name for me."

"Go."

"Vtoroi Solmanov."

"Wait."

I can hear him clicking the keys of his computer. Vultures circle the Mole's body. I will have to bury him here. I can't risk driving the Volga with a dead body rolling around in the trunk.

"Got him," the General says. "Served with a rifle battalion. Now he's a gun for hire. Most recently on the payroll of the Brotherhood."

The General refers to *Solntsevskaya bratva*, the Brotherhood, with respect. Everyone respects the Brotherhood, especially those who warily cruise the same waters.

"Cross reference him with the name Lazar Solovie."

"The nuclear scientist?"

I don't respond. More clicking. The bravest of the vultures lands on the Mole's body. From this distance I can't be sure, but I think it rewards itself with an eyeball.

"Interesting," the General says. "Did you know that Solovie has a contract with the French?"

"No."

"The French like his work enough to pay him an annual stipend of three million Euros. For consulting work related to, quote, the 'safe, responsible uses of nuclear energy and environmentally friendly disposal of waste.' Hmm. The Americans have him under contract as well."

The General busies himself on his computer. Another snow flurry begins. More birds have joined the first.

"Here's something," the General says. We have a bad connection, but still the excitement in his voice carries through the ether. "Solovie spent time at Cambridge. According to the KGB's files, he was feeding MI6 and the CIA information about our nuclear program."

The cold wicks into my bones. It will take hours to dig through the permafrost and bury two bodies. Maybe I'll leave this one, Vtoroi Solmanov, for the vultures. Bury the Mole in Kato's former grave. I don't think she would mind.

"No surprise there," I say. "He worked for the Brits and Americans, now he's on the French payroll."

"That's just it," the General says. "I have the *real* KGB files on my screen, with scans of the entries written by his former handler with the First Chief Directorate. The other files were planted, part of Solovie's cover. MI6 and the CIA thought they'd doubled an agent in place. The First Chief Directorate used that mistake against them. They used Solovie to feed them disinformation."

Intelligence and counterintelligence, truth and lies artfully mixed into a seething brew, impossible to separate into its parts. All these years later, who knows which side Solovie was on in those days?

"Where's Solovie now?"

"Hold on," the General says.

I picture him in his office, lit by the blue screens of his computers, working the phones while the walls around him weep river water. Holding the phone against my ear, I pocket Vtoroi Solmanov's galvanized steel dog tags and trudge across the clearing to the Mole's body. Shoo away the gathered birds. Hoist him over my shoulder. Lug him back the way we came, following our path through the snow.

I'm almost to the bank of the Techa River when the General comes back on the line.

"Solovie's a long way from home," he says. "According to his staff in the Sarov lab, he's working the American half of his contracts now. Advising them on their spent nuclear fuel disposal problems. How's that for irony?"

"Where in America?"

"Las Vegas. They like a disposal site called Yucca Mountain eighty miles north of the city. At least they used to like that location. Who knows about American politics? They might be changing directions."

I dump the Mole's body next to Kato's grave. I'll have to make the hole deeper. I stare at the muddy waters of the Techa.

"I need to go to Las Vegas."

The General sighs. "You don't think I'm already working on that?"

PART V

In the desert
I saw a creature, naked, bestial,
Who, squatting upon the ground,
Held his heart in his hands,
And ate of it.
I said: "Is it good, friend?"
"It is bitter-bitter," he answered;
"But I like it
Because it is bitter,
And because it is my heart."
—Stephen Crane, *In the Desert*

Chapter Forty-four

Stone awakens.

Opens his eyes.

Recoils from the bright light of the sun, blinded.

What the fuck happened? He remembers: Mami Kai, two Tijuana hookers younger than his Scotch, the room spinning crazily. *This has to be bad.*

Hard metal ridges jolt against his back. The bed of a pickup truck, he realizes. When he tries to sit up, he smacks his head on a metal bar.

He squints into the sun. It's high in the sky, a dome of sizzling white radiance cut up by the bars above his head. A cloud of dust spews the air behind them. Through the haze he sees the twin tracks of a dirt road roll away through raw desert, miles of it. Towering saguaros and grasping creosote shrubs rush past on both sides. The bars extend all the way across the top of the truck bed, high enough for him to roll beneath them, too low to sit up.

He's in a cage.

Naked except for adult diapers.

The diapers frighten him. The Mexican cartels often force their victims to wear them while they're tortured. Nobody wants piss and shit everywhere.

The truck bounces over a rut and throws him against the bars. His head strikes one of them hard enough to draw blood. He braces a foot against a crosspiece to hold himself down.

Assesses.

He's in deep trouble. Cotton-mouthed, bleeding, roasting under a winter sun with enough bite to turn his flesh pink. Crusted stains cover the truck bed, thicker between the metal ribs. Dried blood, puke, fecal matter, a bottle cap fused with the crud.

Imagine if it were summer. Imagine a cargo of four, or six, or twelve, packed into this broiling can.

He refocuses. Gets down to the facts. He blacked out in the hotel room at around four A.M. By the sun's position he figures it's early afternoon now. Ten hours. He could be anywhere.

Maybe Mami Kai decided to take revenge for Garcia. Or maybe she believed he was still DEA-connected. But…she wouldn't need to send him on a joyride like this. A word from her and he could have been carved into pieces small enough to flush into the Tijuana sewer system.

Which means Mami kept her promise. She's delivering him to Shakalov. He tries to remember whether he still had on any of his clothes when he passed out last night. Can't recall. Decides the most likely reason he's naked is that Mami's delivery boys dumped him here and took off without bothering to clothe him. He'd have done the same thing in their place.

His problem is the diapers. They send an ugly message.

He looks around for something he could use as a weapon. Other than the accumulated sludge, there's nothing in the back with him. He cranes his neck to see into the rear window of the pickup, but it's tinted black.

The truck turns, slows, and crawls into a canyon. High rock walls painted orange and black by sun and shadow. The truck bobs and lurches like a ship on rough seas.

They stop in a cloud of dust. Voices chattering in Spanish, one argumentative, the other cool and calm. Stone can't make out the words.

A shot rings out.

The sharp sound of it ricochets off the walls of the canyon. Someone screams. "*Compasión!*"

Another shot, another echo off the canyon walls.

Then a low murmur of voices. Gravel crunches as someone approaches. The back of the truck dips as a man climbs onto the rear bumper. He peers at Stone through the bars.

Fat face beneath a black cowboy hat perched crookedly on his head. Eyes narrowed to slits by the folds of his cheeks. A toothpick tucked into the corner of his mouth. Forearms bulging with muscle, a Walther finished with the look of Damascus steel leaking smoke in his left hand, small and deadly as a silver cobra.

Shakalov.

Aged by ten years from the last picture Stone could find on ECHELON. He shifts his toothpick from one side of his mouth to the other.

"You have business with me?"

Shakalov still has a thick Russian accent, fifteen years after he fled to London with the Kremlin dogs panting on his heels. Stone nods.

"What is the nature of this business?"

"The French want a meeting."

"Why?"

"I don't know."

"Take a guess."

"Trade in nuclear waste from Europe."

Shakalov spits a chewed splinter of toothpick at Stone's feet. "Trades like that happen all the time. No problem. Everybody knows. Good business for Russia, smart investment for the West. Nobody needs me."

"The French need you."

"Why?" Shakalov waves his pistol before Stone can answer. "Don't say you don't know."

"Who better to move tons of cargo under the radar?"

Shakalov stares at Stone's near-naked body. He removes his hat and wipes his brow with a brown handkerchief. Contemplates the fiery colors of copper and gold on the rock all around them. Replaces the hat and absently works the slide-mounted safety of the Walther with his thumb.

"How much?"

"I suspect the price is negotiable."

"Why you? Why not one of them?"

"I subcontract for them. They knew I had the contacts to arrange a meeting."

If this can be called a meeting: lying on his side propped on one elbow, flesh roasting in the sun, half dead with thirst, stripped nearly bare before a man with a smoking gun. A man who has probably just finished killing the driver and the driver's partner because they saw his face. Some meeting.

The folds of skin on Shakalov's face ripple with some emotion. Disgust? Anger?

"The story has not been told."

Stone doesn't know what Shakalov is talking about. He doesn't move.

"The Americans are interested in an arrangement, too," he says. He doesn't know that, but the pressure to give Shakalov something worthwhile is building. "This administration makes deals just like all the others"—

Shakalov waves him to silence. "The people who make these deals don't change with administrations."

Stone nods agreement. He's sure that Shakalov can see the pounding of his heart through the skin on his bare chest. This is the moment that will decide whether he lives or dies.

Shakalov aims the Walther at Stone's face. Stone doesn't blink. He's too terrified to blink.

Shakalov laughs. "I don't like people to see my face," he says without moving the pistol. "Now that you know my face, Stone, who comes next? DEA? CIA? Or the Russians? Men from the FSB with radioactive poison for my tequila?"

Stone's mouth is too dry to answer. Shakalov flips the safety to the off position.

"You see why it's easier to kill you, Stone? No worries then."

Chapter Forty-five

On the flight back to Moscow from Chelyabinsk, I dream of a long corridor with no discernible beginning or end. The walls move past me in a stutter of black and white, creating a sensation of rapid motion, as though I am passing through an endless series of lights spaced at regular intervals. The sensation is akin to hurtling forward in a bullet train, with alternating light and dark in the windows.

Valya appears at the end of the corridor ahead of me. Her image wavers like a projection, one moment sharply defined, the next indistinct. Her back is turned.

I call out to her, but she doesn't react.

I run toward her, but the distance between us never changes.

The walls rush by, moving faster as though we are accelerating, although neither of us moves relative to the other. Time passes, but I don't know how much.

Then Valya turns to face me. Recognition blooms in her face. *Alexei! There you are.*

An instant later her joyful expression disappears, replaced by a look of pain so profound my breath catches as though I've swallowed a hook.

The passenger in the middle seat shakes me awake. He looks at me strangely, but says nothing. The plane has landed. I sling my duffel and exit, turning on my phone as I walk. No messages.

I arrive home to find an empty loft.

No note.

No sign that Valya was ever there. Everything she owns is gone.

Sometimes bad dreams come true.

Chapter Forty-six

Stone has looked down the barrel of a gun many times. The adrenaline rush, the icy fear squeezing his guts—those sensations are familiar to him, manageable.

This time is different, because the Walther isn't the most frightening thing. Not even close. The deranged look in Shakalov's eyes terrifies him much more. Wide open, pupils shrunk to dots in the harsh light of the sun, and a maniacal glaze that turns his blue irises into shiny chips of onyx.

"So," Shakalov says without lowering the pistol. "You came here to tell me the *French* want to move cargo?"

"They'll pay."

Shakalov laughs, but it is an ugly sound, like the caw of a scavenger.

"Small change."

From the corner of his eye Stone glimpses men moving. Then it registers that for the last several minutes he's been hearing the scrape of metal on rock and sand. The men are digging a grave. Stone can't see whether it's big enough to hold more than one body. But he knows. He is fighting for his life. If Shakalov thinks Stone is here to barter for clandestine shipping—moving spent nuclear fuel like drugs—let him think it.

"Millions," Stone says. "They'll pay millions to someone who can secretly move their products around the world."

Shakalov stares, his expression cold. "Somebody else will pay millions and I don't have to lift a finger. They'll pay me that just for keeping my mouth shut. And they'll open their borders like a hooker spreads her legs."

The digging sounds stop. Someone thumbs the wheel of a cigarette lighter. Somebody else laughs. Stone can't look away from the Walther and the crazed eyes behind it.

"Who?"

"The Americans."

"Why would they do that?"

"Because they're dirty, they fucked up, and they got caught."

Shakalov lowers the Walther and slides it under his belt. He climbs onto the bars over the truck bed until he is directly above Stone. Gripping two of the bars, he lowers his body until his face is less than a foot above Stone's, dripping sweat.

"Rogues in their Department of Defense cut a deal with the Kremlin. DoD pays the Kremlin to reprocess spent fuel rods from their aircraft carriers and submarines. They pay less than you think because the Kremlin keeps the recovered uranium and plutonium. They make a few practice runs using the Merchant Marine fleet. Okay, no problem. First live shipment was five weeks ago. They pack the stuff into special containers and load it onto a ship."

Still holding his pressed position, Shakalov sticks his face between the bars, baring his teeth in a wolfish grin, forcing Stone to shrink back.

"The fucking ship sank."

His laugh starts deep inside his chest and expands, filling the bed of the truck with a maniacal sound.

"It sank! Three of my men were on board. They were saved. They lived to tell me the story. And guess what? The Americans can't find the fucking thing. They think maybe it broke apart underwater, scattered containers all over the North Atlantic."

Shakalov keeps holding the same position. The muscles on his forearms bulge and jump. Sweat drops onto Stone's face.

"Two of my men got killed in the desert before I realized how valuable they were. The third I keep safe." Shakalov's eyes grow wider, even more crazed. "The Americans will pay and pay.

Whatever I want. Do you know how much proof of something like that is worth? Real live fucking proof! How much is that worth, government man?"

Chapter Forty-seven

Shakalov leaves, driving away in a Range Rover in a cloud of dust. His men give Stone clothes and stale water from a metal canteen. The water tastes like nectar. They squeeze him into the front seat with them and drive him through the canyon to a small adobe house with a tile roof. Give him a room and pallet to sleep on.

The next day they drive him back to Tijuana. The trip takes five hours. Stone figures Shakalov could be as far away as Dubrovnik by now. Stone thinks about the heat, the blinding glare of the sun off the desert floor, the cottony white clouds journeying across the blue ocean of sky. He thinks about everything except Shakalov's last words to him.

"You're the messenger, Stone. Get to the right people and tell them. Set it up, I'll produce the proof. Not some bullshit story. They'll get a statement, but they'll get more, too. My man has a video of the *cargo* being loaded. Tell them that. Tell them I can prove it."

Shakalov's men drop Stone across the street from Adelitas. Behind him a bar called C.O. Jones, someone's idea of a joke. *Cojones*. Testicles. Balls. All around are sleepy streets, gated storefronts, no shouts or music. The place looks sickly in the light of day, leached of life.

Stone stretches. Spots a cab. Whistles to hail it as he starts down the street.

"Where do you think you're going, *imbécil?*"

Stone starts to turn. Stops when he feels a gun rammed into his kidney.

Garcia. The man who took a bullet in the crotch and thinks Stone fingered him. A man with a broken wrist and a grudge.

"You owe Mami twenty thousand dollars," Garcia hisses.

Stone raises his hands to shoulder height. "She owes me a night with two pick-of-the-litter hookers."

"You're missing the point. The only reason I have to let you live is *because* you owe Mami the money. I can't kill you until after you pay. But that doesn't mean I can't take out some of my frustrations."

Garcia shoves Stone into an alley. High walls block the sun, just like the natural walls of the desert canyon. The patch of sky above the walls is a hazy shade of blue. Garcia puts his mouth next to Stone's ear.

"You owe me this."

He clubs Stone in the kidney with his gun. Stone drops to his knees, arched back in agony.

"And this," Garcia says.

He swipes the gun barrel across Stone's face. Bone crunches. Stone tastes the coppery slide of warm blood from his nose and mouth into his throat. Another kidney blow drops him facedown in the gutter next to a wall. Gravel and asphalt rake his face as Garcia drags him away from the wall, then lines up to launch a kick.

Stupid fucker. One big blow and Stone won't feel a thing, no matter what Garcia does.

At least there's that, Stone thinks.

Chapter Forty-eight

Las Vegas looks like a glowing caldera from the air. Fired like the cone of a super-heated volcano, its ejecta colored electric red, blue, and green. White lights like lava spilled at its feet. As the plane banks into its final approach to McCarran, the Day-Glo colors resolve themselves into neon signs; floodlit hotels; colossal replicas of a pyramid, a guitar, the Manhattan skyline, and the Eiffel Tower; ribbons of red and white streets and freeways.

Wheels touch down at 10:39 P.M. Almost twenty-one hours have passed since I left Moscow. Hours of dead time over the Arctic, then a hassle in Atlanta.

The General had made my travel arrangements after pulling the usual strings, but my passport—my *real* passport—raised alarms with the Immigration computers. Two ICE officials escorted me to a small room and left me there for half an hour.

One of them returned with a tall woman dressed in a dark blue business suit, her brown hair twisted into a bun spiked with a pencil. She spent fifteen minutes filling out paperwork, not speaking, not acknowledging my presence at all. When she was done she stamped my passport and glanced at the battered duffel bag at my feet.

"Did you check any luggage?"

"No."

She inspected my Customs declaration. Handed it back to me with my passport.

"Hurry and you might still make your connection."

I stood to leave. She raised a hand.

"Wait. A man named Brock Matthews will meet you in Las Vegas. Do you know him?"

I first met Matthews in D.C. in 2003 at a joint intelligence conference sponsored by the Americans. After the conference he began visiting me in Moscow now and then, "checking in," he liked to say. I contacted him again several years later when I was in Manhattan and needed a favor while I searched for a painting stolen from the Hermitage. Six months after that we traveled together to Chechnya to confront a rebel warlord and, days later, he stood with me in a bunker while I made the fateful decision whether to launch an air-to-surface missile from a prowling drone. And he worked my case in Los Angeles while I chased down an elusive World War II-era cablegram and tried to answer the question whether my father was a traitor or a patriot.

"Mr. Volkovoy?" The immigration official—or CIA officer, or FBI agent, or whatever she might be—tried to get my attention.

"Yes, I know Matthews."

"Good. You are not authorized to travel anywhere without him. Are we clear?"

I nodded.

"I need you to answer audibly."

"We're clear."

"There will be a federal air marshal on board the next leg of your flight. He won't identify himself, but he'll be there. Clear?"

I told her yes, I understood.

Now I glance around the cabin as I take my duffel down from the overhead compartment. Focus on a tow-headed man who looks about twenty-five years old. He spent most of the flight reading *Surfer* magazine, always awake and alert, always with his right arm free. He notices me looking at him, turns, and says something to the passenger behind him.

Brock Matthews waits at the gate. Tall, built with hard planes and angles, radiating tension like a longbow at full flex. He tracks my approach, standing with his arms at his side, his blue eyes cold. He doesn't offer to shake hands.

"This is unexpected," he says.

"Next time maybe they'll send a tall blond woman with poor vision. Perfect for you."

"Uh-huh."

He motions for me to follow him, and we wade through a confusion of racketing slot machines and harried passengers to a light rail car that takes us to the ground transportation area. Once there he leads the way through the parking garage to a white sedan. We climb inside. He rests a forearm on the steering wheel and turns to face me.

"Why are you here, Volk?"

I meet his gaze squarely. "We think we have a rogue on our hands. A scientist named Lazar Solovie."

"I read the report. Why not just haul his ass back to Russia? Why *here* and why *you*?"

My last visit to America led me into a maze of deception and distorted truths. I don't know how much of it was manufactured by this man, and I don't know who won or lost in the end. Matthews might have been part of a conspiracy to mislead Russia's military intelligence, or he might have been conned by a double agent in his own backyard. The espionage business has rightly been described as a wilderness of mirrors.

This time is different. This time I can be more direct.

"We think Solovie had a hand in the murder of a journalist in the Chelyabinsk region."

"Katarina Mironova? Kato?"

"Yes."

He looks skeptical. "You're saying the FSB wants to find Kato's killer and bring him to justice? Give me a break. If you're looking for suspects, start with your own *compadres*."

"I'm not FSB."

"Okay then, why is GRU interested in this?"

"I'm not military intelligence, either. This is a private affair."

"Private? Now we're getting closer." Matthews appraises me. "Truth has a sound all its own, don't you think?"

He reaches a long arm into the backseat, snaps open a stainless steel briefcase, and removes a manila folder. The folder holds several photographs. He angles them away from me, studying them one at a time. Then he separates one from the others and hands it to me.

Eight by ten, black-and-white, good quality even though it must have been shot using a telephoto lens. It shows Kato and me locked together in a Moscow hotel room where we met several times. I recognize the pattern of the comforter. The photographer must have been in a room in the hotel across the street. He or she shot through a gap in the curtains.

Matthews waits a long time for me to say something. When I don't he takes the photo from me and returns it to the folder.

"The question is how you managed to convince the people in power to send you here to resolve your 'private affair.'"

The garage is busy. Cars pulling in and out, travelers loading and unloading their bags, families rolling past our windows with enough luggage to clothe a division. If Matthews knows about Kato and me, then others do, too. The General or someone else will connect the dots between the journalist and her source.

I shift my weight, uncomfortable in the confines of the car with this man who always seems to know more than I do.

"Yes, I have a stake in this. But Solovie is on the payroll of foreign governments, and my people are concerned about having a rogue. That adds a public aspect to things."

"Which foreign governments?"

"French."

"Any others?"

I meet his gaze. Hold it. "Yours."

"One man's terrorist is another man's patriot. Maybe your *rogue* benefits us."

"If he did, he won't anymore. He's no use to you now. Too many people are looking at him."

Matthews purses his lips. "Not good enough. All that tells me is that you want to clean up your mess on my turf. Tell me how this helps *me*."

"I think you have a rogue of your own."

His gaze intensifies. "Who?"

"Two men killed Kato. One French, one American. The American had a shaved head. He was built like a boulder or a rock. The woman who described him to me used the Russian word *kamen*. Stone."

Matthews stares at me without expression. I can see his mind churning furiously behind the rigid set of his brow. Ever so slightly, the skin around his eyes tightens and his lips draw back. All at once he looks like the predator he is.

"*Kamen?*" he says. "*Kamen.*"

He turns away and starts the car, but doesn't back out. Instead, he punches a number on the speed dial of his cell phone.

"Change of plans," he says into the phone. "We're heading to Summerlin."

He ends the call, backs the car out, and chirps the tires pulling away.

"Maybe we can help you here, Volk," he says, steering around the curves of the garage, his jaw set. "Just like old times."

Chapter Forty-nine

Stone hears the whine, beep, and hum of machinery. He sees white light as if through a gauzy haze. He hears voices talking in Spanish. He hears one voice in English.

"Swelling of the brain…massive hemorrhaging…"

He tries to speak.

Can't.

He experiences a vision: dead eyes staring accusingly at him from a mucky hole on the banks of a river. He wants to tell her that it's not his fault, he's just the cleaner, but he's afraid. Afraid she'll notice the three bodies stacked next to her grave, ready to join her in the hole. Afraid she'll know the truth about him no matter what he says.

The eyes track him. They don't blink. They condemn.

Stone craves oblivion.

Oblivion finds him.

Chapter Fifty

We roll along the 215 freeway north and west, Matthews driving fast, his jaw set, absorbed in thought. He exits on a road called Summerlin Parkway. Makes several turns into a residential neighborhood.

We arrive at a nondescript stucco house. It sits at the end of a cul-de-sac, darkness behind it. A golf course, I see when we get out of the car, pools of black marking the location of man-made lakes.

Matthews leads the way inside, past an unsmiling man who stands at the front door with his hands clasped in front of his body. No furniture in the house except for folding chairs arranged in a circle near the front window. Brown carpet, white walls pocked with nail holes and streaked with handprints, and a kitchen with beige linoleum and avocado-green countertops.

Two more men wait inside.

One of them leads the way to a short hall that takes us to an open door and, beyond that, steps leading down to a basement. At the bottom of the stairs are two doors, both closed. Matthews opens the one on the left.

Concrete floors. A steel-framed bed, no mattress, just the wire mesh support. Handcuffs dangling from each corner, dried blood spattering the metal surfaces. Dried blood everywhere, actually. On the metal frame, water-falling onto the floor in crusty puddles beneath the bed, splashing the far wall.

Matthews watches my reaction.

I give him none.

"Looks like an Iraqi torture chamber," he says.

"I wouldn't know."

"Sure."

He opens his manila folder. Selects a photograph and shows it to me.

"Recognize him?"

The photo shows a short, fat man chained spread-eagled on a bed—*this* bed. Still alive. Face puffy, eyes swollen almost shut, gashes above his eyebrow and on his cheek. Deeper cuts on his chest, strips of flesh peeled from his torso.

I shake my head. "No."

"Any reason why he might want to kill two Russian drug traffickers in the Nevada desert?"

"Money?"

"Very funny, Volk."

Matthews removes two more photographs from the folder. He hands them to me.

The one on top shows the remains of a man next to a creosote bush. He's little more than a slab of raw meat, most of his skin scraped away, one foot missing. The second shows the bound body of another man, visible signs of torture all over. Burned flesh, flayed skin, holes where his eyes used to be. No clothes except for stained white diapers.

"Both Russians," Matthews says. "Why Russians here in the desert?"

"Not my territory, Matthews."

I give the photos back to him. Thinking that a Russian gangster named Shakalov is rumored to have aligned himself with one of the old-line cartels. A cartel brought to its knees by Mexican president Calderón's war on drugs and the rise of rival gangs, but one with key lines of distribution through the increasingly monitored and hostile border regions. Several years ago Shakalov began waging a vicious war on their behalf against the host of ruthless new cartels that rose to challenge the established players. A similar consolidation play worked for Shakalov in the Far East, and it will likely work in Mexico, too, unless he's killed first.

If these men were Russian, they probably belonged to Shakalov.

Matthews puts the photos back into the folder and passes the folder back over his shoulder to the man behind him.

"You're not being helpful, Volk. You just failed the first credibility test."

"I don't like tests. What do you want me to say? Rival gangs staking out their turf, sending a message with torture-murders. So what? Would it make you feel better if I told you that the dead Russians probably worked for a man known as Shakalov?"

"Yes, we would appreciate a straight answer from you now and then."

"You know all of that, Matthews. What we're both wondering is what any of this"—I wave my hand to include the bloody room and the photos now being held by the other man—"has to do with Lazar Solovie and Kato."

His eyeballs jitter ever so slightly. He knows something.

"What?"

Matthews dismisses his men with a wave of his hand. He waits in silence until they leave the room.

"We're worried about our own rogues, Volk," he says quietly. "Some of them within the intelligence community, some of them outsiders who play by an entirely different set of rules—people who don't like the policies they see as soft on terrorism."

"Good luck."

"We think Solovie is working with some of them."

Closer, I think. He's getting closer to the truth. As close as a man like Matthews allows himself to come. I nod to tell him to continue.

"We don't want Solovie to disappear. Not until we know more. Meaning you can't kill him and you can't take him out of the country. Not yet."

"Where is he?"

"He spends most of his time in the States right here in Vegas. About a hundred miles northwest of Vegas, I should say. A place called Yucca Mountain."

"What's he doing there?"

"Advising a private consortium on best practices for the storage, reprocessing, and disposal of nuclear waste."

"Best practices? You want to turn Vegas into Mayak and Lake Mead into Lake Karachay?"

Matthews glances over his shoulder. I think he wants to make sure the door is closed. It is. He moves closer to me, standing with one foot in a dried spill of blood.

"Here's the deal, Volk. We passed a law in 1982 imposing limits on how much spent nuclear fuel our nuke plants can store. In return, the government promised to take the stuff off the plants' hands eventually. That part didn't happen. So now those plants are stuffed to the gills, and our Idaho storage facility is damn near maxed out. We have to come up with a plan. Yucca Mountain doesn't work, because Nevada has clout in the Senate. So what are we going to do?"

"Be like the French. Pay Russia."

"We pay a Russian like Solovie to *advise* us, but we can't legally send it out of country."

"I know how important laws are to you people."

Matthews frowns. "Spare me the sarcasm. I'm confiding in you here. Listen." He grabs my elbow and leads me to the far corner of the room. "We need to dispose of our nuclear waste. You understand? But we're going to do it the right way. At least some of us are, because that's this administration's position, and we do what our elected officials tell us to do. There's the problem. Solovie is on the payroll of one of our less than scrupulous factions."

Matthews stares at me intensely. Trying to get a read, I realize. Trying to decide how much of this is news to *me*. I stare back.

"Which faction?"

"Elements within the Department of Defense."

"They operate your nuclear facilities?"

He shakes his head. "Of course not. But they have trouble disposing of their spent fuel rods. A problem they might be willing to pay a covert partner to take off their hands."

"Is that what's happening?"

"Goddamn it, Volk! Aren't you listening? Why do you think I'm so far out on a limb here? I don't *know* what's happening. I'm as much in the dark as you are."

Chapter Fifty-one

Stone comes to. Everything is dark. He tries to move, but can't. He feels as if he's been buried in an enormous jar of jelly, the gelatinous weight compressing his chest until he can barely breathe. His head hurts. Shooting pain starts in his arm and melds with all the other pain in his head. He longs to escape into the warm comfort of the place he was in before he woke up.

Can't.

Instead, the distorted images return, impossible to erase from his mind's eye. He sees misery and death. He watches the stories of his life unfold like a series of still frames lit by popping flashbulbs.

The mother holding her baby, rocking her body from the waist, silent tears of anguish streaming down her cheeks; Lieutenant Daly's head exploding; Jean-Louis leaning negligently against the jamb. "*Associés*? Partners?"

Fatboy bouncing around in the flaming Humvee, the last installment of his life steeped in suffering beyond imagine; a mushroom cloud of black smoke billowing against a dome of white-blue sky; a face hovering above his, lit by the feeble light of a candle—cropped hair, a week's growth of beard, and hard, hard eyes.

The final set of images the freshest: Jean-Louis caressing the woman's cheek with the barrel of his pistol. "Beg, and maybe you can live, eh? It's not so bad. Swallow a little pride. Tell me how much you want life. Maybe your wish comes true. It's worth a try, is it not, *ma chérie?*" And that Russian bitch—God, so beautiful, lifting her face to the muzzle. "Go ahead, shoot, you impotent ape. This doesn't end here." More flashbulbs burst in Stone's mind in quick succession: Jean-Louis baring his canines in a spitting rage, his face transformed into something primordially evil; Jean-Louis spiking the barrel against her temple; Jean-Louis squeezing the trigger.

"You stupid fuck," Stone said. "How in Christ's name are we supposed to find her notepad now?"

Jean-Louis didn't answer. He simply stood over her body, gasping for breath.

Stone stalked away.

"*Kamen!*" Jean-Louis yelled at his back. "Come back and help me with this mess."

Stone did come back. Not right then, but three weeks later, his bank account fattened by a cool quarter of a mil. His fee for "cleaning" Jean-Louis' problem on the banks of the Techa by dumping more bodies on it, spawning a plausible story about students and a journalist killed together, and arranging for a fall guy in the form of an ex-Russian army soldier nicknamed Rhino.

A quarter of a mil. Not bad for a week's work...

Stone jerks fully awake. White room, starched white sheets, an IV drip in his arm. Two other beds in the room, both occupied. A wall-mounted TV tuned to CNN *en Español*.

He's still in Tijuana. Bandages on his face and wrapping his ribs so tightly he can breathe only with much effort.

He survived Garcia's beating.

Now he has to get across the border. Send Mami her money, then deliver a message to someone high enough in the intelligence food chain to understand the full picture and get the job done. Someone able to negotiate a deal to buy Shakalov's silence.

Stone sinks deeper into the hospital bed. Begins to nod off, wondering how many days he's already wasted in this place. Shakalov won't like waiting.

His eyes close. His chin falls onto his chest. He's on the edge of consciousness when the visions begin again.

"*Kamen!*"

Why the fuck did Jean-Louis use that word? A marker like that has a way of pointing at a person.

As Stone fades away, still caught in the moment of that day by the river and seeing it anew in this dreamlike state, he spots a face in the trees. Eyes wide, mouth hanging open, the flesh melted on his face. A fucking goblin, and it's watching *him* walk away, and it's watching Jean-Louis digging on the other side of the fallen tree trunk.

Stone can't distinguish between memory and fantasy. Did he really see that awful face that day? Or is it a figment of his battered brain?

Is he dreaming?

Chapter Fifty-two

Matthews leads me to the other room in the basement. A guard stands in front of the closed door. He wears a badge on his breast pocket that identifies him as an FBI agent.

"How's our boy?" Matthews asks him.

The agent sniggers. "He only cries at night."

Matthews opens the door and motions for me to follow him inside.

This room is bigger than the last one. Empty except for a bed and a man tethered to the bed frame with a two-meter length of chain attached to a choke collar. Matthews regards him dispassionately.

"How goes it, Jimmy D?"

Jimmy D's Adam's apple bobs, accentuating the thinness of his neck and the abrasions made by the collar.

"You can't keep me here."

"His real name is Jarco Dabizha," Matthews says to me, as though the scrawny man isn't in the room with us. "Heard of him?"

"No."

"Killer for hire in Vegas, worked with the *Solntsevskaya bratva* before that. One of your exports. Why is it that we seem to get the worst of your garbage?"

After the wall crumbled, most of the garbage stayed home, in places like Mayak and in the form of people like the men in charge at the Kremlin, like Lazar Solovie, like the General, like me. The kind of people who can spread misery by the gross with the power of the state behind them. But Matthews has it right in some respects. During the period when the oligarchs consolidated power under Yeltsin, some of our most vicious specimens made it out of Russia and found their fortune, the inside of a jail cell, or both in London, Brooklyn, Mexico City, and a host of other places.

Including Las Vegas.

Matthews walks over to Jimmy D and yanks the chain so hard that the collar cuts into the bloody flesh of Jimmy D's neck and jerks his head sideways.

Jimmy yelps and scooches across the bed to try to create slack in the chain.

"Tell the man what you did to the two coyotes in the desert, Jimmy," Matthews says. "In English."

Clutching his bloody neck, Jimmy squints up at me.

"FSB?" he says.

"No."

He waits for me to say more, but I don't.

"You look familiar," he says.

Our paths haven't crossed. I would remember him. "I don't think so."

"Out in the desert," Matthews says to me. "This man and a gang of his cohorts killed fourteen illegals and two coyotes. You know what a coyote is?"

"Not an animal like a dog?"

"No. An alien smuggler. Usually Mexican in this part of the country. But these two were Russians, like you and the sadist here."

I glance from Matthews to Jimmy D. "Why did they kill these men?"

"Good fucking question," Matthews says. "Why don't you answer it, Jimmy?"

Jimmy shrinks away from the sound of his voice. Angles his gaze at me.

"I already told them everything," he says. "Before Delveccio I worked as an independent. Had a list of clients as long as my arm. I've admitted to fifteen murders. Why would I do that and not add two more? Explain it to him."

I turn to Matthews. "What do you want from me?"

"Maybe I was thinking I'd make a trade. Turn you loose on our skinny friend here in return for a little help with your problem."

Jimmy D gapes at us. He darts a glance from Matthews to me.

"One of our more unscrupulous contractors had Jimmy's boss in the other room and worked him over before I had a chance to stop him," Matthews says. "That's the guy Jimmy just mentioned, Delveccio. Even with that, Delveccio claimed he didn't have anything to do with the coyotes. Said he took the heroin and left the scene."

Jimmy D nods in agreement. "How many times do I have to tell you, Delveccio was telling the truth."

I take two steps closer to Jimmy D. Stare into his eyes. Bloodshot. Pupils enlarged with fear. A tic at the corner of his mouth, popped capillaries on the side of his nose. Matthews and his men have drugged him. He's at his most pliable.

The longer I stare, the wider his eyes grow.

I can see the sickness in him. A lack of some essential quality, an emptiness, a fiendish desire to inflict pain. I know the look as surely as I know my own heart. I'm not sure what he sees in me while I stare into his eyes, but whatever it is, it's enough to make him tremble.

"What are you doing?" he says.

Without lifting my gaze from his, I say to Matthews, "I need handcuffs and a blowtorch."

"No!" Jimmy D says. "No fucking way." He wrenches his gaze away from me and appeals to Matthews. "You can't let him do anything you're not allowed to do. I'm not a fucking idiot."

"Handcuffs I got," Matthews says. He opens the door. "Get a blowtorch," he tells the agent outside.

"With pleasure."

Matthews closes the door, and we wait.

"I'm going to have to leave," he says after a moment. "You know what I want from him. Why were those two men tortured? What was it that somebody wanted to know?"

"I didn't do it," Jimmy D says again. I can feel the burn of his gaze on my face, but I don't look at him, not anymore. I shrug out of my jacket. Roll up my sleeves.

"The Frenchman did the dirty work," he says.

Neither Matthews nor I acknowledge him.

"Give me twenty minutes," I say. "You'll know everything he does."

"I don't want him marked up too badly," Matthews says.

"I'll stick the nozzle in every orifice of his body. Roast him from the inside."

Jimmy D—Vegas hired gun—would never succumb to such a trick. Jimmy D has adapted to his new home. He understands the laws and conventions that restrain men like Matthews. But Jarco Dabizha, the man that Jimmy D used to be—henchman for *Solntsevskaya bratva*—that man knows Russia. He knows men like me. He's seen what we're capable of doing.

"I'm telling you!" Jimmy D cries, his eyes wild. "It was the Frenchman. He did it all, and he asked the questions. We heard them scream, but we couldn't hear the questions."

Matthews looks at me. "Maybe you can ask him whether he heard the *answers* to the questions."

"This is bullshit!" Jimmy D screams. "You won't do a fucking thing!"

Matthews rubs his temple, starts to say something to me, then flicks away the unspoken words. *Why bother?* the gesture says. *Let him find out for himself.* I lean against the wall and cross my arms.

"You think we're bluffing," I tell Jimmy D.

"Huh?"

"Maybe you're right, this is a charade. But if you're wrong I promise you this. I won't stop. I don't care what information you give me. I'll keep going and I'll make it last forever. I'll enjoy it. And these people"—I point my chin at Matthews—"these people don't want a witness."

His chin drops. His mouth forms an *O* while he ponders me.

"As soon as he leaves this room, you're done. You'll die hard. Trust me."

He licks his lips. He wipes his nose with the filthy cuff of his pink shirt.

"They talked about a boat," he says. "Okay? I don't know shit about any fucking boat."

"What kind of boat?"

"How the fuck should I know?"

Matthews steps closer, gets right in Jimmy D's face.

"Military? An aircraft carrier, a sub? A rowboat? A fucking yacht? You need to tell me more, or I'm turning him loose."

Jimmy D slides his gaze to me. "A freighter," he says. "The men tortured in the desert were sailors on a freighter."

Matthews wraps the chain around his fists and jerks Jimmy's head closer. "I need the name of the ship, Jimmy? You understand? Without that you haven't given me a goddamn thing."

"I want out," Jimmy says. "Deport me. I don't care where. You can do that. Promise me that and I'll give you the name."

Matthews drops the chain. Straightens. Glances at me. Shoots his cuffs. "Done."

"I need assurances."

Matthews laughs. "This is a fucking negotiation now? Uh-uh. You have my word, now give me the name."

Jimmy D bobs his Adam's apple. Glances once more at me.

"*Chembulk Osaka*," he says, and I stand as still as a statue, pretending I'm deaf, dumb, and blind, too stupid for those two words to mean anything to me. As if I don't know those are so similar to the last two words Kato emailed to her Moscow editor, Mitlov. *Chemical Osaka*, she wrote. She must have heard the name wrong, or lost something in the translation. Or maybe her source got it wrong.

"How does a moron like you remember a name like that?" Matthews says to Jimmy D.

"Did you see the bodies?" Jimmy says.

Matthews looks at him. "I saw the pictures."

"Those poor bastards screamed that name so many times a fucking parrot would remember it forever."

"What else did they scream?"

"Nukes. Something about nuclear stuff. Maybe it was a military boat, I don't know."

Matthews flicks his gaze at me. This is not a topic he wants to discuss in my presence. I can see it in his body language. My usefulness is at an end.

"We'll check it out," Matthews tells Jimmy D. "If it's bullshit, you get the torch."

He starts to leave, but stops at the sound of my voice.

"What did the Frenchman look like?"

Jimmy D shifts his weight on the bed to look at me, wincing when the collar digs into his neck.

"He smiled all the time. A wet smile, like his face was covered with oil. And he didn't move like the rest of us. He *glided*."

"I want facts. Height, weight, hair color, eye color."

"Average. Five-ten, maybe. Brown hair, brown eyes. You wouldn't look twice at him. Or maybe you would, the two of you being the same type and all."

Chapter Fifty-three

"Here's the story," Matthews says a few minutes later.

We're standing outside the Summerlin house, both of us staring into the darkness of the golf course. Palm fronds sway in the wind. The air smells wet with the promise of rain. He shifts his weight uneasily.

"Delveccio's now a protected witness. We didn't touch him, we saved him. A man hired by a rival syndicate cut him up, then we helped him out of a difficult situation. You understand?"

"I know about the *contractors* you people hire for your black ops, Matthews."

Matthews starts to retort, then appears to think better of it.

"We didn't touch Delveccio," he repeats. "And I didn't lie to Jimmy D, either. We *are* going to deport him to Russia. I'm sure he'll end up in the loving arms of one of your countrymen, maybe his ex-partner in the Brotherhood. Bad for Jimmy D, good for us."

Thunder grumbles over the desert. A fat raindrop strikes my cheek, cools my skin.

"I am like one of your contractors."

He gives me a hard stare. "What does that mean?"

"It means I am happy to do your dirty work for you, but I have a price."

"What's that?"

"Tell me about this man called *Kamen*. Tell me about the Frenchman and Solovie. And then turn me loose to find all three of them and bring them to my kind of justice."

The rainstorm hits suddenly. Heavy drops drum on the roof of his car. We climb inside. Soon the rain is coming down in sheets, lit by jags of lightning, twisted by the wind at angles that clatter against the side windows, then the windshield.

Matthews turns on the overhead light and shows me another picture.

"Lazar Solovie," he says. "Taken yesterday at Nellis Air Force Base. DoD flies him in and out from there whenever he comes to the States on their business."

Salt-and-pepper hair combed over on top, black-framed glasses, brown eyes. Pallid skin, almost translucent. Lots of wrinkles. According to the General's files he's in his mid-forties. He looks at least ten years older. He looks like the twenty-four-year-old man I saw in Oteri's morgue—aged far beyond his years.

That's when it hits me. This man is not a lion of science and industry. He's not a globe-trotting internationalist with a lust for wealth or power. He's not the villain.

He's a victim.

Like Glotser, the commander of the troops at Mayak. Like the captain who brutalized the Mole.

Victims all.

Dead men walking, as Glotser said.

Since the first time I heard his name I've been thinking of Solovie as the mastermind or, at the least, a master manipulator. Sitting here in the thunderstorm, quick-and-dirty thinking yields a different conclusion.

Solovie was Kato's source. The man who fed Kato "half-truths and lies," at least at first, but Kato must have turned him.

Solovie gave her whatever information she used for her last story.

The story that killed her.

"Do you recognize him?" Matthews says.

"No."

Matthews takes the photo from me and gives me another one.

Shaved head. Eyes like a crocodile's, hooded and angled up. Grainy skin, thick lips, cauliflowered right ear. The face reminds me of something, a vague wisp of memory, there and gone in a flicker.

"Grayson Stone," Matthews says. "You ever run across him?"

Maybe, but I can't remember where. "No."

"Played linebacker at LSU. Went to Officer Candidate School, tested off the charts. Served five years as an Army intelligence officer. Left there and went to work for the CIA— Intelligence and Analysis. Spent time all over Russia, Asia, and the hot spots in our war on terror. Lost his job when he got crossways with a congressman, but turned it to his advantage by forming Graystone Security. Now he does the same things he's always done, but he makes a shitload of money doing it."

I gesture toward the house.

"He's the one who made the mess in there?"

Matthews nods. He hands me a third photo.

Black and white, low resolution, little more than a shape: the figure of a man framed by the jagged edges of a crumbled wall, a glowing cigarette dangling from his lips.

I hold the picture in the air between us. "This is the best you can do?"

"We think that's the 'Frenchman' Jimmy D keeps talking about. The man's a cipher."

"You must have some information about him."

"Nothing more than rumors about a notorious assassin named Jean-Louis Perrin."

Lightening strobes. In the brief flashes I see suburban houses and manicured fairways and wind-whipped ponds. I see Matthews staring at me with fixed intensity.

"We think Stone has a way to contact him," Matthews says.

"Where's Stone?"

"Tijuana. A border town on the other side of San Diego."

"Let's go get him before he changes locations."

Matthews shakes his head. "He's not going anywhere for a while."

"Why not?"

"He's in a hospital. Rumor is that his past caught up with him. One of the things I want to know is what he was doing in Mexico in the first place."

"Two dead Russians, both probably working for Shakalov, and now this guy Stone south of the border. There must be a connection."

Matthews waits for another roll of thunder to pass before he speaks.

"*You* go get Stone. I'll give you the paperwork you'll need to get there and back. Befriend him. Tell him you're working on behalf of 'interested parties' in Russia. See if you can get to the Frenchman through him."

I think about the email I sent to the General from Chelyabinsk. *Two workers. One mechanic, one cleaner.* The Frenchman and Stone. Those are the two I want. I know I'm being used, but I don't care. I look at Matthews, revealing nothing of the excitement I feel.

"What will you be doing?"

"I'm going to be chasing down the *Chembulk Osaka*."

Chapter Fifty-four

Matthews drives me back to the Vegas airport. Parks in the departure zone. Hands me a ticket to San Diego's Lindbergh Field and an American passport with twenty hundred-dollar bills stuffed inside.

Volkovoy, Alexei. Strange to see my name below the words *United States of America*. Disconcerting to see my photo—an old one taken by the Russian Army, I don't know how Matthews got it—beneath the navy-blue cover of an American passport.

"How long did it take to get this?" I say.

"We plan ahead." He reaches into a bag in the backseat and gives me a phone. "This gives you five hours of talk time, Volk. Communicate—twice a day, at least. More often if you learn something. No fucking around. No private vendettas, no detours."

The passport scan will alert him every time I cross an international border and, as long as I don't ditch it, the phone will locate my position with enough precision to drop a bomb on my head. I understand that part. Less obvious, but still buried in the subtext, I think, is that he wants me to be free to use the kind of methods he can't employ. Otherwise he would assign an agent to dog my every step.

Matthews is using me the same way he uses Grayson Stone and others.

I fly from Vegas to San Diego. Ride forty-five minutes in a cab to the border. Walk into Mexico. Hail another cab and ride it to Tijuana General Hospital.

"Seven stories, very modern," the cab driver tells me in English. He points to a wall pocked with holes on the first floor near the emergency room entrance. "Bullet holes. Drug-runners looking for injured friends who were arrested." He shakes his head. "Things are very bad here, *señor*."

According to Matthews, Stone's room is on the third floor. I go up the stairs and sign a visitor's log. A nurse directs me down a tiled hallway. The door to the room is closed. I push inside.

Three beds, all occupied. One bed covered with a clear plastic tent, its occupant visible only as an ashen face sprouting an oxygen tube. Another bed holds a girl no more than ten years old. Both legs in a cast, an IV drip in her arm, the safety rails on both sides of her bed pulled up to make a pen.

Stone lies in the bed farthest from the door. At least I think it's him. His face is swollen beyond recognition from the photo Matthews showed me. An ugly scar jags from just above his right ear to the top of his shaved skull. Stitches like railroad tracks.

"A decompressive craniectomy."

I turn around, startled by the voice. The man standing there wears green scrubs. Short, not fat but doughy soft, early thirties, wire-rimmed glasses. Not Mexican. American.

"Doctor Hull," he says. "I'm glad to see he has a visitor."

"What's a decompressive craniectomy?"

He wrinkles his nose. "You don't really want to hear the gory details, do you?"

"Yes."

"Are you his brother? A friend?"

"Friend."

"Hmmm."

Hull moves to the foot of Stone's bed. Reads the chart hanging there. After a minute or so he stops reading, but he doesn't look up, studying me from the corner of his eyes instead. Finally, he lowers the chart.

"Do you have identification?"

I show him my passport. He scrutinizes it. I think he's memorizing the spelling.

"Russian?" he says.

"I emigrated from St. Petersburg to California in the nineties."

"Interesting."

"How so?"

"Your friend had another odd visitor a few days after he was admitted."

"Russian?"

"No, French. Quite the international following your friend has."

"What did he look like?"

Hull waves away the question. "I didn't see him. One of the nurses told me."

"Maybe I can talk to her."

"Maybe so, if you can find her. She's missed her last two shifts. That's one of the reasons I'm a bit paranoid, Mr. Volkovoy."

He goes to the head of Stone's bed and reads the monitor on a piece of equipment there, chewing his lower lip. He moves to a second machine and scans the squiggles on a strip of paper dangling from the front of it. That done, he contemplates me for a moment, then seems to reach a decision.

"A decompressive craniectomy is a procedure to relieve the pressure from swelling of the brain," he says. "Pressure brought on in this case by blunt-force trauma. We removed a large chunk of your friend's skull and put it in the freezer until the brain swelling decreased. Then we put it back. There's no helping the scar."

"How long before he can leave?"

"He'll need another two weeks with us, at least, but he'll be sick for longer than that."

"When will he regain consciousness?"

"I can't say."

"I'll wait."

"What?"

I had passed a plastic chair in the hall. Now I retrieve it, place it next to the head of Stone's bed adjacent to one of the monitors, and settle in.

"I'll wait here." I give Hull what I hope is a reassuring smile. "I won't bother anybody."

Chapter Fifty-five

Stone sees the same vision over and over again. That face hovering above his, those hard, hard eyes lit by feeble candlelight in an Afghani's hide tent.

Only now the eyes seem to be boring into his soul.

"Talk to me, Stone. Tell me about you and the Frenchman."

Stone wants to answer. After all, this man saved his life. Stone tries to speak, but he can't make his tongue form words.

Jean-Louis.

"Almost, Stone. Keep trying."

Stone lifts his left hand, the one that doesn't hurt. He feels the grip of another hand, a sensation akin to an electric shock.

"What happened to you, Stone?"

Mami Kai. The desert, the back of the truck, Shakalov suspended over him, dripping sweat. Garcia pistol-whipping him in a Tijuana alley. That's what happened.

"The ship," the face above him says. "Tell me about the ship."

"Sank."

God, what a relief, he can talk.

"*Sank?*" Those hard, hard eyes swim closer. Gold and glowing like a wolf's eyes. "Did you say *sank?*"

Stone fades away.

He hopes the visions don't follow him this time.

Chapter Fifty-six

I call the General on a hospital pay phone. Brief him about everything except the only word spoken by the injured man named Stone. *Sank.* I want to hold that piece of information until the end of the call. The General taps on his keyboard the whole time we're talking.

"There's an advantage to be gained here," he says when I'm finished with my report. "Infighting among the Americans is good for us. We can exploit that. But we need to learn what the fight is about."

"Find out what you can about the *Chembulk Osaka.*"

"I already did," he says, tapping more keys. "She's registered in Panama. Carrying unspecified cargo in the South China Sea as we speak."

"No, she's not. She's somewhere on the bottom of the North Atlantic. Any bets on the nature of her cargo when she went down?"

The line goes silent. Behind me the sounds of a baby crying, somebody coughing, somebody else shouting in pain. "*¡Por dios!*"

"This raises the stakes," the General says.

I don't answer. The person in pain screams again. I can't make out the Spanish words. A nurse clips past me. Looks back, frowns, then continues down the hall.

"Are you there, Volk?"

I want to ask him to find Valya. He has the resources to do it, especially if I tell him about her safe house in Mytishchi. But he'll wonder why she's missing, and I don't want to start his thoughts moving in that direction. The General, of all people, can't find out how personal Kato's death is to me.

"What about Solovie?" I say instead.

"We need to repatriate him," the General says.

"Matthews will trade, as long as we have something to trade."

I don't need to tell him that Solovie's not the one we're looking for, that Solovie is a pawn for somebody more important. But the scientist will be a wealth of knowledge. Names, dates, details about the French and American nuclear programs, and dirt on the General's adversaries in the Kremlin. I'm sure the General is already calculating who he might be able to leverage in Moscow, Washington, and Paris once he has all the information.

"What next?" he says.

"I'll pull whatever information I can from Stone." Including what he knows about Kato's murder, I think but don't say. "I'll find the Frenchman, Jean-Louis. Then I'll bring Solovie home."

I can feel the General nodding across thousands of miles of space. "Do it," he says.

I call Matthews on the cell he gave me. He answers on the first ring.

"You were supposed to call yesterday."

"Stone's in a coma. He may or may not come out of it. If he does, he might not remember any of the things we want to know."

"The hospital staff tells us that he wakes up occasionally."

Just as I suspected, Matthews already knows all about Stone. He probably has someone in the hospital reporting on Stone's condition to him. Dr. Hull, maybe.

"That's why I'm going to wait by his side," I say. "I'll be right here when he wakes up."

"Good. Remember, Volk. Communicate. That's our deal."

I end the call. Go to the nurse's station. Ask the nurse who frowned at me if she speaks English. She doesn't, but she finds someone who can, a young woman as wide as she is tall.

"Has one of the nurses been missing her shift lately?"

"Yes," she says, her eyes narrowed, looking suspicious.

I fan five hundred-dollar bills, then fold them in half and hold them by my side. "I need to find her."

Her gaze follows my hand. Her expression turns venal. "Why?"

"She helped my friend. I want to repay her kindness."

This woman knows a lie when she hears it. But she doesn't want the truth. She wants a way to justify accepting the money. She holds out her hand, and I slip her two of the bills.

"Alejandra Torres," she says quickly. She leans toward me, whispers the address, then steps back and looks around to make sure we're unobserved. "She asked me and another nurse to call her if the American wakes up."

I give her the last three bills. Return to Stone's room. Nothing appears to have changed.

I tuck the phone under his mattress. As far as Matthews is concerned, I'll be here by Stone's side. Before leaving, I stand over the injured man, looking for any sign of awareness.

"Stone? Stone, can you hear me?"

No response.

"Tell me about the ship that sank, Stone."

His eyeballs move beneath the lids, but he doesn't say anything.

I head out of the hospital and into the Tijuana night to find a nurse named Alejandra Torres.

Chapter Fifty-seven

Alejandra Torres lives on Tijuana's southeast side. Thirty minutes by cab through busy streets.

We arrive at a neighborhood of shabby houses jammed together so tightly the roofs appear to be touching. On one corner a strip mall—laundromat, liquor store, hair and nail salon, and a 7-11 next to a Pemex gas station. Across the street a Catholic church, then more houses jumbled together. Cars on blocks. Stray dogs. Men lounging with open bottles of liquor. Children running the poorly lit streets at eleven o'clock at night.

The house at the address the nurse gave me looks like it's made of mud. Stucco troweled on in careless waves, painted a blotchy brown. Yellow porch light, a screen door hanging by a single hinge, the flickering light of a television playing against the drawn shades.

I ask the cab driver to wait outside the house.

"*Sí,*" he says. "But you pay first, hokay?"

I pay him. He drives away before I reach the front door.

I knock.

"*¿Qué pasa?*" A man's voice. Hard-edged.

"*¿Dónde está Alejandra?*"

"*¿Quién es?*"

I've exhausted my Spanish. "*¿Habla Inglés?*"

The door opens. The man scowling at me is unshaven, dressed in a collared pink shirt unbuttoned to the middle of his bare chest.

"Who wants to know?"

I sucker-punch him in the belly. He folds around my fist with a grunt as I use the momentum of the blow to propel him into the house. An elbow to the jaw sends him sprawling. I kick the door closed behind me.

He tries to get up. Slips on a wet spot on the tile floor, lands heavily. I grab his arm and twist it behind his back, holding him facedown while I survey the room.

We're between a couch pushed against the wall and a coffee table. Open bags of chips, empty beer cans, an ashtray sprouting cigarette butts, glossy magazines strewn about. On the far wall, a TV the size of a movie screen tuned to a soccer game.

"What the fuck are you doing?" the man says, gasping for breath.

I hoist him to his feet and crank his wrist toward his shoulder blades until he whimpers, then shove him into the kitchen. Nobody there. Dirty dishes and half-empty bottles litter the counter. Somebody just finished having a big party.

I keep moving, driving him down a short hall to the single bedroom. Inside is a woman cowering beneath the bed sheets.

"Alejandra?"

She says something in Spanish that I don't understand. Eyes wide, pulling the sheet up to her chin.

"Do you speak English?"

She shakes her head.

I wrench the man's arm higher until something pops.

"You're her husband?"

"Boyfriend," he says. He twists his head to look at her. "Sometimes."

"Where did the new TV come from?"

"It's not stolen. I have the receipt."

"Where did you get the money?"

He looks at Alejandra again. Her eyes flash in the light from the doorway as she looks from him to me.

"She got a bonus at work," he says.

I crank his arm. He shrieks.

"What did she do to earn a bonus?" I say.

"Nothing bad," Alejandra says in English. "Don't hurt him anymore."

I shove him facedown onto the bed with me on top of him, one knee in his back. He groans and says something in Spanish. I increase the torque on his arm.

"What did you do to earn the bonus, Alejandra?"

"Nothing. Call a man if one of my patients wakes up."

"Which patient?"

"An American. Named Stone."

"Who are you supposed to call?"

She looks away.

I jerk her boyfriend's arm. His shoulder dislocates with a loud pop. I push his face into the bed to muffle his screams.

"*¡Basta!*" she cries. Enough.

"I need a name and a number."

She scoots across the bed to the nightstand. Hands me a page torn from a prescription pad. All the blank lines on the front of the form empty. On the back, a name and a number.

Jean-Louis. The number has a 702 prefix.

I memorize all ten digits and hand the paper back to Alejandra.

"Burn it."

Still clutching the sheet, she digs a disposable lighter out of the drawer and touches the flame to paper. I pull up on the boyfriend's hair to let him breathe. He gasps for air as we watch the note burn on the nightstand, leaving ashes and a bubbled black stain. I push his face back into the sheets.

"You saw this man?" I say to her.

She nods.

"Describe him."

"Brown hair. Not tall. Not thin, not fat. *Ordinaria.*" Ordinary.

"What else? Clothes? Scars? Mannerisms?"

"*Nada.*" She licks her lips. "He smiled all the time, but not a nice smile."

"Why did you stop going to work? Why stop watching Stone?"

"*Mis amigas*, my friends at the hospital promised to call me." She looks at her boyfriend, reminding me to give him another breath. "He wanted us to have a little fun."

I climb off him. He shudders and tries to straighten his arm, then yelps when fresh pain hits. Alejandra drops the sheet. She's wearing a sheer top that ends above her belly button. She crawls to him and cradles his head in her lap. Both of them stare at me. *What happens now?* their expressions say.

I back out of the room. Four steps and I'm out the front door. I walk across the street to the strip mall. Buy a cell phone and an international calling card at the 7-11 convenience store. Find a kid with a junker car fueling at the Pemex pump. Pay him twenty of Matthews' dollars to drive me back to the hospital.

Stone appears not to have moved. I check the readout that graphs whatever's going on in his head. Wild fluctuations that I suppose indicate that he woke up once. Or maybe just REM sleep. Nothing on his chart indicates that he's awakened during the time I've been gone, but the nurses might not have noticed.

It's one A.M.

Time to call Jean-Louis.

Chapter Fifty-eight

I step outside the hospital to make the call to the Frenchman. A siren wails, closing in. Cool wind carries the smell of cooking meat and exhaust fumes. The flashing lights of an ambulance appear on an overpass. The ambulance follows the bend of the exit ramp to the emergency room entrance. Two paramedics roll out the latest victim of Tijuana's toxic violence—a woman in bloody clothes, her face covered by an oxygen mask.

I walk around a corner and dial.

One ring. Two.

The line connects. I can't hear anything on the other end. I grind the phone against my ear. Nothing but silence for thirty seconds.

"You are a patient man," a voice says in my ear, startlingly clear, the French accent unmistakable.

I don't respond.

"How do I know you are a man?" he says. "Is that what you're wondering?"

He waits for me to answer. Sighs.

"I can *feel* it. I have a *sense* for these things. *Prémonitions.*"

Another siren wails in the distance.

"Do you believe me?" the Frenchman says.

A soldier I knew in Chechnya claimed to have visions. Had one the night before he died, I think, because he gave me a photograph of his wife and son the next morning, a chill winter dawn in Grozny. "No reason," he said when I asked him why he wanted me to carry the photo for him.

The answer is *yes*. I believe in such things.

And right now the feeling of dread is palpable, more intense than the evening I met Ilya in Victory Park. As though something evil bleeds across the miles from his mouth to my ear, something primal, a seeping infection of the human soul. I've never heard his voice before, but I feel as if I have known it for all my life. Embodied in sadistic guards in the rehabilitation center for boys where I spent my formative years. Expressed in the sado-sexual cruelty of the strong toward the weak in Moscow's Isolator-5 prison. Brought to terrible life by the misery of war, where the most inhumane flourish and the most sensitive are trampled underfoot.

"Calling from Mexico, I see," the Frenchman says. "Do you have a message for me, my friend? Has the American awakened?"

Two workers. One mechanic, one cleaner.

"Why did you kill Kato?"

"Russian!" He sounds genuinely surprised by my accent. "Why is a Russian calling me from Mexico? You work for Shakalov, yes?"

"Why did a Frenchman murder a Russian journalist?"

"Ah, yes, that is the question. But not one you want me to answer. You see, if you know the answer to that question, you die. Just like Kato."

Shouts carry from the emergency room entrance. I turn my back to the noise and squeeze the phone so tightly the plastic casing creaks.

"I already know the answer. I know all about the *Chembulk Osaka*. Now, tell me, how am I going to die?"

Silence. Then, "Who are you, *mon ami*?"

"I'm not your 'friend.'"

"No? How sad for me. But I intend to change that. I will make you beg to be my friend. I'll make you beg the same way Kato did. She kneeled before me and pleaded for her life. You know this is true, yes? Close your eyes and make a picture in your mind. You can see it now, can't you, *mon ami*?"

"I'm going to kill you."

He laughs. "So you *can* see it in your mind. Imagination is both a blessing and a curse, don't you think? See this. I *penetrated* her. I inserted my weapon into her mouth and I exploded her skull. Yes, that's it, I skull-fucked her. Picture that."

I disconnect.

My hands are shaking. My visceral need to find the Frenchman—to destroy him—consumes me. So much blood has rushed to my head that I can't see the numbers on the phone Matthews gave me. The best I can do is hit the redial.

"Better, Volk," Matthews answers. "Only four hours between calls this time."

"If I give you the number of a cell phone, can you locate the phone?"

He hesitates. "Maybe. Whose phone?"

"The Frenchman, Jean-Louis. Probably a drop phone, but he had it with him a few minutes ago."

"Give me the number," he says, and I do.

He disconnects before I can ask him how long it will take.

I lean against the wall and rest my head on my forearm. The hospital roars around me in an endless racket of sirens, whooshing vehicles, raised voices of paramedics.

In the day and a half since I left Vegas, Matthews would have learned everything I've been able to learn and surmise about the *Chembulk Osaka*. He will be hunting the men in his own government who made their deal with the French and the Russians. He may have already identified them.

Now he'll do his best to track Jean-Louis.

I don't know what he will do with the information. But I know this much. He will keep me in the dark for as long as he can. Forever, if he's able to.

I don't care about that. Right now, I care about only one thing.

Killing Jean-Louis.

I want to hang him on a gallows and tear him apart.

The evil inside him slithered through space. It wormed into my head and found comfort there, unleashing all the demons in my mind.

Chapter Fifty-nine

Stone awakens to the sound of voices, accompanied by the whir and beep of machinery. He waits until the voices quiet and he hears people leave the room, then opens his eyes. Blinks several times.

A figure looms above him, backlit by fluorescent lights.

"You're awake," the man says in a voice that seems to come from far away.

"Who are you?" Stone croaks.

"Matthews sent me."

Stone's lips crack when he tries to smile. "Keeping his enemies close. Good for Matthews."

"You are his enemy?"

Stone's head throbs. Feels like it's in a vise. He blinks to clear his vision. Sure enough, this is the same man who stared down at him in Afghanistan. No doubt about it now.

"I need water," Stone says.

The man puts a straw into Stone's mouth, and Stone sucks greedily. Water never tasted so good.

"Who are you?" Stone says again when he finishes drinking.

"Volk."

"Russian?"

"Yes. Matthews sent me."

"Yeah, you said that."

Stone flexes his fingers. A cast runs from his right hand to his elbow. Garcia must have broken it during the beating. Stone wriggles his toes and stiffens his legs. They work. He feels weak, but he's going to make it. As he tests his limbs, he studies Volk.

"I know you," he says.

Volk says nothing, just looks at him, apparently waiting for more.

"Afghanistan, summer of '02. An IED took out the Humvee I was in. You brought me to the tent of a friendly Afghani."

Volk stares wordlessly, apparently accessing mental files. Then nods. "I remember."

"Why did you do that?"

Volk shrugs. "I helped a lot of people in those days."

"So what are you doing here now?"

"I want to know what happened to the journalist Kato."

The image explodes in Stone's mind: *that Russian bitch, God, so beautiful, lifting her face to the muzzle.*

Stone considers how to answer the question. He values secrets. Secrets are his stock in trade, and the story of the *Chembulk Osaka* presents the opportunity of a lifetime. No telling what the U.S. government will pay to keep that quiet. But he also values his life. The second he reveals what he knows, Jean-Louis will draw a very big target on his back.

Volk presents a different kind of opportunity. Volk has his own reasons for being here, and if Stone reads the situation right, Volk might be the perfect weapon to launch at the Frenchman.

"Jean-Louis Perrin," he says. "A French assassin named Jean-Louis Perrin shot her like a dog on the banks of the Techa River in the Urals."

Volk's features harden into something terrible. Maybe it's a trick of the light, but his whole face seems to turn black, except for his eyes. His eyes glow as if lit from within by a freshly stoked furnace.

"Tell me about him," he says. "Tell me everything."

Chapter Sixty

Matthews doesn't answer when I call. Neither does Jean-Louis.

Stone improves by the hour. He eats, drinks, endures batteries of tests, sleeps.

I prowl the halls. Dr. Hull and the nurses avoid me. Two shifts of policemen watch me all the time. They know I don't belong here. They probably have a report filed by Alejandra Torres and her boyfriend. But their boss must have been briefed by Matthews.

Leave him alone, but watch him, tell me what he does.

Three days pass. Stone tells me about his company, Graystone Securities. He tells me about Mami Kai, Garcia, and Shakalov. He thanks me for saving his life in the Afghanistan desert. "I owe you, man."

I talk to the General. He's been digging, connecting dots. Officials in the Kremlin worked "off-line" with "special elements" within the Department of Defense in a trial program to dispose of spent nuclear fuel rods and profit from the byproducts of reprocessing. No telling whether the taint spread as high as SecDef, but it goes high enough to matter on the international stage.

Not to mention the international outcry if it becomes known that the waters of one of its precious oceans are endangered by nuclear waste.

The General tells me little about his machinations. This is his game now. His turf. The second time I call him he wonders out loud about whether the sensible course is for me to return to Moscow. "I can take it from here," he says.

But he can't.

Only I can avenge Kato's murder.

I don't use those words, but the idea floats between us, lurking in the pauses during our cryptic telephone conversations. Make money, extract political concessions—that's your part, General. Stone, Jean-Louis, and anybody else involved in Kato's murder—that's my part. He gets it, I think. He won't say as much, but he doesn't order me home.

Maybe he knows I won't obey that order.

Another day passes. Stone is out of the bed, "ambulatory," as Dr. Hull writes on his chart.

I wait until we're alone.

"We leave tonight."

He stares at me. He's not ready. He'll probably aggravate his injuries. I don't care.

"Once we're over the border, pull every string you can to find the Frenchman."

"He's probably still in Las Vegas."

"Find out for sure."

Stone looks away. I can see his mind working the angles as clearly as if the piece of skull was still missing and I could peer inside. Maybe he "owes" me, but this is a man driven purely by self-interest.

"When do we leave?" he says.

Crossing the border north into the U.S. is harder than crossing south. At three A.M. Stone and I wait in a long line. A surge of partiers headed home after a long night, early-morning day workers. Me in the same black suit I've worn since I arrived from Moscow, him in a clean but torn blue suit, a white shirt spotted with brown blotches where the blood didn't come out, and a black knit cap that covers the bandages on his incision.

He looks sick. Pale, worn, pained.

I go through first. The immigration official scans my passport, then studies the screen. I can't see what he's reading. He picks up a white phone and speaks quietly for a minute or so. Two more immigration agents approach the booth from the American side. One of them looks at my passport and at the computer screen. Pencil-thin neck, black-framed glasses sliding off the end of his nose, a name tag that says Gordon Rowe. He takes my passport, motions me to follow him and his companion, and leads me to a corner.

"Mr. Volkovoy, we need to ask you to stand by while we verify a few things."

He seems bothered when I don't say anything.

"Your name shows up on a watch list," he says.

"Fine," I say, peeking at Stone from the corner of my eyes as he hobbles to the counter and hands the official his passport.

"Probably nothing," Rowe says. "But we have to check it out. Shouldn't take more than a few minutes."

The official scans Stone's passport, glances at the screen, and waves him through. Stone passes me without a glance, walking with a staggering gait that blends in perfectly with the loopy steps of the drunks going home through the sliding glass doors on the American side of the building.

"Mr. Volkovoy?" Rowe says.

I realize he just said something I didn't hear. "What?"

"I said, did you enjoy Mexico?"

I nod.

"What were you doing there?"

"Visiting friends."

I don't think his questions are ominous. He's buying time, I suspect, waiting for the official word. Somebody is trying to reach Matthews—or reach whoever is at the phone number that must have appeared on the screen—to ask him what to do.

Rowe and his partner step a few paces away, talking in low tones. I watch Stone through the glass doors. He approaches a line of cabs. One of the drivers opens the back door of the lead cab, and Stone climbs inside gingerly, like an old man slipping into a bathtub.

"How much longer are you going to hold me?" I say loudly to Rowe.

He looks at me, surprised. "I told you, a few minutes."

Stone's cab pulls away from the curb, waits briefly at a light to make a left, then disappears behind a row of buildings.

I take a deep breath. Turn my back to the doors. Try to compose my features into a mask that hides my rage. I'm going to kill Jean-Louis *and* Stone. The mechanic and the cleaner. I will kill them both.

A third man approaches Rowe and his partner. They confer. Moving as a team, they spread out and encircle me. Rowe grabs my elbow.

"We need you to come with us, Mr. Volkovoy."

"Why?"

He scrunches his nose, causing his thick glasses to ride up his face. "You're going to be detained while we clear up a few things."

Chapter Sixty-one

They lock me in a room similar to the one at the Atlanta airport. Windowless except for a portal made of glass-encased steel mesh built into the metal door. Metal table and four wooden chairs. Camera in the corner.

I sit in one of the chairs, staring straight ahead. Hours pass. A man wearing a badge that says Immigration and Customs Enforcement brings me a tray of food. Cold scrambled eggs, hash browns, and two wrinkled sausages the size of my pinky finger.

More hours pass before a shadow darkens the window. Matthews peers through the glass. He signals. Somebody opens the door, and he walks through, jaws clenched, obviously angry. He waits to speak until the door closes behind him.

"You should have told me you were going to cross the border. All of this could have been avoided."

"Where's the Frenchman? Where's Stone?"

"I told you at the start, no vendettas on my turf."

I stand. My chair screeches over the concrete floor as it's pushed back. I close the distance between us until our noses are almost touching. He's taller than me, about the same weight. Probably not as tough as Rhino in a fight, but no easy task. He doesn't flinch or back away. His nostrils flare, his eyes turn a darker shade of blue, the skin around his mouth tightens.

"You're going to do this my way," I tell him.

"Fuck you, Volk. You're in this country illegally. I'll lock you in a cage for years. No lawyer, no hearing, no contact with anybody for as long as I say. Now back off!"

I don't move. "Unless I check in with the General soon, he's going to go public with everything we know about the *Chembulk Osaka* and the cargo she was carrying when she went down."

Matthews doesn't react the way I expect. No rage, no threats, no bluster. He takes a step back, and his eyes glaze as he considers what I've told him. Nearly a minute passes that way. Then his gaze refocuses, and he seems to notice me again. He chews his lower lip. Puts his hands in the pockets of his jacket and wings it open.

"So be it. You rot in prison, the General broadcasts his exposé in the world press, life goes on. America gets another black eye, so what? That's why I'm on the payroll. To deal with things like that."

"Wrong, you're on the payroll to *prevent* things like that from happening."

"Depends on the price." He appraises me. "Do you know why yours is too high?"

"No."

"Because the bills won't stop coming. Every time the Kremlin wants something, it will threaten to pull this ugly little incident out of the bag."

How many times have I wondered how high Matthews resides in the hierarchy of the American intelligence apparatus? I recall a time in the command-and-control center in a hangar at the Budennovsk air base when I had to decide whether or not to launch a missile. *You don't have to do this, Volk*, Matthews said that day, and I wondered if he really had the authority to let me make that decision. I think again about the day Matthews released me from custody at Los Angeles International Airport, handing my knife to me with a wry smile, almost as an afterthought—a knife with a message to Russian military intelligence hidden inside. On both occasions I thought I might have underestimated the man.

Now I know for sure that I did. He's negotiating. He wants to solve the problem of the *Chembulk Osaka* and her cargo right here, right now. And he just may have the authority to do it.

"How many people on your side need to know the truth about this?" he says.

The General. The General's chief political ally, Constantine, a man who has survived in the halls of power in the Kremlin since Stalin's day. Three or four other politicians, including our prime minister, and some of our top navy people. A few more to make things happen.

"Fewer than twenty."

"Anybody big enough to make a statement and issue a press release about a Russian-made environmental disaster in the North Atlantic? One that can be made the subject of international cleanup efforts sponsored and funded by the United Nations, with oversight from various international environmental groups?"

"Russia takes responsibility, the U.S. pays everyone off?"

Matthews takes his hands out of his pockets and shoots his cuffs, then concentrates on the task of straightening his sleeves to avoid looking me in the eyes.

"Right."

Once the official story goes out, the truth won't stand a chance. Investigative journalists like Kato, human rights and environmental groups, and others will dig. Stories will be written and debated on the Internet and in the alternative press. But they'll be dismissed by the mainstream. Unless they're backed by irrefutable proof.

"How many people have to die to make the story work?"

His expression turns bleak, but he doesn't answer the question.

I know part of the answer. The crew of the *Chembulk Osaka*. The people who packed and loaded the cargo. Those who cut the deal and those who implemented it.

"Solovie?" I say.

Matthews doesn't answer immediately. He scrapes a chair away from the table and sits. I sit facing him.

"Yes," he says. "Solovie has to go."

"Shakalov?"

"His man who was on the ship, yes. The one who's still alive. But we can't reach Shakalov himself. We know because we've been trying for years. Him we'll have to buy off until we can get close enough to kill him."

"Me, too. You're going to have to buy me off, too."

"What does that mean?"

"Here is what *I* want. I want the Frenchman. I want Stone. And I want money to clean up the area around Lake Karachay and relocate the people who are most exposed there."

Matthews drums his fingers on the table.

"We don't need you. We have other ways to reach the General."

"I'm here now. You can put your plan in motion in ten minutes. Or you can wait and gamble. Hope you can make a better deal. Risk talking to the wrong people. Lose control."

"I can't meet your terms."

"Why not?"

"We can't pay for a problem that doesn't exist. You understand? We can't acknowledge that we're shipping spent nuclear fuel halfway around the world, and your government can't and won't acknowledge the problem at Mayak. One ship sinks? A problem that can be contained? Fine, the Kremlin will take that deal. A fifty-year-old Chernobyl that's still killing people? No way."

Kato knew.

No light shines in our darkest corners. Governments change, administrations change, the world changes. But the truth about this place remains hidden.

Matthews brushes imaginary dust off the steel top of the table.

"I can't help you with Mayak. But the Frenchman? Stone?" When he looks at me his face seems to be made of frozen iron. "They're all yours."

"How?"

"Stone we can find. The Frenchman will be hard. We've never even been close enough to get a clear picture of him."

"He has a job to do."

Matthews regards me without expression. "What does that mean?"

"He's being paid to kill the people who know about the *Chembulk Osaka*. I'm one of those people. If we set it up right, he'll come to me."

"Maybe."

"Find Stone. Have him arrange the meeting. Jean-Louis will come."

"You're the bait," Matthews says.

"That's right. I'm the bait."

Chapter Sixty-two

Two days later, Las Vegas at its most quiet, three hours before dawn. The darkest part of the night. Muffled freeway noise from the I-15, and a dull roar—car horns, music, the clamor of thousands—from the strip. Rainbow lights from the hotels and casinos in the distance. But there are no lights here. Except for a few isolated blobs of yellow on a row of steel industrial buildings along the street in front of me, everything is dark here in the warehouse district near Industrial Boulevard.

I'm alone. A Beretta 9 mm in the pocket of my jacket, courtesy of Matthews. Fifteen rounds in the magazine and one in the pipe, although I hope to use only two. A new cell phone in my hand. Electronic devices strapped around my waist beneath my shirt. I don't know their exact functions. Tracking. Recording. Signaling—to Matthews hovering somewhere above and behind in a helicopter, and to his people in a van parked near a towering hotel a kilometer away.

The cell phone buzzes.

I answer. "Stone?"

"Who the fuck is this?"

"Volk."

"Where's Matthews?"

"He's not here. This is my play."

Silence. Then, "Matthews has you on a long leash."

"Where's the Frenchman?"

"I told Jean-Louis that Matthews would be here with you. He won't like the change in plans."

"Where is he?"

"You won't see him. You'll be dead before you know he's there."

"I'll take my chances."

My earpiece crackles. "Volk," Matthews says, the sound of his voice sharp in my ear. "The signal is approximately two hundred yards directly ahead of you."

"It's your life," Stone says. "I'll turn on the lights so you can find me."

I start walking down the street between the buildings. A car engine purrs to life on the street ahead of me. Headlights flare. I'm beyond their range. Still, I cross the street and hug the metal siding of a building, the darkness of my body merging with the darker shadow of the wall, advancing more slowly now.

A figure steps into the beams of light.

"Can you see me?" Stone says.

"Got him," Matthews says. "Looks like he's alone, but we have dozens of heat signatures in the area. The area is *not* secure, Volk."

"I see you, Stone," I say into the phone.

"I can take you to Jean-Louis," Stone says. "But I need your help. I'm still having trouble walking. Stairs will be a bitch."

"Where?"

"The building to the left of my car. You see it?"

Corrugated metal sides. Roll-up bay doors, loading docks, a row of windows in the upper level boarded with plywood. I slide closer. One of the roll-up doors gapes open, inky darkness inside. Stone is still standing in the cone of light in front of his car. The white cast on his right arm gleams. I slip into a dark space where the wall of the building jogs to make room for a fire escape.

"We have three heat signatures in that building, Volk," Matthews says in my ear. "Let us take it from here."

Jean-Louis is *not* in that building. Stone may or may not be part of the ruse. But I'm sure that Jean-Louis is not in that building. I mute the cell phone.

"It's your scene," I say quietly to Matthews. "I'll take Stone and get clear."

"You've got five minutes," he says.

I hit the button to deactivate the mute on the cell. "Walk forward fifty meters," I tell Stone.

He hobbles toward me. I unbutton my shirt and strip off the belt with the electronic devices. Lower it to the ground behind me. Let Stone walk five meters past my position.

"Stop," I murmur into the phone.

"Where are you?"

He's talking into his phone, but I can hear him easily enough without it. "Close enough," I whisper. "Don't move the phone from your ear. Use your thumb to mute it."

"Done."

"Don't turn around. Where is he really?"

Stone stiffens at the sound of my voice so close.

"Look down the alley to my right," he says. "See the building with the cell phone tower on top? He's on the roof. He'll snipe you as soon as he sees you."

High ground, good field of fire, impossible to approach without being seen.

"Turn off the mute. Ask me where I am. Then do as I tell you."

His thumb moves. "Where are you," he says again, picking up our conversation as though he'd temporarily lost the signal.

"Inside," I say, hoping that Jean-Louis, who must be listening, believes I'm in the first building. "I'll handle things from here."

I disconnect the call. Stone looks up at the sound of a helicopter. Matthews and his men, preparing to storm the wrong building.

"Walk down the alley to your right," I say.

"Roger that."

While he shambles toward the alley, I slide along the wall to change positions. Cross the street, using a different warehouse to shield me from the roof of the building with the cell tower. Duck into the alley to follow Stone.

A red neon sign illuminates the far end of the alley. Stone is hobbling ahead into the wash of light.

He crumples. Just like that, one moment he is there, lurching ahead, the next he's down. I didn't hear a shot.

I dive for cover against a wall.

Stone gasps. I hear him start to drag himself toward cover.

A searchlight stabs the air behind me. Matthews' helicopter whooshes lower, the roar of the blades blocking out any sound Stone is making. Unmarked cars and vans hurtle down the street and screech to a stop in front of the warehouse next to Stone's abandoned vehicle.

I creep along the alley. "Stone! Can you hear me?"

Behind me, shouts, commands, small explosions as doors are blown open. Ahead, near the neon sign, a figure crosses the gap between two buildings and disappears.

Chapter Sixty-three

Stone is on his back, his black knit cap soaked with blood. I drag him to the shelter of a high wall. Blood spurts from the split above his ear and waterfalls down his cheek. The pumping blood means he is still alive. I can't find any sign of a bullet wound in his head. He must have hit it when he fell. I probe his body, searching for a wound. Find one high on the shoulder.

I rip Stone's shirt off. Tear a strip, wad it into a ball, and plug the hole in his shoulder. Use the rest of the shirt to wrap his head. Dial Matthews, then leave the phone next to the bleeding man.

I scuttle in a crouch toward the space between the two buildings where I saw a figure flit through the haze of neon light. The sign says "King's Wholesale Liquors." I skid to a stop at the mouth of a narrow alley. Like a tunnel, barely enough room to walk between the high walls, wet from dripping drainpipes, fire escape ladders and landings looming overhead.

I stand there with the Berretta hanging at my side, lit by burning neon, facing the darkness.

No sign of the Frenchman.

I squat.

Press my palm against the asphalt to feel for the vibration of running steps. Listen to the low hum of a refrigeration unit, the drone of vehicles on I-15, the throp of helicopter blades overhead, the distant shouts of the men Matthews sent to attack the wrong warehouse. Smell wet asphalt and metal, rotting food, oily smoke from a flue pipe jutting from a roof above me.

Liquid strikes my head and shoulders. Like someone urinating. I tuck and roll against the metal side of a building. Fall to my back and cut loose two rounds—

Just as I recognize the smell of gasoline and watch a flaming book of matches drop in slow motion toward the puddle I'm lying in.

A column of flames explodes with an ear-popping *whoosh* of sound. Engulfs me.

Fuck!

I spring to my feet. Drop the Berretta and run, pulling off my burning jacket as I go. My shirt is on fire at the collar and shoulders. I tear it off, still running, tracked by a dull yellow glow on the side of the warehouse next to me. My hair is alight. The light following me is the reflected blaze.

Pain strikes. All at once, as though somebody flicked a switch. Searing lightning bolts of pain.

Frantic, I blot my head with the remnants of my shirt, trying to put out the fire as I run. Something trips me. I land awkwardly, writhing, still flailing at my head with my shirt and hands, still trying to escape sure death behind me.

I roll against a metal wall. It holds me in place while I extinguish the flames.

Smoke curls around me. I smell burning flesh. I reach for the top of the boot that covers my prosthesis, groping for the knife hidden the mechanism. My blistered fingers find the catch, slip away, find it again—

"Stop that, please."

I freeze. A silhouette cuts across my vision. The Frenchman's right arm appears to be elongated by the gun in his hand.

"I know a little about you, Volk. No knives."

I drop my hand away from the knife. Close my fist on a handful of loose gravel.

He steps closer, raising his gun. Just as Alejandra described him, his face is pleasant, nondescript, average in every way except for the sneer on his glistening lips.

"I warned you how it would be, yes?"

He cocks his head to one side, listening. Shouts. Car doors slam. The rotors of the helicopter change pitch. I think it's lifting off.

I fling the gravel into his face and lunge for his legs.

He reacts like a cat. Skips to one side with a dancer's step, easily avoiding the spray of gravel and my grasp. Levels his pistol. Flame spouts from the muzzle—

Just as Stone slams into him from behind.

Something wallops me in the belly.

Stone and the Frenchman tumble over me. The Frenchman already has the advantage. He went with the unexpected hit, used Stone's momentum to execute a hip throw, and now he captures Stone's left arm in a variation of the *ude garami* judo move, and snaps bone.

Stone screams. Strikes out with his casted arm, but he can't land the blow.

"How do you like this?" the Frenchman says as he drops to one knee on Stone's arm. He must think I'm dead. Otherwise he wouldn't waste time torturing the downed American.

I rock onto my side, clutching my belly. I don't look down. I don't want to see the damage. I have to get to the Frenchman's fallen pistol. The last meter is the hardest, pushing with my feet to wriggle on my back.

Stone screams again.

Sirens wail in the distance.

The Frenchman stands. Dances on his toes to gather power, rams the heel of his boot into Stone's exposed neck. He leans down to inspect his handiwork, then does it again.

The helicopter hovers above us, its downwash whipping trash and grit into my eyes. A spotlight beams down, capturing the tableau: the Frenchman standing over Stone, his face aimed up into the light. He reaches into his pocket. Pulls out a badge and holds it high in the air.

"French External Security!" he shouts.

I pick up the gun. It feels heavy. My hands shake. I draw a deep breath.

Aim for the middle of his body.

Fire.

His head explodes.

I drop the pistol and collapse.

The spotlight from the helicopter wavers, jerks crazily, and pins me to the asphalt. An amplified voice shouts, "On your face! Hands behind your head!"

I can't do that. I can't move at all. I feel as though a great weight is crushing me.

One name. I want to say her name one last time, but I can't draw enough breath to say it.

Chapter Sixty-four

Time passes in a haze of drugs, surgeries, and excruciating debridement sessions in the burn unit at Nellis Air Force Base. Cutting away dead skin until blood flows, covering the wounds with Silvadene, a white, antimicrobial cream. Do it again, over and over. I'm staked to an anthill, nothing to do but suffer.

A doctor reports in dry, clinical terms. The Frenchman's bullet clipped my intestine and tore the wall of my stomach, but didn't do enough damage to kill me in the time it took the helicopter to airlift me to Nellis. The burns will heal, the grafts will take, the pain will pass, for the most part. I'll have permanent scars on my scalp and shoulders and one shaped like a tear under my left eye.

Matthews visits between debridement sessions. Drugs loop my mind. He fades in and out. "The deal is done. You did your part. Why did you drop your locater? We could have helped you."

Two "State Department representatives" interrogate me. I stick to the script Matthews and I agreed to in the Tijuana detention cell.

I was sent to America to investigate a lead in the murder case of the prominent journalist Katarina Mironova. The trail led to the Russian scientist Lazar Solovie, a man also suspected of killing a fellow scientist in Russia several years ago. Solovie appears to have been a rogue working for illegal enterprises. Motivated by greed, by the power of his position, or by some combination of those things or others. Who knows? The CIA must have reams of files on the man. They should do their own psychoanalysis.

Shakalov? Never met the man, only know him by reputation: an animal. Too violent for the Russian mafia, he took his act to Mexico and butchered his way into control of one of the cartels. What does he have to do with all this, anyway?

Stone saved my life. I don't know why. Just another American agent doing his job, I suppose. You give posthumous medals, don't you?

Spent nuclear fuel? I can't help with that topic. Other than one brief visit to the Mayak reprocessing facility, I'm ignorant. I'm a foot soldier with a high rank. I do what I'm told, and I don't look under a rock unless I'm ordered to do so.

No telling what the dead Frenchman wanted. He worked for the French foreign intelligence agency? Maybe I was a case of mistaken identity, maybe that's why he tried to kill me.

They ask the same questions over and over again, looking for discrepancies, for a verbal misstep that tells them I'm hiding something. I tell them nothing they don't already know. I give them nothing they can use in their diplomatic war against the Kremlin.

I'm discharged six weeks after being shot. Spend a night at a hotel near LAX, waiting for a flight back to Moscow. Study myself in the bathroom mirror. Once my hair grows back, it will cover the worst of it, I decide. The small scar under my left eye is in the same place as the teardrop scar on Kato's face.

That seems appropriate.

Chapter Sixty-five

Abram loved Kato with childlike devotion. And she loved him back. I should have realized that. I should have seen the obvious.

Abram fishes the polluted Techa River almost every day.

How many days did Kato spend with Abram? How many times did the Mole draw blood while Kato smoothed Abram's thinning brown hair and told him everything was going to be fine, the pain will go away?

I was right the first time, before I left Chelyabinsk for Mayak. I remember thinking then that the answer lies buried in the mud on the banks of the Techa River, maybe in the form of a spiral-bound notepad with a story inside that someone didn't want the world to know.

I change planes in Moscow and fly direct to Chelyabinsk. Rent a car and drive northwest past Lake Karachay under clear, cold skies, the sun settling onto the horizon. Navigate from memory to the dirt road and the gate wired shut. Open the gate, drive through, and close it behind me. Bounce over the ruts to the shack made of warped gray planks and a thatched roof.

Helen remembers me, but she won't let me inside.

"They found another body," she says through the door. "Near the river. The CIA killed another one. They will come back, I know it."

"You're right," I say. "They'll keep coming back until they find what they've been looking for. That's why I need to talk to Abram."

Several minutes pass in silence. I feel her presence behind the door. I lower myself to the planks of the stoop and sit with my elbows on my knees. The setting sun pours pinkish colors into the western sky. My abdomen hurts, as if the tunnel created by the passing bullet is still open, not yet healed. My head feels like it's still on fire. The pain will go away, the doctor said, but I don't know when.

The door creaks open behind me.

"What happened to your head?" Helen says.

She helps me to my feet, then leads the way inside.

Abram sits by the fire, staring into the flames. The sloughing skin on his face reshapes itself into a grimace or a smile, impossible to tell which. His grandmother rocks in her chair, lost in her private world.

I squat beside Abram. His mother stands at his shoulder and listens while her son answers my questions. His expression is unreadable, but hers is not. She has heard all this before. She knew it all the first time I was here.

Abram tells me about the day on the riverbank when he followed Kato and her two "friends." He watched them lead her to the fallen tree trunk. He saw her drop something into the brush on the way. Neither man noticed. He watched in horror as the Frenchman threatened her with his pistol. No, he couldn't hear what either of them said, but he knew from their tone and the expression on Kato's face that they were "fighting." He put his fist in his mouth to keep from screaming when the Frenchman pulled the trigger.

He thinks the American he calls *Kamen* saw him hiding there.

He was terrified. He didn't go back to that place for a long time. When he did he searched the brush under the trees where Kato dropped something.

He found a small red notepad.

He leads me outside, through a small garden and into a patch of scrub brush where the nose of a rusted wheelbarrow pokes from the brier. He reaches into the bowl and roots through the dead leaves, trash, and unidentifiable metal parts. He pulls out a red notepad and hands it to me.

Mud-streaked, stiff, difficult to open because of the dried mud clotted in the spiral binding, the pages rippled by moisture. I turn to the final entry.

> *Unholy alliances. Enough poison to destroy huge swaths of our environment moves around the world with none of us the wiser. Secret deals trading lives for money and political expediency.*
>
> *A knowledgeable source confirms a deal between the Kremlin and Washington, brokered by Paris, to transport spent nuclear fuel from American ports to Russia's north shore, then route it south to the Chelyabinsk region for reprocessing. Two "trial runs" took place in September and October. The first "live" shipment left port on November 29.*
>
> *The shipment went awry.*
>
> *The cargo vessel Chembulk Osaka, manned by the U.S. Merchant Marine and carrying ten containers of spent nuclear fuel, sank in rough seas in the North Atlantic. The date and precise location are known to certain officials in the U.S., France, and Russia, but are closely guarded secrets.*
>
> *Frantic efforts are under way to locate the wreckage, determine whether any of the containers are salvageable, and decide whether and how to release information about the potentially disastrous consequences for these sensitive waters.*

Cryptic notes follow the final entry. Names, dates, key facts, quotes, snippets she intended to include in the final version of her reports. She used asterisks, check marks, and underlining to indicate important items. She listed things she needed to do.

Call Mitlov. Her editor at Epilogue Publishing, the man sitting alone in his empty office nervously stroking his bald pate like a wasp cleaning itself. No checkmark next to this entry, meaning she never called him. So he must have told me the truth when he said he knew nothing about this story.

The entry below that one freezes my guts.

I look up. Helen and Abram are watching me. Helen sees something in me that causes her to step back. I drop my gaze back to the page.

What's the best way to ensure max exposure? Talk to Ilya about distribution in the old subversive community.

Next to Ilya's name, a checkmark indicating that she had completed the task.

Within days after that, Kato was dead.

Chapter Sixty-six

A six-story building made of Soviet cinder block, no security in the lobby, an elevator groaning away in one of the top floors. I take the stairs to the fifth floor. Walk into Epilogue's empty lobby.

"Who's there?" Mitlov calls from his office.

He startles back in his chair when I walk in.

"What do you want?"

I hand him Kato's notepads. He flips through the pages, pursing his lips when he sees the mud and rippled paper of the notepad Abram found. I stare through the window at the soot-blackened tenement next door while he reads. When finished, he looks at me like a frightened raccoon. Wide eyes surrounded by dark circles.

He gets it. He understands the significance. He knows the danger.

"What am I supposed to do with this?"

"I can't answer that question for you," I say. Then I walk away.

Chapter Sixty-seven

A small, gnome-like man with a grim message. That was my impression of Ilya when we met that night in Victory Park, there in the shadow of the obelisk on Poklonnaya Hill, where Napoleon watched his dreams of conquest turn to ashes. Stooped and bent, with his prisoner's voice and his sad, rheumy eyes. A tower of strength and intellect ready to surrender the field.

That was how I saw him then.

But not anymore.

We're sitting together on the same cold bench. He appears to be wearing the same clothes. This time I break our silence first.

"How did you learn about Kato's murder?"

He stiffens. But only for a moment, then he brings his cupped hands to his face and coughs.

"I don't remember. Everybody knew."

"I didn't. Not yet, anyway."

"Her editor, I think. Her editor must have called me. Why is this important?"

"What is her editor's name?"

His expression turns opaque. "Names are hard for me now, Alexei."

No clouds fill the sky tonight. Without their warming blanket the park seems encased in ice. The waning crescent moon cradles a patch of sky filled with stars.

I reach into my pocket for a photocopy of the last page of Kato's last red notepad. He slowly takes it from my hand.

"What is this?" he says, but I don't respond.

I let him read Kato's notes, her reminders, her checklist. I watch as his gaze stops at the line that mentions his name. He draws a long breath and hunches his shoulders as if fearing a blow.

I look away at the yellow lights marching down the hill. I stare at the moon and the stars.

Years ago I traveled to the memorial at the site of the Katyn massacre. I tried to imagine the final minutes of those murdered Polish officers, POWs, policemen, and intellectuals—handcuffed, taken to a cell with a padded door, and shot in the back of the head like animals in a slaughterhouse. Over 22,000 of them walked through that door, all of them carried out like a slab of beef. Fans ran constantly to mask the sounds of mass murder, but these men knew. They had to know.

So what were they thinking at the very end? A lifetime of love, work, family, and friends, all erased in an instant by men as emotionally drained and physically exhausted—carting so many bodies was hard work—as laborers in the darkest coal mine.

Ilya erased a lifetime of hard work and dedication in a different way. He sold it. I just don't know the price.

"Why?"

He leans back against the wooden slats of the bench. "I'm sick. Dying sick."

"So?"

"I'm afraid for my daughters."

I didn't know he had children.

"They live in London," he says. "But they are not safe. We exported some of the worst of our criminals there. You know that. They still make trades with the Kremlin."

He coughs into his gloved hands. Neither of us speaks for a long time.

"Sometimes," he says eventually. "Sometimes the Kremlin asks them for small favors. This person needs to disappear into the Thames. That one needs a broken kneecap to teach her father back home the difference between right and wrong."

He levels his gaze at me. "What would you have done?"

I stand. Bury my hands in the pockets of my overcoat. Grip the butt of a small-caliber throwaway pistol, considering how to answer his question. A kneecapped daughter, a death threat made against another daughter, a jail sentence on trumped-up charges—all those problems will go away if you tell us when this woman, this so-called journalist who has so many people whispering lies into her ear, tells you she has a story. Simple. She tells you something, you tell us.

I don't know the answer to Ilya's question. I don't know what I would have done.

I turn in a full circle to make sure we're alone. Finish my scan, then look down at him.

"Why me?"

"When I heard the news about Kato, you were the first person who came to mind. I…well, I knew about the two of you. And she once told me that you would protect her like no other."

"So you played both sides. You sold her out and they killed her. Then you primed me to take revenge."

Ilya bows his head in silent acknowledgment.

I understand his logic. All you have to do is point this man, this killer, in the right direction. Let him do the same dirty work he always does. Ilya could avenge Kato's death and salve his conscience at the same time.

I press the pistol against the top of his head and fire. He crumples.

I drop the pistol and leave him there on the hill. A sad, lonely old man bleeding out his life onto the snow, but a man with two daughters still alive in London.

The walk to the metro is difficult.

Everything hurts.

Kato is dead.

Valya is gone.

And I am lost.

Epilogue

"Are you afraid?" a television interviewer asked Kato a year before her murder.

"Of course," she replied.

"So why do you do it? Why not stop, be safe?"

Kato paused. Squared her shoulders. Leaned forward.

"I work on life's edges," she said. "I peer into people's hearts and bear witness to good and evil. To do that I must live on the edge."

She tucked a loose strand of hair behind her ear.

"Do you understand?"

To receive a free catalog of Poisoned Pen Press titles, please contact us in one of the following ways:

Phone: 1-800-421-3976
Facsimile: 1-480-949-1707
Email: info@poisonedpenpress.com
Website: www.poisonedpenpress.com

Poisoned Pen Press
6962 E. First Ave. Ste. 103
Scottsdale, AZ 85251